DRY RIDGE OF REDEMPTION

BAER CHARLTON

MORDANT MEDIA

Rogena Mitchell-Jones, Literary Editor
RMJ Manuscript Service, www.rogenamitchell.com

Published by Mordant Media, Portland, Oregon

ISBN: 978-1-949316-18-6 [paperback]
ISBN: 978-1-949316-19-3 [ebook]

10 9 8 7 6 5 4 3 2 1

CONTENTS

1

ESCAPE

They could have built the shack five years or fifty years earlier. Much past its first birthday on a small island in the middle of the Okefenokee Swamp, no building looked or felt new. The construction of the unregulated land was standard. It was little more than raw vertical boards over a two-by-four stud frame. Boards nailed between the studs provided shelves to put necessary items in a nod to utility and domestication. The white metal kitchen cabinets, in a silent war with rust, helped. The counters of Formica glued to plywood were already rippling from moisture, mold, and where an errant hot pan shouldn't have been put—again.

The rough-woven army surplus blankets thrown over the failings of a couch or chair best described the rest of the furniture found on a curb with a sign reading "free." The beds weren't much more. The government didn't care for spending any attention or money on a remote safe house in a poor state.

Rose set the plate and bowl of food down on the table. Her right hand stealthily turned the phone over, and the short text reappeared. She read it and turned it back face down before one of the special agents caught her snooping. For three days, the man had been getting texts he said were from his pregnant wife. This text confirmed Rose's suspicions about the imminent danger to her and her daughter.

The FBI special agent and owner of the phone came out of the bathroom. He looked at the bowl of beef stew and turned back into the bathroom, closing the door.

The blond agent in the kitchen heard the snick of the lock and swore. He turned and leaned purposefully against the counter, his hands spread on the sides of his guts. Rose walked to the coffee pot and poured another mug. As she turned to stir some sugar in, she added a few drops of eyewash. She had learned the trick many years before from an older prostitute.

She had told Rose, "When you don't want to have sex with your trick, get him shitting his brains out, and he won't have time to think of anything else."

Rose turned as she innocently stirred the added milk. She looked at the special agent. "Here. The cream will help settle your stomach. I don't think those eggs this morning were fresh. Even Sydney's stomach has been giving her trouble. And she has one of those cast-iron teenager constitutions."

The man took the mug and gulped at the coffee.

Rose pulled at her thick jet-black hair flowing from the wide Navajo hair brooch. Her face still held the exotic look of either Japanese or Mexican, depending on how she dressed. Her almond-shaped eyes were full, but the coloring of ultra-dark brown blended with the pupil had always been framed with thick, long lashes. Even on dates as a call girl, she had never needed to wear false eyelashes.

The movement through the sparse forest outside the window behind the special agent caught her eye. Down closer to the water, her daughter had her light blue book bag and Rose's purse. She disappeared behind the water tank to wait for Rose.

Rose looked back at the thin door to the bathroom. She reached out to the wall and grabbed a roll of toilet paper stacked on the shelf. Pulling her face in a look of disgust and impatience, she turned to the special agent assigned to protect her. "I can't wait for him. I'm going to go find a bush. If you do the same…" She jerked her thumb over her shoulder. "You go that way. I'm going down there where the bushes are thicker."

The man groaned as he rubbed his gut. "Good idea."

She tossed him the roll and grabbed one more. The special agent opened the back door with a rush. Rose took the opportunity to grab the cell phone from the table and slip it in her back pocket.

As she walked down through the sparse tossing of trees toward the water tank close to the beach, she watched the lanky special agent moving further out the back. Now it was just a waiting game. But she also knew from the text it wouldn't be much longer.

Approaching her younger self, the alternative plan formed in her head. The boat coming with men sent to kill her needed taking care of as well. A short boat chase of only a couple of miles was not an escape. They needed a head start of at least several hours.

Behind the water tank was a stack of firewood. It was more of a prop to make the homestead look lived-in than something people would use for heat near the Florida border. She looked around among the wood and tarpaulin.

"What are you looking for, Mom?" The teen stood with her bookbag hanging limply at her leg. Her thick head of straight black hair hung in a ponytail to her waist. The silver clasp was a smaller version of her mother's sizable squash-blossom brooch. In a ruffian's hat on her long-sleeve T-shirt, the toothy bulldog mascot was inconsistent with the wide-eyed young face.

Rose stood. She held out the ax and the splitting maul. Her smile was larger than the two instruments of backaches would usually arouse. "Just what we're going to need."

The sound of the airboat caused them to turn and then duck behind the woodpile. Rose shushed Sydney and then explained. "All that texting with agent Roy and his supposed pregnant wife…?"

Sydney nodded and peeked over at the approaching boat.

"It was one of Alex Nyack's guys down at Delta Camp. His name is Don Sykes, a former Marine. He runs most of the canned hunts. If he's coming, he's coming armed, and it's not about being pleasant. They weren't ever going to hide us or protect us. When the men get up toward the house, we need to sneak out the dock. While I try to get the airboat started, I need you to chop holes in the bottom of the aluminum skiff. We need to sink it. Can you do that?"

Sydney nodded as they heard the engine on the airboat stop. She whispered, "Just like chopping wood at scout camp."

They hunkered down further, preparing to sneak around the backside of the pile of wood.

2

DAYBREAK

"Maa Me."

The bray echoed hollow and forlorn.

"Maa Me."

Rocket pulled her eyes wide to break the dry crust of sleep. "Jeez, Baby. Spoiled rotten turd."

Throwing back the blanket and sheet, she rolled on her side and swung her legs out. The large purple bruise, turning yellow and green, caught at the edge of the mattress. She bit at her lower lip.

Sitting up, she slowly rubbed at the bruise spreading from the knee to almost her hip. For the millionth time, she swore she would never train the spoiled pony of a spoiled child. But she knew she was lying. The girl had Crohn's and Down's and was almost blind. The pony had been abused at one time, and the parents bought it without knowing. The girl was already in love when the dangerous habit arose. It was Rocket's job to break the habit, teach the girl how to care for her pony and ride.

"Maa Me. Me. Me."

She looked to make sure at least one window was open. "Damn it, Baby. I'm coming." She scratched under her left boob as she stood. She fell back onto the bed. "Damn!"

Now ready for the pain, she stood, found her balance, and hobbled to the bathroom.

She stood at the mirror as the toilet finished flushing. The wild hair, half-closed eye below the healing three-inch scab from running into a swinging gate, and numerous aches and pains had her grab at the institution-sized bottle of aspirin. She shook out a small handful and then looked at the mirror. "Who knew forty-eight could look and feel so fucked?"

She filled the glass and washed the aspirin down and gave herself a wild, wide-eyed look. "Don't judge."

"Maa MEE."

"Fuck."

Pulling on fresh panties, yesterday's jeans, socks, and boots, she considered skipping the bra and T-shirt. And then she remembered the reaction from one horse on the last trail ride. She pulled out a fresh sports bra and grabbed the shirt off the top of the stack. Standing and walking in the tall brush-guard boots helped to steady her. Or at least she told herself it did.

"Maa Me."

Holding the railing the entire way, she wobbled down the stairs. The front door stood open. These days, with the nicer weather, it hardly ever closed. She whistled.

A large black streak rounded the corner of the barn and met Rocket at the bottom of the stairs. She grabbed at the big floppy ears and gave the dog a full-frontal kiss. The returned tongue was wet, sloppy, and enthusiastic. "How's my Pink? Huh, sweetie?" Rocket started to walk. "Were you out having fun with Auntie Dot? Is she doing something fun?"

Rocket could hear the bellows stoking the morning fire of the forge. Why she didn't run an electric fan in these modern days was beyond Jolie.

Under the large extended roof on the barn, Dot had set up two complete blacksmiths shops. Between forging custom horseshoes, learning wrought-iron work from Fernando, and making swords and knives, her days were crammed.

Many days when Fernando came to visit, Rocket liked to sit on the fence watching the two working—Fernando creating art deep in the back smithy, while Dot created custom shoes for difficult hooves in the front. Watching Dot delicately work her way around the long-nosed anvil at the edge of the corral calmed Jolie's soul. The nose was so long, the small end at the tip was perfect for creating even the miniature shoes for the thirty-inch tiny horses. She was even getting a reputation big enough to call for the brown truck to stop by.

Rocket called out as she heard the mechanical bellows pause. "Hey, Dot."

Dot's muted call of good morning was interspersed by the sound of a large hammer taking heavy hits on the anvil. Thousands of hits measured her days.

"Maa Meeee."

"Stop it, Baby, or you'll suck your tongue down your

throat." The cathedral-like space of the barn was dark but warm from the several horses. And one spoiled donkey.

"Maa Me. Me. Me."

"Yes, Baby. Mommy is here." Rocket opened the door to the first stall, and the donkey shot past and spun. Rocket turned to embrace the head as the donkey pushed its forehead against her entire body. Rocket's hands scratched back along the sides of the head and jaws. The sound of the soft bray sounded like a cross between a cry and purring.

Rocket leaned forward and kissed Baby between the ears as Pink wove in and out of the four stationary legs. "What would my morning be without turning you loose?"

She laid her head sideways on the bony head between the ears. She remembered the phone call from an old friend running a pack station near Yosemite. The call was random but started Broken Ride Acres.

There was a seven-year-old pack donkey, kicked in the head by another. It set off a behavior they couldn't break. The donkey refused to be in a pack-line, even if she was the lead donkey. She was kicking out stalls during the day but also hated the corral overnight. At night she was only content locked snug and safe in a stall. She was only happy during the day following the pack station's owner around like a lovesick puppy.

Following him into the office and then kicking apart the front counter had been the last straw. It was either dog meat, the glue factory, or someone who could deal with a ruined pack donkey.

A couple of days and Rocket had figured out the broken donkey. First, the name Zelda had to go. It was too close to zero. Any donkey who could haul hundreds of pounds of supplies up the Sierra Nevada Mountains was no zero—even if a darker-gray circle surrounded the one eye. The next was figuring out where and when she was happy. Roaming free to see what was going on by day was good, but she was only secure closed in her stall at night unless they took her out for a trail ride.

Rocket was teaching the city-raised Dot to ride by taking trail rides. Most were only a day or two, but they had taken a few into the mountains separating the Santa Ynez Valley from California's Central Valley.

Rocket enjoyed the quiet of the long rides but loved watching Dot find out about muscles her knowledge of mixed martial arts had never exposed her to. Rocket never gave up a hint she was relearning about the same muscles. She had stayed in shape during her seven years in prison, but the muscles from weightlifting weren't the same. Turning forty-seven hadn't helped her ego, either, but the trail rides also helped ease her Jolie-Rocket split personality. The rodeo gave name to her wilder, burning-balls-to-the-walls, tougher-than-an-angry-steer side. Even before she found her last rodeo champion mount, Thunder, she was known to launch from the chute like a rocket. Drunk in the bars, she took to a fight just as fast. The burn, heat, and explosive nature fit the name. But she had her nurturing side, as well. The side that preferred teaching little girls on even smaller ponies. Getting a grasp on controlling the beast and holding fast to the gentle was always a struggle.

"Hey, Jolie?" The call came from the closed-in section of

the barn. It was the large room where Dot kept her grinding equipment for making knives and swords.

Rocket turned toward the open access door from the barn. "Yeah, Dot?"

"Mike texted he was starting out."

Rocket snorted breathy into the donkey's head. Mommy time was over. "Okay. I'll go start the bacon."

Dot stepped into the doorway. Her natural hair of twisties was standing straight up through the broken top of her grinding helmet. "We're out. I think we're down to just elk steaks and bubble gum."

Rocket laughed at the old joke. "Nope. Chewed the last bubble gum three nights ago when Punchy was home." She looked down at the large black cane corso dog. "Well, Pink. Looks like you have to suffer eating some elk trimmings."

The dog's large, floppy ears slapped as she turned and shot through the barn door before Jolie. The donkey followed. Jolie threw some hay in Baby's trough, then made her rounds through the barn. All nine horses had come to her with a problem the previous owner no longer wanted to deal with. Head shy, flinch kicker, saddle shy, bit shy, or just turned mean for no reason, Jolie had taken them in. Only one horse in a year and a half had she ever judged to put down. A horse turning ornery because it's filled with painful cancer can't be changed. Painkillers and other drugs can only do so much.

As she walked past the doorway into Dot's grinding room, Jolie stopped and frowned. "Hey, Dot?"

Jolie could hear the steel come away from the grinding belt. The silence was only broken by the dull hum of the powerful motor. Dot probably still had her grinding helmet down covering her face, but she could still hear. "Did Mike say if he was riding or walking?"

The woman in the stretched black tank top stepped back into the doorway. Her cut muscles already glowed with sweat from wielding the heavy hammer and the hot forge. She raised the helmet from her face as her eyes danced across empty air that Jolie knew to be the text on her phone. Finally, the woman pulled the phone out of her back pocket and thumbed it open.

"He just say he startin' out." She looked up with a frown, and then her face cleared except the black freckles across her walnut face. "I wouldn't be no hurry. Until that gelding, Stonewall gets used to his new thicker horseshoes, he gonna be shy 'bout putting rider weight on his hoof."

Rocket sucked her lower lip in and squeaked her teeth. The horse was a mix of thoroughbred and Bashkir—a curly-coated dray horse. The breeder was trying to make a riding horse that was hypoallergenic. The result of his experiment was the frog in the horse's hoof was prone to damage. "Well, I hope he has enough smarts to at least lead him over here and make him walk on those new shoes. Standing around in his corral doesn't do anyone good."

Jolie looked down the alley of the large barn at the heads out of their stalls. All fine-looking horses—and one way or another, all broken rides.

She turned toward the large open doors. "I'll go cut some meat."

In the sunshine, she looked back at the wrought iron letters over the barn doors. The sign needed a few more letters and flourishes, but in her heart, the sign had always been there. Broken Ride Acres meant just as much about the horses as the two women.

The seven years of prison had, in some ways, instilled more than it had taken away from Rocket. But the years were a constant reminder of her mother no longer here. After, it was a reminder of the worst kinds of betrayal—that of a life-long best friend. Friendships would never come easy. Trusting others would take the same trail. But every day she had Dot and Punchy, it got easier, or at least she knew she wasn't alone. Mike had always been a constant in her life. His renting the new house she was building for him kept him closer than ever.

Dot had given up her title and career as a mixed martial arts heavyweight champion. The last seconds of the last round of her last fight had made headlines in the sport around the world. The blow was her signature move of Dotting her opponent's eye. Unfortunately, that night her opponent was her best friend. And what they didn't know was she had a brain bleed. With the single blow to the head, Dot had won the title but lost her friend. Soon after, she would lose her father, who had taught her how to make knives and swords, to a random shooting in a liquor store.

Both women shrouded themselves in their friendship and the quiet nature of the ranch's four-square miles. Or a quiet trail ride. It wasn't lost on the men in their lives—the initials of the ranch weren't about testosterone.

3

GALVESTON

The twin-engine airplane turned west in a lazy, gentle curve over the open water of Galveston Bay. Rose smelled the rank fumes rising from the sun-cooked dead water. The century of oil, diesel, and gas pollution only got flushed out every few years by a hurricane. This was not the year the toilet got flushed.

The cloying stench reminded her of the dead oil fields hidden in the southwest industrial stretches of Los Angeles. Only the coppery tang of blood and rendering around the Jimmy Dean sausage plant in East Los Angeles had repulsed her more. It was old death versus active death. The bay water was a slaughterhouse. As they flew along the bay, the lack of any boats sailing or anyone fishing confirmed the death of the water.

The white wings cast a slight shadow as they crossed the pollution choked Pelican Island. Even the low-lying creosote bushes were the color of old oil on the landscape.

The pilot, Jerry, pointed out his window. "Galveston." His

headphones hung on the hook between the door and front windshield. He hadn't pulled them over his large blond curls the entire time since leaving his dock east of Mexican Beach on the Hidden Coast of Florida. Rose wondered if he ever flew anywhere that he had to talk to flight control of any kind. She knew the stack of three instead of two radios was unusual except for smugglers. The third radio was a short-band used by those standing on empty dirt roads or boats out past the three-mile mark.

His narrative of sight-seeing had sprinkled the long six-hundred-mile flight. He had pointed to the distant land they were skirting and explained. "Loo-see-anna." And then minutes later had broken into a lengthy lecture of, "NoLins up that-a-way." It had been entertaining in its own way.

The single-engine plane groaned as Jerry pulled up and over the Gulf Highway Bridge and then let back down on the other side. As they skimmed the southern edge of a small island, he lowered the left wing and swung back, heading southeast. The flat land on both sides was lightly dusted on the left and coated on the right with buildings—docks on the left and submerged sandbars on the right.

The battered and faded reddish ball cap turned. The large dark glasses were mirrors reflecting Rose's face in double miniatures. "Offatts Bayou."

As the bayou widened out into more of a bay to the south, the plane hugged along the northern shore with its bleached homes, small warehouses, and tight docks. The large pontoons of the aging Cessna 195 inched closer and closer to the water surface.

As the bay seemed to run out, Jerry eased back on the

throttle. The hiss of the pontoons slicing the surface of the water soon became a thump as the water took hold. The seatbelt pushed dully at Rose's chest and then released.

Jerry pushed in power, and the plane surged forward, taxiing toward a small, weathered marina.

The slips were less than half-filled with boats or something partially floating. Nothing was sparkling white fiberglass. The bleached gray wood was the contrast to the oil-stained boats, pilings, and water. When people talked about their boat down at the marina, this was not the kind of marina they were referencing.

As they approached the end of the first dock, Jerry fanned the prop and turned off the engine. The man who had been sitting on the back deck of his boat, two slips down, stood and sauntered toward the plane.

The airplane floated the last few feet toward the dock as Jerry opened his door and stepped out onto the pontoon. Bending, he grabbed the rope out of the bucket-hole in the pontoon and tossed it to the man dressed in cut-off work pants and stained wife-beater. The rope hit him at the hole just above his distended belly button. A slow swirling slash of his hand and the rope was secured to the worn metal cleat on the dock.

Jerry grabbed the back rope, stepped onto the dock, wrapped it to a bollard, and secured the back. He walked forward and opened the backload door for Sydney and Rose to climb out.

He turned to the man quietly standing watching. "They need a ride up to wash town. Buy a car, maybe."

The man nodded and started slowly walking up the dock.

Rose stepped onto the dock, watching the retreating man. She reached her hand out to the pilot. "Thanks, Jerry." She pulled a fat crinkled yellow envelope from her oversized purse. "Fifty thousand. And, Jerry, I wouldn't deal with Nyack or my husband anymore if I were you. After today, they'll be radioactive."

The man ticked his head up as he slid his hat back an inch. "I figured. I ain't liked the business they been doing lately. This is my last run south." He waved his finger at the plane. "I'll probably jus' sell Pepe to one of the guys in Belize and let someone else fly me to a new home."

Rose patted his shoulder. "Good thinking." She glanced at the man halfway up the dock.

Jerry sighed. "He okay. Slip him a couple a hundreds, and he'll take you where ya want ta go. By tonight, and half a bottle, he won't know nothin'."

She grimaced as she glanced at her daughter. "Thanks again, and take care." They turned to follow the man.

The pilot turned back and untied his plane.

As Rose and Sydney reached the man at his sagging truck, the plane roared overhead and wagged its wings.

The three snuggled into the cab. The smell of rust was more pungent than the sweat leaching out from the man's lack of hygiene. The man held his hand on the key in the column. "What kind of car?"

"Cheap but will get us to Chicago by Friday."

He looked at Rose. "Today Monday."

Rose's face deadpanned. "I don't drive fast."

The man pursed his lips and started the truck. Pulling

back away from the railroad tie, he put the truck in first and headed for the sketchier side of town.

———

AN HOUR LATER, Rose stood close to Sydney between the two cars. Sydney held a map of Louisiana the car dealer had provided her. Rose held a map good for her trip through Colorado and into Minnesota.

Rose pulled two more maps from her purse. Handing one to Sydney, she looked her in the eyes. "You sure you're okay with a map that doesn't talk to you and tell you every turn?"

Sydney's arms were close to her side as she looked around. "I think I'll be okay. If I get lost, I'll stop at a coffee shop and ask directions."

Rose hugged her. "It's pretty easy. Stay on forty-five and go north on sixty-nine. From there, you should see signs directing you to the airport. I'll be standing out front of the departure gates for American. Only touch the steering wheel and then wipe it all down with the baby wipes. Don't forget to leave the keys under the mat."

The young girl nodded. "Okay. I'll see you in about an hour or so."

Rose held her head between her hands. "I know you're scared. I'm scared too. But we'll be okay. We'll get through this."

The tear slipped down the girl's cheek. "I know, Mom. Live to fight another day." The quiver of the chin was slight but there.

4

CHORES

Jolie had learned early to stick only a pound or so of elk steaks in the microwave to defrost at a time. Her first impatient try had been a stack of four large steaks. She hadn't believed the half-hour the microwave read for the five or more pounds and kept opening the door every five minutes. Dinner was an hour late that night. Punchy and Mike laughed in the necks of their beer bottles when she wasn't looking.

The women got their laughs when Jolie swept the legs out from underneath the former rodeo clown and deputy sheriff. As Mike laughed at Jolie's boyfriend lying in the dirt, Dot swept his legs out as well. Shaken beers spraying had ruled for only a few minutes before they all realized nobody had gone to town to pick up more beer.

Her razor-sharp knife sliced off the gristle. The point pricked into the end and flipped it in the air. The flash of a black head with floppy ears snapped it out of sight. Jolie loved watching Pink acting like a puppy. She wasn't old, but

Jolie knew the cane corso wasn't a long-lived breed of dog. Every day was a gift.

The microwave dinged, and Jolie took the next steak out. Not fully defrosted, but enough to allow Jolie to slice it up into finger steaks for a quick fry when Mike showed up.

The back screen door squealed. Jolie didn't have to turn to know it was Dot. She let the door hit her butt so it didn't slam.

"He just hit the crest. He walkin'. I heard him swearin' at po' Stonewall." She grabbed a small piece of the raw steak and sucked it into her mouth. "I'll check his frogs later."

Jolie pointed at the steak. "You do know it's not healthy for you to be eating that raw meat."

"Ain't hurt me none yet."

Jolie lowered her eye at her friend. "It ain't the meat I'm talking about." She slapped the back of Dot's hand with the flat of the large knife. "It's the cook you have to worry about. Now go wash up and set the table out on the porch. We don't want to make Mike walk farther than he already has."

Dot pointed out the window, and Jolie looked. Dot's other hand grabbed a piece of meat and popped it in her mouth. "Hmm, my bad. I thought it was someone coming up the drive." She looked down, laughing at the tip of the large knife pointed at her belly.

Jolie laughed. "You've been warned."

Dot rolled her eyes. "Jeez, Rocket, just like last week and the week before. Admit it. I need raw meat." She turned on the water at the sink and scrubbed her hands and arms. She sniffed at her pits and shrugged.

Jolie focused on the steak strips. "Punchy said he'd introduce you to a couple of the better deputies…"

Turning off the water, Dot grabbed the towel and slowly wiped her hands as she stared out the back window. "I saw those boys at the barbecue. None of 'em would last a single round in the ring." She hung the towel on the hook. "No, thanks. I'll find my own." She nodded her head at the window, looking up the hill. "Mike's here."

Jolie turned to see the man walking with his left fist in the halter of the large horse. At eighteen hands and almost a full ton, the horse was a monster. But next to the six-foot-four former surfer, they were a match. Jolie giggled at how the curly dark blondish coat of the horse matched the man's hair where it wasn't going gray. The man wasn't sure of the analogy but had come around to have a soft spot for the giant horse with delicate feet. Jolie hadn't seen him use a cane in over a year.

With a flick of his wrist, the reins whipped around the hitching post. Jolie had only seen one other person use the underhand whip of the reins, and she knew Mike had never met the pro rodeo bronc rider from Oklahoma. Where he learned the technique was beyond her.

She stepped over to turn on the range. Her right hand shot back with the knife. As she turned her head, Dot laughed. Her hand was inches from the meat but separated by the tip of the knife.

It was a constant game with them, the little sparring that led up to the late afternoon workout. The martial arts ring was in the barn, but most of their real fights were in the dirt of the barnyard. In real life, there were no corners, ropes, or rules. Their knife fights were with knife blanks and body pads. But the effort and training were as real as death.

Dot brought her experience from years of professional mixed martial arts. Jolie brought her years of horse wrangling, pig hunting with a knife, and seven hard years of staying alive in prison. The two knew all about clean fighting as well as staying alive dirty.

Mike breathed deeply through his nose as he walked through the door. "Something smells good." The tall man bent slightly to nuzzle into the back of Dot's neck. "Yup. Already fired the forge. Now there's a perfume a real man can get used to."

Dot spun and slapped his chest. "Get out, smooth talker."

"Okay." He turned back toward the front door.

Dot grabbed at his belt and hauled him back as Jolie laughed. "I think she meant for you to keep sweet-talkin' her."

Dot growled at Jolie. "I meant if he here, he be workin'." She pointed at the silverware drawer. "We eatin' Al this mornin'."

Mike pulled the drawer. "Well, I'm always a sucker for Mr. Fresco." He looked at Jolie. "Punchy here?"

Jolie shook her head as she dredged the steak strips through the egg, flour, and into the hot skillet. The oil bubbled and popped. "Just the three of us this morning. Punchy's still up in Sacramento at some Department of Justice conference on sexual equality and harassment."

"Learning new tricks?"

She side-eyed him. "Teaching. Obviously, he learned many tricks jumping in and out of the barrels at the rodeos."

"He's a good man. You better make good on that boast about marrying him soon. I saw Skeeter Thomas down at the feed store eyeing his backside."

Jolie laughed. "Skeeter can eyeball his backside all she wants. She's fourteen and wondering about riding bulls, broncs, or just jumping barrels. I watched her try to run the gymkhana barrel races this spring. It wasn't a pretty ride."

Dot flattened her pushed-out lower lip as she nodded. "She not pretty either. I think when she figure it out—she be chasing girls."

Jolie shrugged, Mike rolled his eyes as he leaned on his one heel toward the door, and the two women worked in silence.

Dot grabbed the plates and mugs. "I'm jus' sayin'."

Jolie stood poking at the steak strips as she thought about the young girl on the cusp of womanhood. Despite being the owner's daughter, she pulled her weight more than most of the men. She never shied from bucking bales, humping sacks, or sweeping out. If it weren't for the bumps sprouting under her shirt and the ponytail dancing across her belt and back, her daddy could be proud of his young son becoming a man. But she also knew the man was proud of his child, no matter what came—she just wasn't the typical rodeo rider her mother had been.

THE PLATES WERE CLEARED, and the second carafe of coffee was near the bottom. Pink spread out against Jolie's boot.

"What do you think?" Mike worried about his horse. He

had heard about the giant horse who had been happy in the soft pasture, but the minute weight was applied on a hard dirt surface, the horse became anything but his namesake.

Dot thoughtfully moved her finger along the crack in the table. "Fernando say it take some time for big Stone ta get used to less pressure on his feet. Da shoes be almost ha' inch of hard rubber married to aluminum shoes. He gots high heels. They takes time. You try four-inch pumps some time."

Mike looked at Jolie. "But you gals don't think he could still hurt his frog?"

Jolie leaned back. "This is where I defer to the farrier or a vet. If he blows out the frog, you might as well shoot him right there. We can always find you another large horse to ride…" She leaned on the arm of the chair and looked down at her constant companion. "Or we can even find you a large dog to follow you around." She looked up with a smirk. "Or you can have a giant of a dog following you around while you just walk everywhere. Your choice."

"I don't want to put him down just because he has poor feet…"

Jolie rolled her head down and watched as Pink adjusted her body firmer against her master's boot. "They don't come here to be put down. They come here for salvation and to live out their lives as long as we are blessed to have them. You of all people know I don't need to make any money, and they can take all they need. The BRA is here for them, any way they need support. Even at the end, we're here to make it peaceful and loving."

"Bra?" Mike's face didn't know whether to frown or laugh.

Dot snorted softly as her body rocked. "Broken Ride Acres. We all be broken one way or tuther. So who better to understand damaged horses and mules?" She nodded her head at the donkey, rubbing her ear against the hitching post.

Jolie pulled at the edge of her wide brim. "I told you Baby's a donkey. A mule is a cross, and Baby could only mate with a horse her size or smaller."

Mike chuckled. "There are those little, tiny house-sized horses…"

The steely eye slid sideways, glowing like a hot iron from the forge. "You better be glad I have a dog on my foot, or I'd kick your bum leg halfway to Santa Barbara."

The man glanced under the table. "Good girl, Pink. Take a nice long nap. Protect your Uncle Mike and his bum leg."

Jolie's sigh matched Pink's. It was then the dog farted a small toot, breaking the moment. Jolie turned to Dot. "When you're getting the coal and ordering a load of hay, can you see if they have any fart-less dog food?"

Dot pulled at one of her twisties. The thumb rolled the end along her finger. "She be farting in the bed?"

"No."

"Then why worry? You can't smell anything out here with the rest o' the horseshit and Baby."

The half-asleep donkey shuttered at her name. "Maa, maa…"

Jolie snorted. "It's okay, Baby. Mommy loves ya. Go back to sleep."

The diminutive donkey leaned her side heavier against the hitching post.

Mike thought with his finger up.

Jolie growled softly. "Feeling for the wind? There's no surf out here."

His eyes slow blinked with a soft snort. "No. I was trying to think of what I needed in town if Dot's running in for feed."

"For the house?"

Mike rocked his body and nodded his head with one eye closed in disgust. "Right. I need a large blowtorch to fire those builders up. They weathered in the walls and roof a week ago, and I haven't seen a plumber or electrician yet. These are the slowest builders I've ever seen."

Jolie reached for her satellite phone and thumbed up the antenna. "Why didn't you say something before? If I don't have a completed house for my renter, how will I charge you rent? Are you still out in the tent?"

He pushed his lips as he shook his head. "I moved up onto the porch the last rainstorm. With the deep porch, I was out of the rain, and I get the better view."

She rocked back in understanding as she fished for the right number. She cut off the answering voice. "Paul, Rocket. and I'm red-hot. I was just over to the house. Your boys weathered in over a week ago and then left. If I don't see all the trades on that build by ten o'clock, you're fired, and I'll let everyone in the valley know how unhappy I am." She thumbed the phone off.

The block of plastic and metal vibrated as she sipped on her coffee. Her eyes were on the gigantic horse tied off on the corral rails. "Leave Stonewall here. I'll work him on the lunge line and hot walker. Let's see if he can get used to walking and maybe at least my weight."

The three eyed the vibrating phone. It had moved three inches with the urgency as if the contractor could reach out and touch the device.

Suddenly the air filled with the beginning bars of the Beachboys Wipeout. Jolie held her breath. "That's your butt, not mine."

He rolled up on his right hip as he fished out his satellite phone. Thumbing the antenna, he answered, "Go for Mike."

He listened as his eyes sparkled at Rocket. His smile was wide and toothy. "No, Paul. I left shortly after the sun came up. You know, the only place I can be dry and safely sleep faces right into the sunrise. So I started walking over to Rocket's to get a shower that your plumber guy promised me a month ago. But I just got here to the Broken Ride and haven't had a powwow with her. I think she might be out exercising one of her horses… or killing something. Why do you ask?"

5

REPORT

Alex? This is John Perlmutter, down at Delta Camp."

At the other end of the phone, the large man swiveled in his chair and looked out across his view of Atlanta. He never liked the city as much as he loved the potential it held. "Yeah, John. Tell me some good news."

The usually forceful voice of the former Navy SEAL thinned. "The only good news is they didn't kill anyone getting away."

"Who got away?" Alex sat up and turned back toward his desk. His eyes were searching the few papers. He was trying to remember what hunts they had scheduled.

"Stanley's wife and daughter. They escaped."

Alex's eyes stopped and narrowed. This wasn't about a quarter-million-dollar hunt for a Cuban or Haitian. This was about his life. "But you had them stashed on an island with those FBI guys. Who did you send over to kill them?"

"Don Sykes and Teddy McConnell. They're two of our

best. Both former marines and have done jobs for us before. They slipped up on this one."

Alex closed his eyes and sighed with his chest against his desk. "Slipped up how?"

"They left the key in the airboat. The girls put a splitting maul through the bottom of the FBI's aluminum skiff and sank it. Then they took off in the airboat. When they got back to the dock in Olustee, they hotwired the SUV and stole it."

Alex stared at the key fob on his desk that held two keys. Complacency had gotten the better of them, and it caused him to hang his head. "No, she had the keys."

"But it was one of the new ones we got for Camp Delta."

Alex's attention shifted to the small wet bar across the room. He rarely drank during the day, and this might be one of those exceptions. "She kept all the books. We ordered the new rigs to be all keyed alike. Open one will open them all. Either that or she knew where they hid the emergency key." He looked at the wet bar again. "Who was driving the SUV?"

"Sykes."

"Who drove the airboat?" He knew he didn't need to ask. The day just kept getting better and better.

The man on the phone stalled. "Um… Sykes…"

Alex wanted to throw something through something. "Because he always drives the airboat. The key was on the same ring."

The voice was small on the phone line. "Shit."

Alex's voice had turned to more of an angry growl. "Find out where they went and have Sykes and McConnell ready to go to wherever they are. That whore grew up in Los Angeles. That's a big fucking city to go searching. You better hope you find them before they get to some big city like that."

"Yes, sir."

6

SORRY ABOUT THE WORK

Mike stood and walked to the edge of the porch. Looking out across the valley, it was like he could see the other man talking. Except, the man was over the distant hills in Santa Barbara.

"What's up, Manuel?"

"I wish I didn't need to ask, boss, but I have some serious trouble."

Mike thought about the young man. The tattoos were in the process of removal as if to erase his troubled youth. Mike had taken a chance on the ex-convict and former gang member, and the man had never let him down. He had worked hard and turned his life around. He never went back to Los Angeles, even to visit what little family he had left. His life was about work and fixing up the shack he had bought in the squalid neighborhood of north Goleta near the University of California.

Mike rubbed the back of his neck, trying to figure out any

code the man might be speaking. "Is this something we need to discuss at the office?"

"Sir, I took the liberty of moving the trouble out to the rocket range. I should be there within the hour if you can join me."

Mike turned to look at Dot and Rocket. "I'll let them know you're on your way, son."

Jolie squinted at the stilted speech of the man and dipped the brim of her black hat, allowing it to dance over her eyes in acknowledgment. Whatever was going on, she would back his play.

Mike turned to look back out across the valley. "You have clearance. What are you driving?"

"A survey pig, sir." Most knew this to be the common nickname for the company's SUVs used by the crews. Like most fleet vehicles, it had started white. But as the dings and dents gathered, the patches of various colors of primers made them look like multicolored pigs at the county fair.

Mike's thumb slid the phone off. He left the antenna extended as he laid it on the table. He picked up the coffee carafe and headed for the door. Slinging the remains of luke-warm coffee out into the large dirt wagon yard, he said, "I think this is going to be a-lot-more-coffee kind of day."

Jolie looked at Dot. "I guess I won't be working over at Norm's today."

Dot stood. "Buttercup needs a good rub down. I rewrap her legs. Blinker needs time on the hot walker…" She sniffed a couple of times. "And yo daughter seriously need a bath."

"Which one?"

Dot glanced under the table where the two mud-encrusted hind legs were sticking out. The two four-legged children, Pink and Baby, were almost inseparable. If one rolled in the shit pile, the other was about to start or coming out the other side. "Both." She stepped down the stairs from the porch. "I be back in a couple hours. Try to stay outta trouble, Rocket."

Jolie fluttered one eye. "Always."

JOLIE STOOD on the edge of the large porch. Pink sat, attentive to her left leg. They watched as the mostly gray-primer-splotched SUV slowly made the turn at the end of the driveway and into the large wagon yard. Not for the first time did Jolie wonder what it must have looked like when the four- and six-mule teams of her grandfather's made the same turn. The hard turn was by design. The two large rocks, forcing the awkward turn, were placed, and partially buried by her grandfather. There were more accessible places to build the driveway or approach, but this forced a wagon or car to slow down to a speed that made it an easy target for a rifle.

She found traces of the access cut to bring the giant wagons in with long logs used to build the lodge and lumber for the large barn. Five trees, each about a hundred years old, grew in the middle of the trace. Jolie had planted more.

No sign or badge represented the company. Just a beat-up and brush-scratched old work truck. She was surprised it didn't wheeze or knock as it pulled up quietly to the porch and parked next to the battered green truck. In her Rocket

days, Jolie referred to the type of truck as Rodeo Ready—
beat to shit and ready to run all day.

It would appear the company had adopted her philoso-
phy. The doors only squealed lightly as they opened. Manuel
stepped out and closed his door. The black-haired woman in
the passenger seat hesitated as she opened the SUV's
passenger side door. From behind her dark glasses, she eyed
Jolie's tall moccasins, jeans, her wide-brimmed hat, and the
large dog.

A young girl stepped out of the SUV's back door as she
pulled on the inevitable teenager's backpack. Her hair was
the same jet-black as the woman's hair was in the front
passenger seat but longer. Her moon-round face and almond
eyes probably matched the older woman too. The girl's
yellow rough-out work boots had never seen a day of work.
All she needed to be a cliché was a cell phone to occupy her
nose and fingers. She looked around at the weathered barn
and house with casual disdain.

Manuel leaned his hand on the nose of the SUV as his
right foot kicked softly at the dirt. "Que pasa, Rocket?"

Pink leaned minutely, lessening the weight on the paw
nearest Jolie. She recognized Manuel as a friend who usually
had a treat. Jolie's finger snapped softly behind her leg.
"Hiza." The Japanese command to heel was nothing more
than a sharp breath.

Pink rocked and adjusted. The gentle weight against the
tall moccasin increased. Her attention returned to the work
of watching the two unknown women.

"Rocket, this is my... Aunt Rose and her daughter,
Sydney, like the city."

Relatives would make them Mexican or Latinas instead of Asian, as Rocket had thought.

Both of Jolie's first index knuckles remained hooked in her front pockets. The appearance was her hands were stuck in her pockets, but the truth was loosely curled fists ready for combat. The trick she had learned in prison but perfected with the mixed martial arts instructions of Dot. The brim of her head bobbed slightly. "Howdy. Welcome to Broken Ride Acres."

The woman nervously stepped forward with her hand raised. "Thank you for the hospitality on such short notice…" Her hand and soft southern accent hung in the air and then fell, embarrassed.

Jolie's sized up the woman with an eye honed by seven years of prison. The espadrilles looked relaxed and low-key, but the tiny gold button screamed designer. The jeans were only available in someplace with the word *boutique* in its name. The blouse was cotton but fitted. Her makeup and hair were a minimum of an hour to get the right casual look. Her skin and features said Asian or Mexican, but the rest was all pampered city—but not Southern California. Jolie guessed Midwest or eastern seaboard—Baltimore or Atlanta.

Jolie's gaze slid back to the young man now kicking nervously at the dirt. "Manuel, why don't you go show Sydney the barn and feed Baby. Or at least make her eat some oats. Rose and I'll be in the kitchen getting some coffee. Take your time. And don't let her touch anything that might hurt her."

Manuel knew he was dismissed but also let off the hook. He turned and took the girl by the arm.

"But I don't want to go see some smelly old barn…"

He leaned in with his face angry next to her ear as he kept walking her toward the barn. "Hush. Do everything you're told before Rocket turns her dog loose. Don't you complain or whine or snivel like a spoiled little girl. If you haven't gotten it yet, your life depends on you fitting in here." The girl glanced back with large eyes at the scary woman with the scarier dog.

Jolie turned toward the door. "Coffee's in here… unless you need to also grab your purse." She watched the reflection in the one window as she took a slow step. The woman hesitantly reached out to the SUV's door and then drew it back. Jolie resumed her normal ground-gobbling gait.

In the kitchen, with her eyes watching the reflection in the side of the toaster, she carefully measured the recommended spoonful's of coffee grounds into the coffeemaker and pushed the button. Turning, she studied the woman standing inches from the other side of the doorway. She was uncertain and guarded. She glanced back into the large living room. Then her eyes swept the floor of the kitchen and small, empty dining room with only four rough stools at the counter.

Jolie leaned back against the counter. Her voice was slightly gravelly from too much dust the last few days. But then, this wasn't a time for the voice of a debutante either. "Pink is out watching the kids. Making sure they don't get into trouble. Sit."

The woman hurried just a bit too fast to do as she was told. Jolie thought about where she had seen the response before. In prison. The tiny younger prisoner nicknamed

Mouse came to mind. If any of the white gang barked, she whimpered. Jolie's cellmate, Mary, had explained the beating, taking of food, rape by mop or broom handle, and lesbian sexual abuse until she was compliant and cowed.

At the sound of the final bubbling of the coffee into the pot, Jolie removed her hat and set it flat on the counter. The brim darkly spread nearly front to back. Opening the cupboard, Jolie brought down two hand-thrown earthen-ware mugs. She had bought them when the potter took three standard white restaurant mugs and poured them into one of his. There was still plenty of room for cream. She bought his entire table full and asked about plates. If one broke, there were boxes more.

She filled the mugs and placed one in front of the woman, whose eyes hadn't stopped bouncing all over the room. As calm as she appeared, her eyes gave away how afraid she was.

"I don't drink coff—"

"I didn't ask if you did. It's not poisoned, and there's the cream and sugar. If you need the fake city sugar, the nearest store is eleven miles back down the road."

The woman only flinched at the two words *city* and *fake*. But her pupils dilated as she realized their isolation. "I didn't mean to be—"

Jolie cut her off. "Look. Let's get one thing straight. The only thing that counts right now is honesty. Manuel called and warned us he was bringing trouble. That's all we know. Since you arrived, I can only go on what I see. I'm guessing you aren't any kind of blood to him. I know his background, where he grew up, how he grew up, the trouble he got into, and the prison time he served. He's a great kid. He works hard and is a straight shooter. He's turned his entire world around. But a couple of years ago, he didn't know me, but he put his life on the line for me. I owe him. I'm guessing you now have your life in his hands… and he's getting ready to drop you in my lap. So, let's start with who you really are."

The woman hesitated. She thought for a moment and finally heaped a few spoons of sugar into the coffee and stirred slowly. Finally, she filled the last inch of the tall mug with cream. Removing the spoon, she looked where to put it.

Jolie pointed at the counter. "We don't stand on Chaucer's Points of Etiquette around here—but the counter gets scrubbed clean many times a day. We live on this counter. We roll dough here. I butcher animals here. I haven't slaughtered a human here, but also none have died on it." The implied *yet* hung in the air.

The woman put the spoon down silently. "Thank you." Her left eye winced at the still bitter taste.

"It takes a bit getting used to. If you're here past today, we can get you some tea in town."

Rose put down the mug. "No. It's fine. It's been a while since…" She looked up at Jolie. "Since I grew up in Boyle Heights. East Los Angeles. I used to steal sips out of my father's mug. He was what they called a roughneck. He worked on the oil wells and pumps around Los Angeles. He had a fourth-grade education and then went to work doing anything to help feed his family in Mexico. When his mother died, his father fell apart and into a bottle. He had eight hundred dollars for the coyote to bring him to the United States. He heard if you joined the army and volunteered for

Vietnam, they would give him citizenship. They never did. But he worked hard until the day he died."

Jolie watched over the brim of her mug, studying the woman through the steam. "But you're not Manuel's aunt."

The woman paused and looked hard at Jolie. "Why is this only a one-way street?" The insertion of spine was hesitant.

Jolie put down the mug. "What do you want to know?"

"You said Manny put himself at risk for you two years ago…"

Jolie nodded at the easy answer. "I was fresh out of prison. He gave me a gun."

"He wouldn't do that."

"There were reasons."

"Where did he get the gun?"

Jolie smiled at the game. She had played it for keeps in prison. This was the kind of game children play before it counts, with lives being lost or saved. "You're not his aunt."

The woman sat back. Her fingers were pinched at her lips as she thought. "Did you know he has a sister?"

Jolie nodded. "She's up in Vacaville, I think."

The pulse in the pupil told Jolie the woman hadn't known where. But she knew about the sister.

"We were like sisters. We met in the third grade. If the nuns hit one hand, they hit both of our hands. We were trouble for each other from the start. When we were in the eighth grade, we were shoplifting and selling pot. When we were fourteen, we boosted the nuns' station wagon and drove it to the beach. By the time we were sixteen, we would give hand jobs to construction workers for a fast twenty. The next summer, we learned what a fifty looked like and how to give a blow job. After school, we drifted about, picking up money and having a great time, until one night a guy tried to rape her."

Jolie nodded. Her voice was husky and low. "Is that the guy she killed?"

The woman's eyes darted to Jolie and around the room, looking for a safe answer. "It's why she's…"

Jolie sipped on her coffee. Rolling the mug between her hands on the tabletop, she ignored the unspoken truth. "But that was more than twenty years ago."

The woman's face hardened. "Justice isn't the same for someone who doesn't have blond hair and blue eyes."

"What did she get?"

"Twenty to life."

Jolie had heard the same story several ways. "And when she got jumped in prison…?"

"Aggravated homicide."

"She expanded to life." Jolie's lips rolled tight.

"What were you in for?"

"Murder. I served seven."

Rose rolled her head, evaluating the other woman. The hard lines on her face and hands hadn't come with just age and working horses. It was the kind of aging she had worked to avoid. "Did you do it?"

Jolie's eyes turned to lines of pure Rocket. The anger was still there, just below the surface. "Twelve people in this valley thought so."

"But did you…?"

Rocket took a long, smooth pull on her mug until her heart rate calmed. Jolie softly set the mug down and smiled as she cocked her head. "How did you get out?" Both knew she was talking about the life of prostitution.

The woman sighed. "When I was twenty, I was doing a call. One out-of-town businessman became a regular. It wasn't long before he wanted to meet outside of work. He took me back to Atlanta and set me up in an apartment, but I wanted more. I'd seen that movie with others. You're the kept woman until a younger one comes along." Her voice faltered and softened. "Eventually, I got more."

Jolie nodded her head toward the barn. "Sydney."

The woman rocked and looked down at her hands in her lap, the thumbnail flicking on the other. Her voice was as soft as the waves in her black hair. "Sydney."

Jolie sensed the woman would need more of her Jolie side rather than the hard-pounding Rocket. It was time for some fresh air.

Jolie stood. "I've gotta pee, and then I need to go walk a horse. Why don't we continue this outside?" She pointed through the living room. "There's a bathroom straight down the hall."

She left the woman at the counter and went upstairs. She didn't know why, but she felt naked under her T-shirt. As she topped the stairs, she heard the stool scrape the floor. It's hard work facing your past, but she figured the woman had come this far…

7

WHERE ARE WE?

Jolie watched Rose's face from the corner of her eye. They rounded the barn, and Stonewall stood dark charcoal in all his glory. The white blaze down his nose matched the blaze on his chest. Everything else was a deep gray down to his black hocks and hooves. Even the thick shoes were quenched black to match his hooves.

The horse wasn't vain, but Jolie thought it was worth the extra hundred to have matching shoes. She would have worked extra jobs to do the same for any of her horses back in the day if she had known about it.

"Holy mother of…"

Jolie snorted. "Nope. Stonewall is all male. Well, what's left of him, that is."

Rose turned with a frown. "Stonewall, as in Stonewall Jackson?"

Jolie smiled. "Nope. As in the stone wall of Hadrian that divides England and Scotland. Hadrian had it built to stop the Scots from jumping the wall on their tiny Shetland ponies. Years later, during the wars between the two, the English knights on their giant Friesian war horses found they couldn't jump over the wall either. So, where the foot soldiers could scamper over any part of the great stone wall, the knights had to ride through the passages every mile or so. It stonewalled any large-scale formal attacks at the border."

Rose wagged her head at the gentle giant lowering his head to Jolie's hands. "He's as big as those horses on the Budweiser commercials."

The black hat tipped. "Nope. The Clydesdales are commonly a couple of hands taller. They're called dray or draft horses. Dray means wagon. And that is also their job—they pull wagons. They are also too wide across the back to ride comfortably, even for a tall man. But they bred the Friesians short and stocky to carry the knight and his armor, which, with the horse armor and tack, was usually close to four hundred pounds."

Jolie opened the gate, and the horse joined them. She turned and started walking with the horse following. After a few yards, she stopped and looked back at the other woman. "Are you coming with us?"

Rose blinked a few times. "Are you going to put a leash or whatever it's called on him?"

"Why?" She turned to pet the side of the massive jaw. "He knows I'm going for a walk. He can either come with me or go back to the corral. He's bored in the corral, so the better of the two is to come take a walk with me."

The horse turned his head to look at the other woman.

Jolie snorted softly. "He wants to know if you're coming with us or not."

Rose moved. "Where are we going?"

Jolie bumped the brim of her hat up the hill. "Back two."

"Back to where?"

"Nope. Walking on the back two miles. We have to stay where the trail is soft on his feet."

Rose had caught up and looked up at the large head. "He's got delicate feet?"

Jolie stopped and thought. She wondered if the woman had ever been around any animal in her life and figured not. She leaned in next to Stonewall's front leg, patted him low, and then held up the hoof between her legs. The shoe was the size of a dinner plate. She scraped her thumb to clean out around the frog in the middle. "This lump is soft. It's called a frog, but to us horse people, we know it as the horse's second heart. When they step, the frog compresses, and the blood in it pushes back up his leg. Each step is another push. It's like a heartbeat, except it does what his heart can't do, pump the blood back up his legs to his body. So, the heart sends the blood around and down the leg…"

Rose smiled. "And the frog pumps it back up to the heart."

Jolie smiled and let the leg ease back down. "Right. But this big guy's frogs are excessively sensitive. So we gave him the special thicker shoes. We walk him to get him used to the higher shoes, and we hope he adjusts to the feel of walking enough to carry a rider."

"What if he doesn't like it?"

Jolie shrugged her face. "He bucks and then kicks. He broke the last owner's hip. Knocked him off the back and kicked him in midair. They thought it was the corral post he went through that broke his butt, but the surgeon saw the horseshoe bruise right where he needed to cut."

Rose's hand elevatored up and down. "And here he is, following you like a puppy."

Jolie turned on her heel. "Horses are smart. You can show them your sweetest side, but they can also sense the other side."

"If he didn't behave, would you beat him?"

Rocket stopped. Her teeth clenched tightly. "No animal deserves to be hit." She turned and walked.

The silence was thick as they walked. Rose followed slightly behind Jolie but away from the dark beast.

As they neared the crest where a large live oak spread near the edge of the cliff, Jolie glanced back. Rose's jaw hung wearily to one side. She wasn't panting, but the armpits on her blouse were darkening. Jolie was sure she hadn't shown this reaction to exercise in many years.

Jolie stopped near the tree that shaded the crest. She leaned into Stonewall's head and muttered at his nose. The horse moved slightly and started cropping at the dried grass.

Jolie smiled at Rose. "This is his favorite time. I take a rest, and he gets to eat." She stepped under the large branch and into the depth of the shade. The heat only came under the tree during the hottest times of the late summer. She sunk to the ground and leaned against the gnarled trunk.

She removed her hat as the other woman timidly joined her on the sparse dry grass. Nothing lush grew in the deep shadow. Jolie lightly held the brim with the fingertips of both hands. The other edge curled slightly at her boots. Her chest filled with a mix of memories. All the good times growing up, coming to this tree with her father and at least a half-dozen dogs, throwing the hard red ball for the black mastiff, carrying young puppies, who tired on the way up, only to be packed back down in a makeshift shirt sling, her childhood had been about her father, the dogs, and the meaning of family. Even the hard times carrying a shovel while her father carried the rifle, all her life seemed focused around this tree—even getting shot by her best friend the year before. It all seemed like a full circle. It was where she drew her strength.

"Penny for your thoughts…"

Jolie didn't even flinch. She kept her eyes on the thin curl of smoke across the valley. It was the winery burning down the logs to coals before burying the pig for a strange cowboy luau. She knew probably nobody else in the valley could see the smoke, but from more than a few miles, she could. Her father had taught her how.

She growled softly, clearing her throat. "Pick up that acorn near your right foot."

Rose leaned over and picked the nut from the ground. She held it up. "How did you know there was a nut there?"

Jolie rippled her brow and slowly ground her head around. "Seriously? Look again. What if I had said to pick up two dozen nuts?"

Rose looked with a new sight. "Oh." She now could see the ground was all nuts. This year's layer lay on top of last year's and those over the previous year's. She turned back, holding the nut she chose. "What about this nut?"

"Throw it."

"Where?"

"Anywhere you want."

Jolie watched the nut land about twenty feet past where Stonewall was cropping the grass as she thought about the shovel. It was a new one. Her grandfather's shovel had worn with the years and finally broke. It now hung from the metal on the wall of Dot's blacksmithing shop. Dot honored the soul of the old steel and the generations it had worked.

Jolie took a deep breath and let it out slowly through her nose. "That would be Hondo. He was mostly an English mastiff with some rottweiler and Pitbull mixed in, maybe. He would always go for a locked jaw grip on a pig's snout. First in and last off. He was close to two hundred pounds but would still take the fight to a boar three times his size. He was just over thirteen. He had passed quietly near the front door during the night. It was the only time I saw my father cry. He told me to get the new shovel. And then he kneeled and lifted Hondo, draping him on his shoulders, and carried him the whole way—never stopping. Mom followed. She didn't cook or clean or nothing for almost a week."

"Pigs…?"

Jolie twitched and looked over. "European wild boars. These hills are full of them. They survive on those nuts. We hunted them for meat on the table, same as you go to the supermarket."

"But you said they were… That would make them six hundred pounds."

Rocket smiled her broad, rodeo-winning smile. Her front teeth would make most horses proud—the pearls were pure shining glory.

She nodded and spoke. "Yup. My father took me hunting for my sixteenth birthday. He was hoping for something easy, like two or three hundred pounds. What we found was a couple of suckling pigs about thirty or forty pounds. The dogs jumped and tied them up. Dad just stepped in and slit their throats. But while Dad was kneeling and skinning them out, Hondo triggered. Hondo was never wrong. He spun and faced the brush. I grabbed the pig knife out of the sheath on my dad's back and turned just as the mother broke through. The other dogs hit—but were too late. Only Hondo was ready and took the nose. The pig was already at her stride and moving like a freight train. I squatted in the stance. As Hondo and the head moved past, I buried the knife into the lower shoulder. Stepping on the handle, I went over the top. But the knife levered through her heart—cutting it in half. Her tusk hit the dirt and cut a trough for three feet. She stopped less than a hand width from my father's foot." Jolie leaned back against the tree. "We packed her all out. Dad wanted a correct weight. She was six-seventy-eight. Her guts were another thirty or so. It was the biggest pig ever killed with only dogs and a knife."

Rose's eyes shaded in disbelief. "What kind of knife?"

Jolie's hand and arm flashed through the air as she leaned forward. Sixteen inches of silvery steel floated in the air. Jolie studied Rose's enlarged eyes and the flash of fear. The woman paled from her throat to the shine in her black hair. "You can ask Dot at lunch. Her father and mine designed it. It's not shaped like a Bowie and too fat for a dirk… so I don't really know. But it works great on pigs."

She fed it back under her shirt and leaned back. "Throw

another nut. I haven't done this in years. It's good to remember where you're from."

The nut landed. Jolie laughed. "Whiskey. Great donkey but walked like it was drunk."

Rose flipped a nut with her thumb. It landed between them and the edge of the cliff. Jolie got quiet. "Blue. Pure Australian cattle dog. He went for one last lunge after my father had called them off. He was in the way of the bullet. The rifle jammed with the next round, and my father drew the knife. It was his first knife kill and the last time he carried a rifle. If Hondo had his heart, Blue had his soul. I think that was the only year we ever bought meat. Dad just couldn't bring himself to hunt without his buddy."

"But you don't seem sad talking about all these buried dogs and a donkey. Why? How?"

Jolie harrumphed softly. "Hell, this is the happiest place on earth." She pointed just past her left foot. "Dad is there. Mom is out in the sunshine because she always liked it there. Grandpa and grandma are on the other side of the tree. She liked the east, so they get to look at where she came from. Hell, even that cliff has its happy part." Jolie kicked out her right foot. "I was just about there when my best friend shot me. I lost my footing and stumbled out there and over the cliff. The wall brush, dirt, and sticks tore me up, but they also slowed me down. But the time I was at the bottom, I lay covered by the cliff, and she didn't get a clean second shot."

Rose was gawping at the air. "That… well, that can't be true. Where did she shoot you?" She stood and stepped close to the edge. "That's… that's…"

Jolie stood and started unbuttoning her shirt. "Yup. About

eighty feet." She slipped her shirt off. Rose could see the harness over the sports bra. Jolie turned around so the woman could see the massive scar from the reconstruction. She also knew the masses of scars from her years of riding rodeo stood out too. Sometimes a visual was the most convincing statement.

"Holy…"

"The bullet entered just left of my spine. A 30-30 bullet is soft lead and slow. It cracked my scapula but slid across and blew my shoulder apart. I only survived because of who I had become, my future boyfriend Punchy, and my longtime friend, Manuel's boss, Mike. You'll meet Mike at dinner." She pulled the shirt back up and started buttoning.

"Do you wear the knife all the time?"

Jolie shrugged her eyes and rolled her head. "Depends." She leaned over and recovered her hat. She flipped it onto her head and started walking. "Come on, Stone."

As they walked, Jolie stopped and picked up a rock that fit her hand. She bounced it a few times to adjust it and figure out how she wanted to throw it. She finally skipped it through the air underhanded. Her hand was already pointing as the rock hit the large bush. There was an explosion as a dozen quail flew out. Jolie laughed to watch them fly.

"Do you hunt them?"

Jolie looked around, laughing. "For food? You get three ounces of meat, a pound of bones, and five or six pellets of buckshot and a chipped tooth." She snorted and smiled. "I'll show you tonight at sundown. Them chuckers are much more fun to just feed." Jolie chose the level trail. It would give Rose a rest. "So, what happened back east?"

Rose paused and looked around at the ground. Finally, she found an acorn from a few years before. She held it up for Jolie to see.

"It's an old acorn…"

Rose threw it as hard as she could up the trail they were on. She looked at Jolie.

"This is the demarcation trail. It runs across the middle of my property. It separates the lower hectares from the upper hectares."

Rose smirked with a snort. "How many of those hectares in each?"

Jolie knew the woman couldn't see her one eyebrow raise. She hadn't asked what a hectare was. "About five hundred in each. There's a little more in the uppers than the lowers."

Rose worried her lower lip. "So, you're saying you own four-square miles. Thereabout."

Jolie had a distinct feeling there was butt-sniffing going on. She dipped the tip of her hat. "You've heard of a homestead?"

"Sure. It's a mile square or a square mile. The government checkerboarded the railroad right-of-way with them. Selling the homesteads paid to build the railroads. California history in the fourth grade." Jolie continued for Rose with what schools didn't teach. "And every twentieth mile, the squares were two on one side and two on the other. If they laid the railroad, they built a station in the center. This trail would have been cut for the railroad. Half of the township would be downhill, and the rich folk would be uphill for the better view."

"But it didn't make it?"

Jolie turned and pointed across the valley. "See the one hump of a hill that seems bluer than the rest?"

"Just to the left of the smoke?" Rose nodded.

Jolie smiled at the woman seeing the smoke. "At the base of that hill, the rich hacienda owner paid off the officials to bring the railroad to him. He paid to build two rail spurs. One to his ranchero and livestock, and the other to the village of Buellton. My grandfather paid less for this township than he would have had to pay for a homestead over there."

"Why not just buy a homestead over this side? Who needs this much land?" She looked around. "You don't even do anything with it."

Jolie's smile pulled back almost to her ear. No teeth were showing. In her rodeo days, this was when most smart cowboys got up and left the bar or knew they were about to lose a roping competition.

Jolie turned up the trail. Stonewall followed feet from her back. "So, again, what happened back east?"

8

UNTIED

"It all came untied."

Jolie looked back. "What did?"

"Everything." Rose threw up her arms and spread her hands. "His business, our marriage, our friends, everything I thought was great and wonderful. And then there was Sydney."

"Husband…"

"Stanley. Sydney's father. He made an honest woman out of me between my water breaking and Sydney showing up. It was a two-minute business deal. Sign here, here, and there." She rolled her lower lip and then spat as if she had eaten something foul.

Jolie glanced at the sound but kept walking. "Was there ever any romance?"

"Some… but not particularly. Not the kind you read in romance novels or see in movies."

The black hat tilted up and then resumed the flat. "There never is. It's a lie. Even people deeply in love with each other don't act like those in books and movies. It's like summer rain in the night. You must be listening. It's the soft dance on the tin roof, not the thunder and lightning."

"You've been there…"

Jolie stopped at two large rocks outcropping from the side of the track. "We call these boulders the two lovers. They never say a thing to each other. They never touch. But they know through hell, high water, sunshine, fire, or the dead of night the other is there beside them."

Rose leaned her thigh against the one stone. "Yeah… kind of like that."

"So why are you running from it?"

"Because I know everything." Her head hung as she ran her finger over the stone. "I did the books for his business. He's a contractor and developer." She looked up shyly. "That's why I knew what a hectare is and how many to a mile. We did a development once with 250 hectares."

"That's a big development. How many houses?"

"It wasn't. It was all commercial land for car parts manufacturing. They cluster and share labor and shipping." Rose combed her hands through her thick head of hair. "I think that's when it all started getting sketchy."

"How so?"

Rose looked out across the valley. "This is a beautiful view. You're right. The rich folk would build up the hill, but their homes would get more wind and storms. Your grandfather chose well to build down there in the shelter."

Jolie threw her right leg over the other stone and wiggled into a comfortable seat. "Sketchy." This was the conversation she needed.

Rose blinked and looked at Jolie. She rolled her lips in resolution and mounted the rock. "With that development, we started cooking the books. By the end, we were running three sets of books. The ones we could show the IRS, the ones we could show his partners, and the actual set. After that, I knew I needed to have copies of all the sets." She looked up, her face hardened. Jolie had seen the look in prison—resolve.

"So this is about the business? Is he asking for a divorce?"

Rose held out her hands in a stop. "Easy there, cowboy. We haven't even got close to the fun stuff yet."

Jolie pushed at her hat just above her forehead. It moved back. "So, the business is only the start?"

She nodded. "A guy named Alex Nyack owned the property we developed. Stanley and Alex became best buddies. Three or four nights a week, Stanley would call from Alex's country club or a nightclub or who knows where. They were, in his words, out talking business. If there were other women involved, I didn't really care. By then, he was sleeping most nights in the pool house, close to the liquor and where he could come home late without disturbing Sydney or me."

Jolie took off her hat and looked out at the transparent curl of smoke in the distance. "Many people drink more than they should."

"Yes, but do they kill people?"

Rocket's head snapped around. But what she saw was not an accusation but a tired confession. "Kill?"

Rose shrugged her eyes and face. "Alex got Stanley interested in paintball. I went a few times, but soon it was time at the club's shooting range. What started as a drawer full of pistols soon became a refrigerator-sized gun safe. Next, he tore out a section of the basement to build a safe room filled with everything up to machine guns and an RPG or two."

Jolie frowned. "RPG?"

Rose's lips rolled in disgust as her hand waved at the air. "Missile things they fire from their shoulders. They kill tanks and trucks and stuff with them. Every action movie these days has at least one. It's why he got one." Her hands drew quotation marks in the air. "Because he saw one in a movie and thought it was cool."

"And this was because he was a developer?"

Rose picked at something on her pants and then dusted them off. She glanced back at Stonewall, cropping at some green grass he had found. "When you develop property, and the project is in the tens of millions or hundreds of million dollars, and you're cooking the books, the skimming can easily be a million that has to go somewhere. At one time, the gun safe was half-full of bricks of hundred-dollar bills. Each brick was a hundred thousand dollars.

"One evening when I knew he was out of town, I counted it. There were three and a half-million dollars in the safe alone. There were only five pistols he had probably forgotten were in there. The new gun safe was a room twenty by twenty in the basement. He was rapidly filling the walls, drawers, racks, and chests. I think the value of the stacks of money had become chump change. But while my husband was arming for World War Three, Sydney was starting junior high school. The social requirements of the right school, right country club, right sport, and proper families to associate with were growing. And the books were becoming even more complicated, and I needed help."

Jolie put her hat back on. Adjusting the brim, she thought out loud. "I don't suppose you could hire just any accountant to take over."

Rose softly snorted as she flicked her long hair back over her shoulder. "Alex to the rescue."

Jolie scratched at her arm. "I think I see where this is going."

"Ha." Rose's bark was vapid. "Not in your wildest dreams. The club wasn't enough for the boys. Next came the camp up in the Smokies. At first, it was just a camp to play soldier, dress up in camouflage, and wear guns. Then there was the serious militia factor and the whole prepper issue. But worrying about zombies and the coming apocalypse wasn't enough for Stanley and Alex—they wanted to hunt. And I don't mean deer or pigs. So they bought an even more remote tract of land. Something more like ten times this size. They wanted to shoot something and never be heard."

"What were they hunting?"

There was real fear in Rose's dark eyes. Jolie had seen it in prison also. She had even seen it in the stainless-steel sheet passing for a mirror.

Rose swallowed hard. This was the cliff. The leap of faith. The trust in what Manuel had told her was her only salvation. "It started with homeless people. But people who are starving and beaten down by life have little fight left in them. You might as well do them a favor and just shoot them to end the misery. They even tried feeding them and training them, but it didn't work. They still just walked out in the bush and stood until they were killed.

"Next on their list were runaways. Alex and a few of the guys liked the young girls turning tricks blocks from where they got off the bus to the city. They would have their way with them and then see what they had in the forest. Some had more grit than they had bargained. But in the end, it was just a chase of an hour or so—just no sport."

Jolie felt the cold sweat run down her spine. "They wanted a threat more like themselves, but still a canned hunt."

Rose drew her rolled lips back, almost white, as she dipped her head. "They skipped college athletes because they were too high profile, and some had kids of their own."

The black hat tipped up on the right side. "Let's see. Athletic, trained, but not all that smart. Not the typical person you find at the regular bars."

Rose rocked. "And that is where I drew the line. Alex had connections for girls from Haiti and Mexico. They were already turning tricks when he got them. They just needed better driver's licenses to make them able to go into the bars. What dumb country boy doesn't want to try a colored girl? Once they had them back at the house and away from friends, they drugged them, and Alex took over."

Jolie checked her watch. She knew Dot was back by now and would want lunch. She slid off the rock. "What did you do?"

"Stupidly, I went to the FBI there in Atlanta. If I'd been thinking straight, I would have gone up to D.C. or anywhere but Atlanta. But… I didn't know how the system worked. Or, at least, how deep their connections went."

Jolie snorted. "Connections." She waved for her to follow.

Rose jumped off the rock and dusted off her pants. "Connections. I promised them evidence of everything. I even gave them copies of records, enough to prove my worth. They promised to put Sydney and me in the witness protection program if I testified. I moved some funds around offshore because, by now, I was an expert at it. And then about a month ago, while Stanley was away with Alex, we ran."

Jolie reached back and rubbed the enormous nose of Stonewall plodding along behind them. "But if you weren't involved with the camps and such, how did you have evidence?"

The short chuff broke Rose's stride. "If you turn on a light, you need power. You either install solar power and all the equipment, or you call Georgia Power. If you go off-grid, which they did a lot, every panel, inverter, rack, battery, and screw creates a receipt. If you pay Georgia Power, you get a receipt. If you buy a thousand gallons of diesel fuel, you get a receipt. If you got receipts for one price but paid another and a bribe, you got two receipts with three records in the multiple books. We were using Alex's bookkeepers, but Stanley only trusted me to review all the books and keep the control books only he saw. I made copies of everything."

She looked in the air with her head cocked as she recalled numbers.

"A battery bank of a hundred twenty-four-volt deep-cycle batteries sells for just over ten thousand dollars. But if you shop around for rebuilt batteries, you can skim a few thousand off the top. Fifty thousand for a top-of-the-line new array, but cycled-out utility panels can trim the cost in half. Mexican girls are worth five thousand, but Haitian girls the same age are only two. And the list goes on and on. Half of my time was to find how and where Stanley could cheat his partners, customers, and the IRS. The FBI showed more interest in the money than the trafficked girls or soldiers hunted. It was obvious from the start—nobody cared about the several dozen homeless taken off the streets."

Jolie pointed at the branch in the trail leading down the hill. "So, what was the problem with the Atlanta FBI? I mean, don't they have to report to the main office or something?"

"At the office, everything was good. Except I should have figured something was wrong when there was more interest in the figures of how Stanley was cheating his partners. It wasn't until we disappeared when the problem showed up."

"But you were with the FBI, weren't you?"

"Sure, but that was the problem. They put us up in a safe house out in the Okefenokee Swamp just south of Waycross. In theory, it should've been safe. But I also knew there was a camp less than fifty miles away down in Du Pont. One agent kept getting text messages supposedly from his wife. They weren't. They were from the camp across the swamp. One night at dinner, I slipped some Visine in their waters. While they were leapfrogging each other the next day for the toilet, I peeked at his cell phone. The stupid ass didn't even have it pass protected beyond passing his finger down the screen. I had done the same the day before, and it opened. The text messages were from one of Alex and Stanley's friends. They were coming in an airboat. When the boat arrived, Sydney chopped a hole in the other boat, and we stole the airboat. We've been running ever since."

Jolie stuck her fingers in her mouth and whistled. A series of sharp chirping whistles returned. Stonewall nudged his way through the women and headed down the trail to a reward of oats and hay. Jolie laughed as she glanced at Rose. "Men. All you have to do is mention food, and they come running."

The two chuckled at the truth. Jolie squinted over with a frown. "So, you're across the country in a stolen FBI car… how did you get to Santa Barbara?"

"We ran to the Hidden Coast in Florida. It's a series of islands off the southern coast near Pensacola. But I dumped the car at a chop shop in Jacksonville. I'd used them before, but Stanley thought we just dropped cars in the ocean."

Jolie laughed. "He taught you about skimming but never guessed you could skim him too?"

Rose chuckled and smiled evilly at Jolie. "There was a lot that man had no idea—like Manuel. You were right. We aren't related. So as far as Stanley knows, I don't have any more family after my mother died. I only knew I still had family because I would get an occasional Christmas card, even when he was in jail. When he got out, I reached out from a friend's phone and then mailed him some money to get him started."

"How did you get from Florida to California without Stanley tracking you?"

"There's a drug runner on Santa Rosa Island. He runs to Mexico all the time. He has a long-range seaplane. He flew us to Galveston, and then I bought a truck with cash. It's still registered to my elderly uncle Festus Pomeroy in Galveston. Last I saw, the key was in it, parked on Figueroa Street near the Jimmy Dean sausage plant. It probably hit Mexico before dark. Chevy trucks are popular down in the truck farms." She winked at Jolie.

Jolie rocked back with a bark. "Shit, ol' Stanley never had a chance."

"Nope." She pulled a small phone out of her back pocket. "I bought this burner in East Los Angeles. A hundred bucks. It doesn't text, but it came with two hours of untraceable airtime..." She looked at the screen. "Damn, no service. The FBI took away my cell phone when we ran. They told me they didn't want it traced... Little did I know it wouldn't matter anyway."

Jolie opened the back door. "I was wondering why a teenager didn't have a cell phone glued to her hand and nose."

Rose rolled her eyes. "She's been missing her friends a lot. The problem is those friend's fathers are Stanley and Alex's friends."

As they stepped through the back door of the house, the voice was more of a bark. "About time. My stomach thinks my throat's been cut."

Jolie swung her hat at the freckled face. "Rose, this is Dot, my partner on this spread and the person responsible for most of the ironwork around here. Dot, Rose, Manuel's aunt."

Dot reached out her hand. "I met your daughter already. I had to explain how to use a pitchfork."

Rose raised an eyebrow as she shied her face. "She touched a pitchfork or just pitched a fit?"

Dot smiled as they shook. "Pink be behind her, growling. Not really. She just grabbed da tools and open dem stalls like it be old school. She be mucking stalls and brushing down horseflesh since."

Rose's eyes were huge. "This I want to see."

"Well, call 'em in. We 'bout ready to throw burgers at the grill." She leaned over, sniffed Jolie, then wrinkled her face. "Eww. You done gone skanky. I needs ta hose you down."

Jolie rubbed her middle finger along her nose. "We walked Stonewall up to the tree and across the break trace. Good for him, and good for us."

Manuel and Sydney came through the back door. Rose turned and put her arm around her daughter's shoulder. "Hi, honey. How…" Her face crumpled into revulsion. "What did you fall into?"

Sydney grumped. "Horseshit. Is lunch ready?"

Dot pointed the large restaurant-sized spatula at the girl and Jolie. "No. Flat-assed no. You two go shower now." She pointed at Rose. "If 'n you walked wid Stonewall and Rocket… you take one too. Lunch be in twenty minutes. Now scat." She waved the steel blade around in the air. Then her gaze landed on Manuel.

Laughing, he raised both hands in self-defense and then put his finger over his lips as he leaned to watch the young girl walk back toward the distant bathroom. Finally, he lowered his hands and closed on Dot. "I supervised Sydney. There's no way I was getting close to all the horseshit. I've smelled you two after a day of only tending to the horses."

He leaned against the counter. "But I've got to give credit where credit is due. The last time I saw them, she was just a spoiled brat. So, either this shit they're in has her in shock, or she is starting to grow up."

Dot glanced back over her shoulder. "She's how old?"

"Seventeen."

Dot chuffed and then laughed. "Dude, you was womaned. She be the same little shit you remember. She played you."

He shrugged and raised his eyebrows as his head leaned. "Maybe. But those stalls are clean and scrubbed. I told her they used to be racehorses. They're used to the muck taken out, swept, then mopped, and finally, fresh straw layered in two inches evenly. She then brushed each of them down before she put them back."

Dot lowered one eyelid. "She gots horse back home?"

He reached for a strip of kimchi-pickled zucchini, and the spatula came down flat. He withdrew. Holding his hand, he looked at Dot's mischievous black eyes. "I don't know, but she had to have learned that attention to detail somewhere. She mentioned something about a horse camp or something."

Dot pointed the spatula at the food with a warning look on her face. "One, you gets one, just one zukki or I sick Pink on yo' ass."

Manuel snatched his bounty and nibbled. "Yes, ma'am."

9

PLANS

The evening's fire glowed like a dim memory in the embers. Only the stars and distant lights of cars coming through the pass invaded the dark. Most of the talk finished a while before.

The long-faded bib overalls struck Rose above the ankle and the small tattoo. Even the rubber barn boots hadn't fit her. Jolie gave her credit for walking into the barn and forge area barefoot. She had been right about the simple little espadrilles and the boutique they came from. It was a far cry from the Broken Ride Acres. Thank goodness for the stretchiness of T-shirts.

Jolie and Rose had snickered at the T-shirt Sydney picked out of Dot's stack. Some had burned holes that could probably sell on Rodeo Drive in Beverly Hills if it weren't for the sentiment printed on the shirt. The entire stack was swag from her years of championship fighting in the mixed martial arts, some clean enough to wear to town, but most offensive enough to only appear in the forge area. Those who bought Dot's swords and knives understood the edgy art and sentiments of her shirts.

Sydney's choice touted an event called The Brick Stack. The graphic was a solidly built outhouse. Jolie and Rose both knew the young girl's chances of privilege knowing what it was were slim to none. The over-the-knee spandex fighting tights were thick and durable but stretchy enough to fit the young girl snugly. Her thighs and gluteus maximus were smaller, but she was taller than Dot.

Sydney jumped at Dot's comment on fit and a slap on her butt. Or, as Dot put it, the moneymaking muscle. If Dot's legs got a lock on an opponent's neck, upper chest, or arms—one dot from her fist and the fight was over.

The only standard part of the leggings was the MMA regulations. Dot was glad to see the leggings come into style as streetwear. The only clothes she had more of than fight leggings were offensive T-shirts.

Mike sighed and opened his eyes. "Those steaks were perfect." His head rolled to Dot. "Your mother can send you more of that rub, or I'll drive down to Glendale and pick it up, anytime."

Dot laughed. "Mike, you be cute and all, but you also be stone-head dumb. Dat rub ain't momma's recipe. Dat be pure Haitian rip-out-your-neck-and-grab-your-tongue Voodoo. Princess's husband stole the fixin's from his grandmother, a true Voodoo goddess. She buried seven husbands, and each married to her fo' over twenty happy years."

"That would make her over one hundred fifty or sixty years old." Rose frowned her a jaundiced eye. "I call bullshit."

Dot roared as she slapped Mike on the chest. "See. Dat white people monopoly crap rub off on people like Rose. We need to move in and live in sin, so it jus' stop." She leaned forward and looked at the ghostly visage in the low glow of embers. "Nobody ever say nothin' 'bout her getting a dee-vorce. No, ma'am. Dat be one big happy house."

Rose turned to where Jolie had curled into Punchy hunkered down into the oversized chair. Only a low rolling growl of a snore gave proof he was alive. "She's not playing fair."

Jolie held up both of her palms. "Hey. Don't point that fight over here. We just be broken-down rodeo folk living in sin. Besides, I don't think I could handle a second husband. Punchy, Mike, and Manuel are enough boys in my life."

Mike raised his still almost full beer. "Hear, hear." His head flopped over to Dot. "But I might take you up on that offer of a bed for at least a night."

Dot opened her mouth to make a smart remark and then looked at his face. "Do I get to have my ways with yo' body?"

He didn't trust his voice. He nodded gently.

She reached out and rubbed his arm. She was sure he had also taken some of Jolie's Dilaudid to kill the pain in his hip. "You really needs ta get that looked at. I kin only do so much."

His lips rolled tight as his eyes closed. His nod was more of a wave of his upper body.

There were many stories about them naming the ranch Broken Rides.

Jolie nudged Punchy awake. He looked around and silently got up and went to bed. Only he and Jolie knew he needed to be up at three in the morning to drive back to Sacramento. He had stolen the afternoon to drive down for dinner and talk to Rose.

"Rose." Jolie's voice lowered as she settled down in the seat next to the woman. "I need to go work with a horse and rider over past Solvang tomorrow. If you want to come, we can pick up some clothes that will fit you better." She nodded at the bib overalls.

"Why, honey child…" Rose's voice was a breathy, terrible impression of someone trying to be Southern. "Whatever do you mean. This here gala attire is classic and haute couture."

Jolie snorted. "Yeah, it's hot *something,* all right. It was couture when my mother bought it thirty years ago."

Rose gave her one raised eyebrow. "But at least it fits my butt and thighs."

Jolie pointed at Dot's and Sydney's leggings. "So would those."

Rose growled. "Not in the deepest bowels of hell would I ever wear those twerky tights. I know they're all the rage on the West Coast and even Atlanta, but they are still nasty."

"So we'll just pick up some jeans to fit in."

Rose thought a moment. "Some work shirts would be good too. Do they still make denim shirts with snaps?"

"I think we can pick it all up at the feed store."

Rose leaned her head away from Jolie and looked at her hard. "Underwear too?"

Jolie chuffed. "Maybe not that Kevin Bacon stuff, but don't count them out. I get all my sports bras and panties there, and Punchy hasn't complained yet."

Rose looked back at the front door where he had disappeared minutes before. "That man is a sweet saint. I'm willing to bet he hasn't complained once since you two met. You don't find that very often in a cop."

"Deputy. He's a sheriff's deputy. I think he complained years ago when the calf I'd roped knocked him and the barrel he was in for a running loop. But other than that, we've had no complaints outside this recent gig he's been doing up in Sacramento."

Rose crossed her leg over the other knee. "He mentioned the teaching."

Jolie nodded. "He only has five more months up at the DOJ. He'll get his sergeant stripe out of it as well as the bump in pay. I told him I wouldn't marry him if he didn't make sergeant."

Rose leaned her head and looked through her fluttering eyelashes.

Jolie held her nose up. "A girl has to set standards, you know. I'm not marrying just any old broken-down rodeo clown that comes along."

Dot stood and helped Mike to his feet. "Come on, surfer boy. It startin' to get deep here." She leaned over to Sydney. "You in the room on da main floor. Jus' right of the toilet. You momma kin bunk upstairs. G'nite Syd. Mornin' come early when Baby start to cry."

The girl looked in horror. "You have a baby?"

Dot patted her on the shoulder. "You find out soon enough."

Manuel strolled out of the kitchen back door. There were some slices of elk steak layered with zucchini kimchi. His smile was as wide as a boy could get. He stepped off the porch and approached Dot and Mike.

She turned in the dark at the smell of the kimchi. "Dat gonna burn rat through yo gut."

His smile glowed in the dark. "Taking the boss to bed?"

Dot weaved her head. "I'm gonna be working his hip. You best take the couch in the big house. The screams don't reach in there."

He saluted with two fingers as he watched Jolie and Rose get up. Sydney looked lost. He crossed and sat next to her. He chewed on his sandwich of meat and vegetable as he thought about the looseness of this family of his.

Inside, Rose stopped Jolie at the bottom of the large log stairs. "Why did you take us in? I mean, what do you get out of it?"

Jolie turned. The small nightlights on each stair heightened the hardness of her marble-like eyes. They didn't twitch. "*¿La verdad?*"

It had been a lifetime since Rose had heard the term to tell the truth. Even in the barrio, deception was only part of discretion. "*Si.*"

Jolie blinked, slow and careful. "When I most needed someone to have my back, the people I thought did were so much smoke in the wind. I trusted in the system, like you. But twelve scared people in this valley sent me away for seven years. When I got out and proved who really killed my mother, there was still not a peep. By the end of an extremely noisy trial to send who I thought was my best friend since the third grade to prison, the last two jurors had moved. Nobody wanted to admit they had been wrong. The only person who had my back for the next seven years, and believed I was innocent, was my cellmate and now a close friend. She will never get out. She's in her sixties and has another forty-eight to serve. But I know she's in my corner. Today, up on the ridgeline, I knew you two needed someone in your corner."

Rose shifted awkwardly. "One more?"

Jolie sighed, then stifled a yawn. "Short one."

"Mike, Punchy, and Dot call you Rocket. But Manuel calls you—and you introduced yourself as—Jolie. Which is it?"

Jolie snorted as she swung her arm out large and turned the woman up the stairs. "My name is Jolie, Jolie Jet Richards. My mother had a small necklace made of jet. It's a gemstone that was originally wood. I grew up on horses and rode rodeo. Everyone earns a nickname at the rodeo. Mine was Rocket. My horse was Thunder. We used to break time records. The name stuck. But these days, I'm slower and in for the long ride. I work hard to get back to Jolie. But Rocket is still there when I need her. Sometimes she comes out leading with her mouth, and other times her attitude. Some-times it's at the wrong time, but other times…" Her voice trailed off as she waved the oversized hat in her hand.

"Hence the Broken Rides Ranch."

"Acres. Broken Rides Acres. It spells bra for a reason. There's just us women." She pointed at the two doors at the other end of the landing. "The bathroom is all yours. I made up your bed. Sydney is just under you. Sleep tight—you two are safe here."

Rose stopped at the corner newel post. She turned with her hands splayed across the top. "Jolie?"

The voice floated softly from the room with the open door. "Yeah?"

"Thanks."

Jolie stepped out. She was already down to just her sports bra and panties. She nodded. "I got ya." She stepped back through the door as if she were just a wisp of smoke.

1 0

SWAMP CAMP OMEGA

Simpson stared at the large Camp Omega sign hanging from the two tall telephone poles. He raised his right arm in a mock Nazi salute and then slapped a juicy snap with his left at the armpit sweat pond. He smirked more inwardly than he dared show his amusement. Sergeant Kunkle never had a sense of humor about body sounds. The AR-15 rocked sideways across his bulging gut. He slipped it back to the proper placement. Reaching down with both hands, he pulled his pants back up and over his watermelon-sized ass cheeks. He cringed whenever any of the officers referred to him as *Meal Team Six*. It wasn't his fault. His mother had told him that she'd had a thyroid condition when she was pregnant with him. His birth weight was only seven pounds, and he had been compensating hard since then.

"Watch the road, Meal Team." Sergeant Kunkle's voice filtered down from the high perch in the large tree.

The militia camp had many of them. Simpson had never been up. He begged off about getting spasms at heights, but everyone knew it was more a fear the ladders couldn't support his four hundred and eighty pounds.

He turned back to face the half-mile of road leading up to the camp, his mind still rolling over the meaning of Omega. He knew many of the birds and animals of the Okefenokee Swamp, but none of them called omega. The waitress at his favorite Waffle House tried to explain something about a country named Greece, but he just figured she was trying to be impressive with a bunch of bullshit.

He stood with his index finger in his nose as a large black car rapidly approached. The dust cloud behind filled the space between the stands of trees.

His finger dropped out of his nose and smeared snot on the butt of his weapon. Only when the car was a block away could he focus well enough to recognize the black Escalade of the man everyone called the commander.

Simpson stepped out of the middle of the road and pushed down on the counterweight. The barricade rose as the SUV never slowed down. The man behind the smoke-tinted windows never raised a hand or nodded his head in acknowledgment of the two men guarding the gate.

The rail-thin older man stepped out of the small guard shack, providing weather protection for the radio and phone. His head turned against the swirling dust cloud and faced the dust cloud where the black SUV had disappeared. He leaned over and spat a large gob of greasy chew. Wiping his mouth on the suntanned and tobacco-stained arm, he mussed more to himself than the other man. "I don't think the commander is having a nice day."

The older guard couldn't know the half of it.

The early morning had started with a phone call.

Stanley slid the Escalade to a gravel stop. Hitting the "off" button, he burst out of the vehicle and stormed his way into the building. Glancing around, he stomped through the empty administration office. At only five-foot-seven and a hundred and five on his heavy days, the stomping went unnoticed. He hadn't thought to wear his heavy boots with metal heel plates.

The rough-sawn floorboards ended at the heavy door. Every other door on the compound was rough-sawn boards nailed with a Z-cross bracing. This door was solid, sound-proof, and two inches thick with a metal plate buried in the middle.

Stanley paused for only a second and then opened the door. The green carpet was lush and the exact color as money. The door closed with a dull thud. Stanley stood staring at the man behind the desk with the phone to his ear.

The khaki sleeves on the campaign shirt hung folded above his elbows and hinted at the massive biceps. The flattop haircut looked cut with a straight-edged ruler. The thumbprints of silver at the temples only heightened the severity of the man's features.

"Stanley is here. I'll call you back. Keep me posted." He softly cradled the phone, his elbows spiked on the top of the large cypress desk, his right fist socketed into his left hand. "Stanley?"

The man took a slow breath and let it out through his nose. He finally walked to the side chair and slumped into the deep padding and leather. "What the hell, Alex? You said she was secure with the FBI—she escaped just as the team got there. You said she couldn't get off the island—but she stole their boat. THEIR FUCKING BOAT. And then she hotwired their SUV. Their BRAND-NEW SUV."

The larger man blinked.

"Then she uses OUR car dump and our pilot. And the fuckhead takes her to Galveston. What the fuck was he thinking? They take two cars and head in different directions, and now some fucking brainchild calls me at my mistress's house at five in the morning to tell me they've lost her. After four fucking days—THEY LOST HER?"

Alex gently turned the chair and faced the man. "Stanley, if you insist on yelling and swearing at me like I was your cheap whore of a wife, I'll just shoot you here and now and solve all my problems."

Stanley read the larger man's face. There was no bluff, just cold resolve as Stanley collapsed back into the chair. "Jeez, Alex, I'm sorry. I just don't know what to do. I've got the FBI working up interstate charges or something and the one person I thought I could trust…" He washed his hand over his face.

Alex stepped to look out the two-inch-thick bulletproof window. His hands spread loosely over his hips. "Look, Stan, as far as we know, Sydney still has her phone. You know how our daughters are. Heck, they couldn't go to a class in school without texting each other. We can't trace texting, but we know they're in California. It's where Rose grew up, and it figures that even with no family left, she would go where she knows or semi-knows the old neighborhood. We have several friends out west ready to pounce once the girls talk."

Stanley sat up straighter and turned. "But what if she turns her phone off again?"

Alex snorted softly at the window. Turning, he gave his partner a condescending look. "Seriously? Y'all know we special chipped those phones when we gave them to the girls a few years back. I know you thought they were good girls, but even good girls like to do bad things and go where they aren't supposed to. Even if they take the battery out, the moment they re-power up, the tattletale calls us."

Stanley opened his mouth only to have Alex stop him with his palm up.

"It's infallible. Once the tattletale is turned on, only we can turn it off. If it has power, it's going to tell us where it is."

"What about aluminum foil?"

Alex leaned into his face and whined. "Ooo… What about kryptonite?" He stood and stepped back to his desk. Sitting, he toyed with his cell phone that was sitting on his paperwork. "Think about it. They're only seventeen, and they're girls." He jerked his head toward the camp gate. "Only Meal Team is dumber. He still thinks his ear mic is connected to a real radio and is waiting for his orders to shoot something."

The two snickered softly at the man's expense. They also knew about half of the lower level of the militia were in the same illiterate category. Many struggled to stay in school until the fifth or sixth grade. Some built character by toughing it out. Others quit when they didn't pass for the third or fourth time. Some confirmed their truancy with the pregnancy of a classmate. Their income, from lower-skills manufacturing jobs, spent eating, drinking, and buying more paramilitary gear and clothing. The lucky ones still lived at home with their parents. What was going on at the camps was far beyond their imagination.

Alex moved his cell phone and fingered through a few sheets of paper. "Which reminds me. We have a couple of dark runners coming up from Miami. Do you think the good senator is skilled enough to track a..." He scanned the encrypted report. "Looks like a twenty-two-year-old busboy."

Stanley rubbed at his unshaven chin. "I don't know. The senator is getting older and slower. They have him on those blood thinners and all. Maybe if the boys beat the fight out of the kid first. Is he Cuban or black?"

Alex squinted at the report. "Maybe both. Just says dark. Beating him makes sense. Lord knows we don't want the target to turn around and get the senator with his gun or anything."

Neither laughed. Both remembered a canned human hunt not many years before, resulting in an embarrassing bloodbath for another company in Louisiana. The homeless man turned out to be a former SEAL down on his luck. The days of transporting him, and keeping him ready to be hunted, had resulted in him sobering up. He had turned the hunt around, resulting in the death of a sheriff, the county's district attorney, and his mistress. It had taken seven of the militia two weeks on foot to track the man down. They killed him on the tourist-filled streets of Shreveport, Louisiana—steps away from the Veteran's Administration clinic and safety to tell his story.

Canned hunts of animals were quasi-illegal. Canned human hunts, on the other hand, while highly profitable, carried extraneous charges of conspiracy, murder, depravity, torture, and the taints of racism and deprivation of civil rights. But bodies rotting in the bowels of a swamp carry none of the baggage—just fat offshore bank accounts and leverage over powerful people.

GO OR STAY

Sydney slumped heavily into the chair.

The snow-blue center slipped to the corner of Jolie's eye as the steam from her coffee curled out of the mug and into her unbrushed hair. She sipped and waited for the teenage complaint. The barbed swipe at county life expressed as a question.

"Does Baby always get up so early?" The sigh almost flattened the girl's chest.

Jolie licked the coffee from her lips. "Rough morning?"

The girl looked off toward the barn. "It's Saturday. I wanted to sleep in."

Jolie's thin-lipped smile pulled back on the side the girl couldn't see. The prisoner in Jolie wanted to lash back, but the horse whisperer reined in her tongue. "And yet you got up, cleaned stalls, fed horses, and hugged Baby like the rest of us. And get ready… Baby knows nothing about the sanctity of a Sunday morning."

"Except Dot." Sydney stood and looked down on the

expanse of the black hat. "Is there any..." She thought. "Coffee left?"

The right front tip of the hat bumped up. "Sure. About twelve miles that way. Watch out for the rattlesnakes. They're breeding this time of year and easy to piss off."

Jolie could sense the girl biting hard on her lower lip. She had watched it before and knew the retort would come later. She listened to the sound of the rubber boots retreat into the kitchen.

The bare feet were more hesitant. Jolie wasn't sure if it was Rose's routine yet or not. Out of the corner of her eye, she watched Rose's feet standing on the edge of the porch. The toes curled over the edge and then flared wide as if feeling the morning air.

"Should I start rustling up some breakfast? Or do you do that?"

Jolie dipped her hat down on the outboard so she could look up at the woman. "Do what?"

"Rustle. Rustle up a meal."

Jolie looked out across the wagon yard toward the barn. "Hmm." She sipped her coffee and thought. "I never thought about it. We just cook it, grill it, or peck at what's in the cold box. I don't ever remember rustling."

Rose chuckled as she sat. She looked at Jolie and started laughing harder.

Jolie sipped on her coffee as she watched the morning over the corral. "What?"

Rose snickered. "Really? You peck at the food in the refrigerator? You don't pick?"

Jolie caught the laughing. She put her thumb and finger

together and mimicked a bird pecking. "Like a bird pecking for worms or grubs."

Rose burst out laughing and pointed at Jolie's bird.

"What?"

"My favorite salsa goes by two names. Most people call it salsa cruda. It's made of crudely chopped onion, cilantro, tomatoes, and jalapeño peppers. But the proper name is pico de gallo." She bounced the tip of her index finger on the tip of her nose. "It means the pecker of the bird."

Both were laughing so hard that they had to put their coffee mugs down. Neither had noticed Dot crossing the wagon yard.

"Your laughing be scaring the livestock." Dot's growl was only an edge of laughter herself. "Best be mo' coffee."

Rose stuck her finger up and called. "Sydney was just rustling up more." This set the two off even harder.

Jolie stopped suddenly and grabbed at Rose's arm. "Uh oh." She nodded toward the barn.

Even across the wagon yard, both women could see the pain. Mike was walking slow, but the hip wasn't swinging as much as being dragged.

Rose leaned nearer Jolie. "He really needs to get that hip fixed. That must be killing him."

Jolie's voice was more into her gravel register. "He probably took a dozen aspirin an hour ago when Dot woke him up. She must have been working him over to work out the kinks."

"Arthritis?"

"Some. But several years ago, he got drilled at the Trestles. When the lifeguards went in, they were certain it was a recovery, not a saving. I remember it was touch-and-go for a long time. His wife and I traded time at the hospital. Most of those early days, he couldn't tell us apart, so he slept knowing she was there for him."

"I'm guessing by drilled and Trestles, you were talking about surfing. But his wife…?"

The brim of Jolie's hat floated back and forth. "Died of cancer while I was in prison." She looked up and smiled. "Looking better this morning, Mike."

He leaned forward and circled down onto the top step. "Don't worry. I called your favorite jerk. He'll squeeze the peckerhead in tomorrow. Dot's throwing me out. I think it was past one when she—"

"I should have just shot you." She handed him a mug of coffee. "How many did you take this morning?"

"None." He looked up at her. "I called Jerk before. He said he wants me off aspirin for at least a day. He figured Rocket still had some Dilaudid floating around." He looked over at Jolie with expectation.

Jolie nodded and stood. "How much to get you rustled?"

He sucked in a breath and slowly sighed it through his nose. She knew the answer wasn't out in the trees he was looking at. He just wasn't used to anything close to admitting real pain.

"Let's start you with a couple of deuces and see if you make it through breakfast." Jolie caught the nod from Dot.

Tiny bits of omelet washed away from each plate by the delicate but large pink tongue of the ranch pre-washer. Rose giggled when Pink also washed a smear of strawberry jam from the back of her thumb.

"So, you're related to this surgeon, and he did some magic on Jolie's shoulder, but you still call him a jerk?" Rose was incredulous.

Jolie snorted and put her hand on Mike's arm. "I've got this. Jerk is Mike's nephew, like Mike is my big brother or uncle. Family isn't always about blood. But as for the jerk, his name is Jewels Nerkelzelinsky." She smirked at Mike's shocked face.

Mike closed his mouth as his eyebrows raised, and he gave Jolie a nod. "I'm impressed. You rolled out that name like you were his mother."

Jolie slugged his shoulder with her left hand. "Peckerhead. Jewels is easy to say. They're a girl's best friend…" She winked at Dot. "In the city."

Rose frowned. "So it's because nobody can pronounce his name… He becomes a jerk?"

Mike chuckled. "No. His father was Jerk. Jewels is Jerk junior."

Rose turned on him. "And the peckerhead is…?"

"I used to ride longboards made from balsa wood instead of foam. I hated the weight, but the ride was smoother, like an old Cadillac or Lincoln. It wasn't slower but felt more forgiving. The nickname started as Woody Woodpecker, shortened to woodpecker, and finally just peckerhead. By the time I hung it all up, I was the last wood board on the central coast. Kids were taking over the surf with faster shortboards turned out in China. For me, the heart and soul were gone. I just hadn't realized it until Rocket here made me an offer I couldn't refuse. *My* jerk is gone, but my nephew carries on. Even his nurses can't pronounce his name."

Jolie looked at the bottom of her empty mug and up at Dot. She took off her hat and started winding her hair into a tight bun. "I need to get skunky before I clean up to head to town."

Dot wheezed a laugh as she stretched. "Damn, bitch, you don't knows how ta gets skunky. Yo jus' lays in da corner and whimper."

Rocket rose slowly, flexing her muscles. "You think, bitch? Loser does dishes."

Dot bulged her chest and arms into a curtain of ripples as she stood. "Fuck you. My girl Syd do them dishes. You gonna clean my forge." She looked at the silent girl, whose eyes were huge at the unexpected blow up. Dot gently back-handed the girl's shoulder. "Ain't dat right, Syd girl?"

The girl gently nodded as her face drained with the knowledge she had just been dragged into whatever was happening. She looked to Mike for guidance.

Mike smiled with a chuckle and reached out. "Leave the dishes. Pink already cleaned them enough. Help me out to the back barn. This is going to be good."

Sydney and Rose helped Mike stand and get down the stairs as they all watched the two women and dog strut toward the barn. The trash-talking had intensified and turned fouler. Mike found himself having to blush for all three. He figured the two holding him up had heard the same or worse.

Halfway to the barn, Sydney squeaked out a soft voice. "Did I miss something? Why are they mad at each other?"

Mike chuckled. "Nope. Best of friends." He looked down at the young girl at the crest of womanhood. "You cleaned the barn. Didn't you see the fighting ring down at the end?"

"Sure. But it didn't make sense. It's in a horse barn."

Rose looked around the large man's chest. "Dot was a fighter in mixed martial arts like what your dad likes to watch."

Mike snorted. "Dot was a champion. But she also trained Rocket up to compete in a few fights too."

Sydney's face opened in shock. "At her age?"

Mike focused on the barn door. "Age is only what you make of it. They usually just spar at each other in the stalls. A foot trip here, a toss there, but when it's time to really blow off steam, the ring is the only safe place."

1 2

BLOW

The raised standard competition ring shone as bright as a prizefight. Both fighters were in black fighting leggings and sports bras. Only the gloves and headgear were different: red for Rocket and blue for Dot. Both sets showed plenty of wear and tear.

Sydney's eyes were enormous and only occasionally blinked. Rose's eyes danced from hand to foot to head and body. The blows were not ceremonial. The sound vibrated through the rafters. Sydney jumped with the first body slam as the dust fell like a soft rain from the timbers above.

Mike watched while keeping count with each successful leg sweep, a clean blow to the head or body, grapples, and throws. His index fingers rose or fell as the match ping-ponged back and forth. Either Dot was losing her edge, or Rocket was maturing into hers.

Mike kicked the bell to end the fourth round. Sixty minutes of solid battle with only a minute between rounds.

Dot showed her time at the forge. Her arm and upper-body work were superior. But Rocket was faster and deadlier with her legs, jumps, and sweeps. Only once had Dot connected with a leg. Rocket had swept Dot to the mat five times and even driven Dot to the mat by jumping up and wrapping her legs in a spinning headlock.

The spinning motion twisted the trapped fighter off her feet as her body spun erratically with the extra weight of the other fighter. The intent was to force the fighter's head to a face plant, but Mike noticed Rocket's stop of the rotation, so Dot landed with her head supported by the thigh. It would have gone unnoticed in a genuine match, but Mike had seen the move dozens of times. It was always the final takedown. Both women panting—exhausted.

Dot would now be calm and ready to pound out fresh steel or grind on her backlog of knives. Rocket, after a shower, would be ready to be Jolie with her head ready for dealing with the town. Mike figured this had more to do with shopping for clothes than a fight.

The two rolled out of the ring and hugged. As Jolie walked away, Dot took a swipe at her ass. The contact was just a fingertip touch, but Jolie looked back with her large toothsome smile. The touch was as wasted as a miss. Rocket had scored the last punch or blow.

Dot laughed and washed her gloved hands about Pink's ears and head. She kissed her on the nose and waved her at Rocket's retreating backside.

Mike and Rose remained sitting on the hay bales. Rose looked at her watch as Mike watched Sydney get up and follow Dot. "Is it always this way?"

Mike thought and nodded. "This long and violent? Pretty

much. Jolie is still working Rocket out of her soul, and Dot… Well, let's just say Dot has her own demons."

"It seemed fast, but that was an hour of fighting. How long are martial arts fights, anyway?"

Mike shrugged his face as he looked over at Rose. "The rounds are three minutes. They say each feels like an hour. Normally, in a title fight, there are five rounds with a minute rest between."

Rose's eyes grew as round as her agape mouth. "But they just fought for fifteen minutes each round."

Mike shrugged and smiled. He draped his arm over the woman's shoulder. "It's how they roll. They are all in. I was told to butt out in the early days when I tried to stop them after a half hour. These days, I just kick the cowbells. It's up to them to comply."

He nudged his chin at the barn door. They started walking.

"When she was about twenty, Jolie came down to the Trestles one morning to compete in the big wave surfing competition. She told the judges she needed to win by nine o'clock or withdraw. She had an invitation to enter the Levi Ride and Tie being held twenty miles up the coast."

"Did she win?"

Mike twitched his head as his upper lip sucked in past his lower teeth. "Nope. True to her word, she pulled out at eight-forty-five. As she was climbing into her truck, the only competitor with a higher score lost his left foot and skidded into a wipeout."

"Ouch."

"I'll say. When she dropped out, I didn't have to take the wave. I had won. But the wipeout busted me down to third."

Rose laughed. "But what about the Levi thing? And what is it?"

Mike paused in the sunlight. "It's a marathon: one horse and two riders who also run. One rides ahead and ties the horse. While the horse catches its breath, the other rider is running to catch up. That rider gets on the horse and races to the next tie-off and takes off running. They keep leapfrogging that way until one team crosses the finish line."

Rose turned with a frown. "Why not just ride the whole twenty-five miles in a single shot? I mean, wouldn't that be the fastest way?"

Mike nudged his chin at the house. "I need to take care of some coffee." They started walking again. "An average person can run a horse to death, and in the early days, they did. Now, they have several health checks. The medical teams check the heart and blood pressure, give them water, and make sure they are safe to continue."

"What about the horses?"

Mike laughed. "That's who we're talking about. The humans usually get a little water and stand around antsy to be racing."

"Why not just leave the horse at the vet check and take off running?"

She helped him up the single step of the back stair. Mike shook his head. "Not allowed. Whoever brings the horse in must take them out. Even if they tie them off a hundred yards later, they must stay through the health check. It saves lives." He opened the back door. Leaning just inside was one of his canes. He limped into the kitchen and the hidden bathroom inside the pantry.

"Where was I?" He sat splayed on a stool at the counter as he listened to the coffee brew. "When it started, there would be a serious runner and a long rider on a hundred-dollar horse. Only the runner made it across. Then there were people like Rocket who raised hell about throwing away horses. So, the rules changed."

"And Jolie rode in these races."

Mike nodded. "Her and a guy named Bert Sails or something…"

"Stayless. Bret Stayless." Jolie came into the kitchen and snapped her shirt at Mike. The harness holding her large pig knife up the middle of her back was over her tan sports bra. Her long blond hair hung still damp in a dun-colored rope. She turned and sat on the stool in front of Mike. "Braid me."

As Mike worked, Jolie continued. "We weren't especially competitive, but we were there to shame the city slickers there for the money and fame. Bret ran in his boots, and I ran in moccasins. I tried those track shoes once. Once. If I'm going to cover ground, I'll take feeling what's under me."

Rose poured coffee in three mugs. "What about the horse?"

Jolie nodded thanks. "Bret had a great horse. He was usually in and out of the vet checks in a heartbeat. His horse was a cross between Arabian and a Paint—American Paint Horse. If you ever saw a cowboy and Indian movie, the Indians were usually riding Paints. Bret used to ride him on hundred-mile endurance races. He won a twenty-thousand-dollar bet once. He road Checkers from Malibu to Santa Cruz in under a week."

Rose's mouth gawped open, and then she frowned as she cocked her head. "That's a long way."

Jolie smiled. "It is—if you're driving." She sipped her coffee. Putting down the mug, "If you follow the coast, it's even longer. California has a fat belly. But the coast range is reasonably straight. Get up onto the coast trail, and it's almost a straight shot. It trims off almost a hundred miles." She pointed back toward the back of the house. "We were on part of the trail yesterday. The ridge trail is essentially a spur dropping down into my property. But the coast trail is higher and straighter, and we're an hour drive from the surf. The fat of the belly is only starting.

"The hard part for Bret was getting up and out of the city and onto the trail. Once he was there, they only stopped to eat, drink, and take a nap. Bret slept in the saddle, but Checkers just kept going. They made it in a little over five days."

Jolie stood and looked at Mike. "You want us to drop you at your car now or when we get back?"

He cocked his head and listened. "I don't hear Dot pounding steel. She must be grinding the stack of knife blanks she needs to finish. I'll take a little nap and then get her to work a bit more on my back. You can drop me over after lunch."

Jolie pulled her shirt on over the harness and bra. "Okay, we won't be long." She looked around for Pink. "Pink?"

Mike smiled and nodded toward the barn. "I think she's still curious about Sydney."

Jolie gently wagged her head as she looked at Rose. "Slut. She's a slut, I tell you." She looked at Mike and smiled as she pulled on her wide-brimmed Storm Rider and shoved it to ride low over her ears and eyebrows. "She must get it from her momma."

She glanced at Rose. "I need to have a talk with my daughter."

As they walked into the grinding room, all three females jumped at Jolie's voice. The errant child spun and raced to her knee and acted like she had been there obediently, as always. Jolie thought about the other two but let it go. When they were ready, she would beat it out of Dot with a six-pack or a bottle. Something was there, and it probably wasn't her business.

She knelt to fluff the big floppy ears of the large Cane Corso. "Is my widdle girl behaving? Do you want to stay here with aunties Dot and Sydney?" She roughed up the giant head. The tongue became a large pink slab as the smiling mouth hung open and slopped with saliva. "Who's my girl? Huh?"

Jolie stood. "We're only going to the feed store. You need anything, or is there an order in?"

Dot grabbed the table with both hands and leaned her butt against them. "No. No, I good. Gots plenty o' coal and steel."

Jolie nodded as she screwballed her face at Dot and her acting like a misbehaving ten-year-old. She looked over at Sydney. "Syd, they have ranch clothes too. We're getting your mom some bib overalls and boots that fit. Do you want anything?"

The girl shied. "No, thank you." Her eyes peeked at Dot for half a second. "I'm… I'm good."

Jolie could sense the hands had been in the cookie jar but didn't know what the jar was, much less the cookies. She let it go.

She waved and looked wide-eyed at Rose. "Okay, ladies, we'll be back for lunch. Mike's on the couch, but he wants you to beat his back with a rock or stick or something."

"Pipe." Dot watched as the two turned at the door. "An iron pipe. He want me to roll out the knot he get on his left side. Only a pipe get it out."

Jolie looked conspiratorially with enlarged eyes at Rose. "Scary. Scary, I tell you." They waved and left.

Dot and Sydney both sagged in relief.

The black hat appeared back in the doorway. "Oh…" Both women snapped back to attention. "I'm leaving Pink here to watch you two. So, no funny business." The hat disappeared.

The two listened to both doors as they squealed and then slammed shut on the truck. The engine roared to life and, with a slight kick of dirt, nosed out and down the drive.

Sydney barely whispered. "Do you think they're really gone?"

13

NEW TACK

Dot felt the belts on the largest grinders. Years of experience told her she had a couple of hours left in the grit before she would need to change them. She pulled the sizable red striker buttons on both. The belts on each machine jumped and soon were traveling at forty-two miles per hour. She wanted to remove metal but not overheat the knife blanks. She had heard of other knife makers who rocked their six-foot belts at over fifty miles, but she felt it tore up the belts faster and unduly overheated the blanks. Her reputation had nothing to do with speed these days.

She pointed at a wooden tray heaped with blanks. "Grab dat tray. I be showing you what you do."

She walked over to a sink with a handful of wire brushes. She turned on the water as she smiled at the grunting coming from the girl. Dot figured the only heavy item she ever picked up was a book bag—if that. The girl quietly rolled with the punches or just assumed someone would lend her clothes and feed her.

Dot felt the water. The water from the well was bone-chilling cold. The heater was working today, and the water was slightly warmer than temperate. The girl would have her hands in the water for the next couple of hours. Dot didn't want to hear any whining about cold water freezing delicate hands. She pointed at the one sideboard, and Sydney put the weight down with a thud. No complaint. No comment. She just waited for the next direction. Dot smiled.

"Jus' let da water run. Well pump fifty-gallon every minute. We have plenty. The wastewater go to a tank we water with." She grabbed a blank and a wire brush. Dipping the tips of the wires in the large cake of soft soap, she started scrubbing the blank. "Cutting the blanks make nasty. I suggest you use dat gloves." She nodded her chin at the wood rod hung with heavy-duty kitchen gloves. "Da lye soap take off skin fast as nasty."

She rinsed the blank and examined the dull gray metal. "Clean go here." She leaned the blank in the wood drying rack. She looked at the girl. "You got?"

Sydney nodded and reached for a blank. Dot silently watched her pick up the blank barehanded. Sydney stuck the blank down in the soapy water and scrubbed. In seconds, the hands and blank came up out of the water. Dot watched the frozen agony on the girl's face. Dot stopped her. She held her hands out, palms up. "Show me yo hands."

Sydney put her tender white hands with the two now broken, angry red blisters from the day before next to the scarred leather of Dot's. The two sets of palms were a universe apart.

Dot reached out and grabbed a pair of gloves from the

rack. She slapped them into the girl's stomach. "Don't be stupid. Dat Baby's job. When a body smarter dan you tell you sumtin', you pays attention or youse never learn." She stepped back over to the grinders. "And day best be clean."

Sydney flared meekly and watched out of the corner of her eye. "Or what?"

Dot's head ground around. The face was stone hard. "Or I kick yo ass, and you only get roadkill fo dinner."

Sydney turned back to the sink. She didn't want to know if Dot was messing with her or would truly serve her roadkill.

The two worked in silence. Only the high singing of steel turning to grit and clicks of rough ground washed blanks racked to dry filled the air.

Dot hoisted her wooden box full of rough ground blanks and carried it to the sideboard. She moved the other box out of her way. Taking the last six nasty blanks, she put the box on the floor, turned on the second faucet, and grabbed a wire brush.

When their shoulders or hips bumped, Dot could feel the small jump of the girl. Dot continued until the reaction stopped, and a few times, Sydney bumped back.

"So, who be beating on you?"

"Where?"

Dot's hands froze for a second. "We start wid school?"

"Other girls."

Dot eyed her up and down. "You not small. Why?"

The girl scrubbed quietly.

Dot bumped her with her hip. Sydney stumbled a step. "Why?"

She glared at Dot and then looked down at the water running over her hands. Her response was quieter than the water.

Dot turned off both faucets. "Why?"

"They think I'm gay."

Dot turned on the water and went back to scrubbing. She rinsed and handed Sydney the clean blank to put in the rack. Grabbing another, she started scrubbing. "Is you?"

The girl twitched hard and looked with horror at Dot. "Why'd you say that?"

"Well, you be quiet. Don't want to attract no attention. Do what you told." Dot shrugged her head into her right shoulder. "Kinda…"

Sydney didn't blink or move.

Dot kept scrubbing and lazily looked over. "Well? Be you?" She stopped scrubbing. "That be a simple question. Jus' yes-or-no kind o' question. Okay, yo jus' nods."

The girl looked back at her hands, and her nose didn't nod more than a half-inch. They scrubbed in silence until the rack was full and the box was empty.

Dot turned off the water. Drying her hands, she hip-checked the large red buttons on the grinders and then flipped the towel onto the sideboard and tossed her head. "Come on. I show you something."

A small rack of knife blanks stood on the bench. She picked one up and held it out to Sydney, pinched between her thumb and finger. "Only touch where the handle be. It called the tang."

The girl took the blank and admired the reflecting polished blade. "It's beautiful."

Dot pointed. "Dat you. You and blade look like any other." She took the blank back, opened a jar, and stuck the blade into the clear liquid. Sydney's nose wrinkled at the smell, and Dot laughed. "Dat ferric chloride. It be acid and ex-sta cute shiny face." They watched as nothing appeared to happen, and then, gradually, the blade darkened.

Dot pulled the blade out and let it drip into the jar. She put the glass lid back onto the jar and carried the blade back to the sinks, where she ran the blade under the water and scrubbed. After a minute, she dried the steel with the rag.

She stuck the tang into a clamp at the benches and grabbed a block of wood wrapped with black emery paper. Spitting on the blade, she worked the block and emery paper over the face of the blade. As Sydney watched, a wavy river of dark and lighter steel appeared in the polished blade.

Dot flipped the blade over and polished the other side. Finally, she withdrew it and handed it to Sydney. She pointed at the hidden grain of the two different steels, and then she lightly tapped the girl's chest. "Dis be who you be in here. Ya show da shine like all da rest, but only let in here da special ones."

The girl looked up with wet eyes. "Do you have a special one?"

Pink nosed at the two. Dot chuckled. "Pink be my special one now."

Sydney smiled down at the goofy, lovable dog. "But before?"

Dot kneaded at the large black ear, and Pink leaned into the hand. Dot nodded quietly.

"What happened?"

"She dead." Dot rubbed at the sting at the side of her eyes. "How?"

Dot looked up in the face of innocent curiosity and the brashness of youth. "An accident."

"Car?"

Dot's head wagged as she gently took back the blade. Opening a metal box, she stuck the blade down into a slurry of wet coffee grounds. "We go through lot o' coffee round here. Da acid in dem grounds turn the dark lines darker."

She looked up at the girl. "No. During a fight. She had a problem wid her brain. We didn't know. She supposed to win… I hit her one last time on the head." Her lower lip sucked in under her teeth. "I never fight again."

"Except with Jolie… err, Rocket."

Dot nodded.

The sound of the truck making the last turn into the wagon yard ended the moment. Pink spun and bounced off their legs as she shot out the door.

Sydney laughed. "Goofy dog. She sure loves her mother."

Dot bit at her lip. "You got it wrong. Pink be da mother. She lay down her life for Jolie. Don't let goofy confuse you…" She pointed at the row of polished blades waiting for their acid bath to expose their true nature.

The potential glistened in the girl's eyes. She shifted her weight as her eyes danced along the rows of knife blanks. "Will you teach me to fight?"

Dot bit on her lower lip as she hung her hand on the taller shoulder. "And how to make knives. But first, it's lunchtime."

14

CONDITIONING

There's nothing in there to rake." Rose frowned at Jolie.

Jolie snorted with her wide, toothy smile. "Sure there is. There's a mess over there, one in the far corner, and look at this mess just here by the gate. Here, turn around." Jolie grabbed the woman's hips and spun her. She pulled two large carrots from the back of the golf cart, bit off the tip of one, and offered the other tip to Rose. The woman took the offered bite. This was all a new game, but even if the rules weren't obvious, she would at least play along.

As Rose scanned the empty dirt of the small corral with the two horses, Jolie jammed the carrot tips first into Rose's and then her own back pockets. The long greens hanging seemed like green extensions of the women's long hair.

Jolie opened the gate. "Now remember, they're more spooked of you than you are of them. But they are also curious. So move slow and lazy. Move your butt from side to side so the air gets plenty of that good-smelling greenery.

But only poke at the ground with the rake. Don't really rake anything."

"There's nothing to rake anyway."

Jolie shrugged her face under the brim of her hat as she closed the gate. "They don't know that."

"What if I poot?"

"If you what?"

"Poot." Rose stared at her. "Fart."

Jolie snorted and hunched her shoulders. "Cowgirls don't poot."

"Well then, what…?"

"We fart." Jolie raised her knee and slung out her hip like she was about to blow the backside of her pants out. Her face screwed into a tight knot. Then with a jerk of her head, she stood back straight. "Nope. Guess it's gonna be beans for dinner tonight."

The two laughed as they pretended to rake. Occasionally, one or the other would slip a carrot out and take a bite. Rose was demure. Jolie knew her breath carried a long way and chewed the carrot with an open mouth. She watched for the twitch in the ears of the horses as they caught the scent.

"I done raked that section this morning early. Now you're just messing it all up." The deep voice was smooth as molasses on a stack of hotcakes.

Jolie didn't even look up. "Ellen, this is Norm. He's the shit shoveler around here. Norm, this is my friend from up Frisco way, Ellen. Don't get any smart ideas, though. She's spoken for and already carrying his seed."

Rose looked up at the handsome black man dressed in a starch-pressed white shirt. The smile was warm and friendly, but the jeans and scuffed boots said "work." She nodded. "I'm sure there's plenty of raking to be had out here, Norm. If you want, you can find another rake, stuff some carrots in your pockets, and join us."

"Well, Ellen. I would. In fact, I've got a huge hankering to come out there and rake like the devil. But Rocket don't allow it. Only women can join her with the new horses until she needs a sucker to try putting on a saddle for the first time. So you will be the only person to stand out there, poke at the ground with a rake, and wave those sweet-smelling carrots around."

Ellen rolled her eyes and looked over at the smile pitched under the tipped hat. "You weren't joking about shoveling shit. I think I should have worn hip waders. What did you say his real job was?"

Jolie leaned on her rake as she thumbed up the front of her hat. Her smile gleamed in the morning sun. "I don't know what his real job is—if he even has one. But he used to shovel out stalls for his daddy. When I gave up ponies for quarter horses, he started learning how to be a groom for some of the best racehorses on the West Coast. But since he spruced up his daddy's farm and told everyone he was the owner, I haven't seen him do a lick of serious work."

Norm laughed. The sun sparkled off the white at his temples and his smile. "Says the woman poking at the dirt and waiting out another couple of mustangs."

Jolie shrugged her one eyebrow. "Did we ride in the Labor Day Parade?"

"You promised the Fourth of July."

"You didn't trust Golly in July."

"She bit me."

"You gave Molly the bigger carrot."

"You didn't hold up your end of the contract."

"And you paid me what?"

"Nothing."

Jolie pulled down her hat and turned. She side-eyed Rose with a conspirator's smile. "You got what you paid for."

Norm bounced the heel of his hand lightly on the top of the fencepost as he turned to leave. "I just sold them to the Shepard twins. They'll be calling you. They want to learn team roping."

Jolie ground around on her one heel. "I don't do boys. Besides, those two are useless. One's a loser, and the other can't get his nose out of his math books."

Norm stopped and looked at the building going on out in the pasture to the south. His customers had complained long enough about the thirty-seven days a year of rain. He was building a sheltered arena.

He looked at Jolie. "The world is leaving us behind, Rocket. That 'loser' made more money than you and I combined. All the computer time he spends playing games pays him some serious money. His dad said he is probably going to be a millionaire before he graduates high school."

Jolie spat.

Norm shrugged his face. "Say what you will, but he works long hours at his skills. But about the horses—Golly and Molly are going to the girls."

Jolie growled deep in her clearing throat as she looked up at the curl of cloud. "Shit."

Norm started walking back to his office. "Yup. They just

turned ten. Same as you when you started. It's about time we had a reason to go watch rodeos again." He waved his hand over his head. "Nice meeting you, Ellen."

Rose watched the man as Jolie fumed and kicked at the dirt.

They left their carrots on four widely spaced fenceposts. Sitting on the round second rail, they crossed their arms along the third. Jolie's brim was only a couple of fingers above her hands, held down by her chin.

Rose laid the side of her head on her hands. "What's wrong with the twins?"

Rocket's teeth muffled her reply. "Nothing."

"The horses?"

"Nothing."

"Then what's the problem?"

Jolie sighed and rolled her head. "Nothing, really. They're a nice family. I'd heard about the one boy. I just don't understand computers. The girls… Well, they're cute. But I knew they would outgrow the ponies and doing pony dressage. In the barn, when they got their tack, they looked at the western tack and saddles. Many times, I caught them running their hands over the heavily carved parade tack. Little girls usually grow up and find boys or clothes or the beach. But some… the smell of horseshit and sweat is the best-smelling perfume you can buy. The feel of a thousand pounds of hot quarter horse muscle twitching in the chute is a drug more addicting than heroin."

Rocket looked back at the two mustangs. "The dark brown mustang…"

Rose looked. "Yes."

"If he's lucky, some serious rancher or ranch hand will snatch him up. I've seen him turn at a full run out in the field. He can zig, zag, and zig again faster than a heartbeat. If he were a breed stock, I would guess he had Doc in him. Doc was an amazing cutting champion back in the sixties. But this boy is fresh off the range, and his blood has run free with the wind for twenty generations. Only the best and strongest survive and breed."

"What about the tan one?"

"She'll be fine. She'll make one of the local ladies happy to ride a few times a month. The rest of the time, the woman will pay Norm a bucket of money to keep her fed, clean, happy, and ready."

Rose looked back at Jolie. "And where does Jolie fit in? I get you retired from the rodeo, so Rocket isn't there anymore. But where does Jolie fit?"

Jolie wound herself out of the fencing and stood. "Jolie is where she wants to be." She nodded toward the truck. "I worked hard all my life. So did my folks. I'm not sure if Dad really knew how set up we were. I could lie on the porch and eat bonbons if it were in me. But that's not me. I work the horses I want. I train the people I want. I'm happy."

"Only girls."

Jolie nodded as she squealed open the driver's door. "Boys are hardheaded and are only there to look good or get the glory. You watch girls around horses. They lean in when they're brushing. Some, as I did, bury their noses in certain parts, where the neck folds into the shoulder. Even after a warm wash, their smell is powerful. By the time a girl knows her horse's smell and dreams of it in the night, the horse can smell the girl the moment she enters the barn. They smell each other and build a bond boys will never understand."

Rose rocked forward and back.

"I've seen Sydney do that. I thought it was just one of her… Sydney things." Jolie nosed the truck up onto the road. "Now there's some deep water running there."

"Syd?"

Jolie nodded and looked over. "Yup."

Rose continued to rock as her lower lip curled into a roll. "You have no idea."

Jolie nudged the truck onto the onramp and headed onto the freeway. "Oh, I've got my ideas. But what was that this morning? I've never seen Dot act so weird. They looked like two little kids with their hands in the cookie jar."

Rose hummed. "Try catching them on her bed with their hands down each other's pants while swapping uvula gum."

Jolie took her foot off the gas as she coasted down the off-ramp. "She's gay?"

Rose hung her elbow out the window as she thought. "I've been fairly sure for a few years, but I'm not sure about her girlfriend, Bunny. I think she might have daddy issues."

"As in…?"

Rose looked out the window at the alley where they were parking. "Hard to say. She's always been an adoring daughter, but these last few years… I don't know. It's almost like Bunny's more attentive to her father's needs, getting him a beer before he asks, serving him before offering to help her mother, and even Addie, her mother, has changed. She's shrunk into herself like she's been replaced by Bunny. And I think it's more than just her day drinking."

"And Sydney?"

"I don't know. It's tough." She looked over at the sinewy rock of self-confidence. "She's always been a good girl. Maybe too good. She does her homework, chores and helps with cooking and clean-up without all the usual teenage sighs, groans, and tantrums. It's like she's working hard not to draw attention, or..." Her voice drifted off as the idea escaped her.

Jolie pushed her door open with her boot. "Avoid confrontation that might bring out heated words? Maybe exposing the truths?"

Rose paused with her door half-open. Her voice was soft with realization. "Yeah. Like that."

Jolie looked at the quiet Rose from the end of the truck. "Come on. Let's get you some Broken Ride gear you fit." They both glanced down at the mid-calf bib overalls. The laughter was soft and accepting.

15

NEW SHOES

Nah. Maybe the length, but the foot looks wrong."

Jolie was still looking down with her jaw in her chest. "Wrong how? Too short, too long, too many toes, or just the wrong color?"

Rose looked up at her, squinting with one eye jammed shut and her mouth twisted. "Not enough toes?" As Jolie laughed at her, she finished with the famous line from an old movie, "What hump?"

Jolie rested her arms on Rose's back as they continued to laugh. "Hey, Herbie?"

The owner looked over the top of the counter without leaving his chair. "Yeah, Rocket?"

"Is Chester here today?"

The man rolled his head back and yelled at the ceiling. "Chester, Rocket needs your body."

Rose ground her head around to look up. Jolie only crossed her eyes and stuck her tongue in the corner of her mouth like a bad cigar—a bad imitation of Groucho Marx. "Wait until you get a load of his hump."

The two were still laughing when the first boot landed in front of them. The other dragged across the worn board floor and came to a rest next to the first. Jolie stood with a smile. "Take your boots and socks off."

The young man squinted and jammed his one toe on the heel of the other boot, slipping his foot out. There were no socks. The other foot left its boot. The two feet looked like someone had stolen them from two separate people and stuck wrongly on the young man. The big toes were on the outside with the little piggies together. But they also weren't the same size.

Jolie smiled and stepped behind him. Sliding her foot between his, she rested her hand on his shoulder. "Don't move." She leaned around and looked at Rose. "Well, Ellen? Which foot looks like Sydney's?"

Rose studied the three feet. Jolie's were a size ten and a half. The other two were at least an eleven and a thirteen. Rose bent over and looked closely. "That one."

Jolie stood and glided her foot out. Stepping beside the young man, she bent over. "Which?"

Rose pointed. "The one with only six toes." She stood and blushed at the man's smile.

Jolie stayed bent over. She knew the effect the wrong feet were having on Rose. "Are you sure it's not the one with the seven toes?" She stood with a smile. Chester had been only twelve when Jolie went to prison, but he was already making pocket money, betting people couldn't guess how many toes he had. Eight years later, he was still ready to show off his wrong feet. "What size, Chester?"

"Eleven. What kind of boot?"

Jolie smiled warmly and shook her head softly. "Not this time. Moccasins. Prairie runners."

The man turned on his heel and strode toward the back. "High-top. Triple Conchos. Light or dark?"

Jolie looked at Rose. "Ellen?"

"Light?" She looked at Jolie. Then called louder at the archway where the man had disappeared. "Light please, Chester."

"Heard you the first time." The voice sounded disjointed and eerily echoey.

Jolie shrugged her face. "They hide them way in the back." She raised her voice as she side-eyed the owner. "It's as if they're ashamed of them and their heritage."

Herbie put up both his hands as if to say, "I only work here."

Rose frowned. "Heritage?"

Jolie smiled. "The original design is Navaho or plains Indians like the Paiute. But the hippies in the sixties found the shorter single-Concho height lent to rough scratches and chiggers. So, they started sewing the bushwhackers. Someone tired of gluing on new soles all the time, so they glued on tough rubber soles, bringing you back to boots. Eventually, some surfer talked to some hippie about shark-skin, and…" She spread her hands out, palms up.

"Two pair of light bushwhackers. Size eight and twelve. Inserts to match." Chester dropped the boxes and bags on the floor next to the chairs and low stool.

Jolie pointed at the chair.

"But I'm only a seven…"

Jolie and Chester snorted. Chester ripped open a bag. "Not with these inserts. Now you're an eight."

Jolie bent and dug the rolls of soft leather out of the box. She unbuttoned the Conchos and stuck an insert in. Handing the tall moccasin to Rose, she pointed at the chair again. The woman looked at the soft black leather sole and then sat as she slipped out of the rubber boots.

Jolie scoffed at Rose's thin socks. "We need to get you some working socks too. You can throw those city socks in the trash."

Chester reached into his back pocket and produced a pair of thick white socks. "Your size."

Rose buttoned the three Conchos at her calf and turned her foot back and forth. The soft, rough-out leather felt more like suede than anything tough enough for the mesquite and brush. "Oh, my gosh… Oh, honey, where have you been all my life?" Her smile grew broad as she looked up.

Jolie's smile was a full brace of pearls. She handed Rose the second moccasin.

Rose took the moccasin. "I bet Sydney ends up sleeping in these."

Jolie smirked. "We need jeans and work shirts too. Do you know her sizes?"

"Sure. I buy all her clothes for her. She only goes to the store when she needs shoes." She stood and started walking. Her eyes were large as she looked back at Chester and Jolie. "And this is the leather of a real shark?"

Jolie laughed. "My pair is almost fifteen years old with the original soles. The stuff wears like iron."

Chester snorted. "Yeah. Fifteen years of prison, and you wearing them damn rodeo shoes all the time."

She pushed her hip into his shoulder. "Shut up, child, before I have to switch your feet back."

He looked up with crossed eyes and a goofy look. His voice slurred like Igor in Frankenstein. "Try it, master. Whatever could you screw up this time?" His favorite Halloween costume was drawing stitching all over his face and hands and going barefooted. The kids squeal with delight, and the feed store is a must for trick-or-treating.

They piled the bags of clothes in the back of the truck among the larger bags of carrots, oats, and bird corn. Rose looked at the filled bed. "Good thing we brought a truck, and the dog didn't come."

Jolie looked across the bed. "If Pink had come, it would be you riding in the back." The stare was hard but informative.

They were both quiet as they got in. Rose pulled her door just to the cab and snugged it closed. Jolie watched and only smiled on her offside. "Buckle up." She knew the door wasn't closed.

As they turned left at the end of the alley, the door swung open, scaring Rose. Jolie laughed. "Here. Let me help you with that door." She jogged sharply toward the sidewalk, startling a couple of tourists. The door banged shut.

Rose looked over with a blank, wide-eyed look.

Rocket laughed. "It's a fucking truck. Beat to shit but will run all day to Montana and back. She's Rodeo Ready."

"Rodeo Ready?"

Rocket nodded. "Beat-up so much nobody with any decency would want to touch it. So it can sit at a rodeo or anywhere with the key in it, and nobody will ever drive off with it. But we maintain the mechanical, so it's ready to drive anywhere you need to go. Rodeo or hunting." She glanced over. "There's nothing worse than to hear the hunting in Montana is a slugfest of elk, and your ride is in the shop with a bad carburetor."

Rose frowned as they dropped onto the freeway. "Slugfest? As in snails?"

"Nope. As in slug your bullet out there anywhere, and it's going to hit any of a thousand elk."

As Rose recognized the turnoff they were at, she thought about Chester. "Were his feet really sewn on wrong?"

Jolie peeked over as she nosed the truck over the holes in the start of her long driveway. "Did you notice his eyes or fingers?"

"What about them?"

"His eyes aren't level for one. But one is pinkish brown, and the other is blue with a teardrop for a pupil. And the fingers are all the same length."

Jolie pulled the steering wheel, and the truck nosed into the wagon yard. "I'll even bet you didn't notice his left hand has a fifth finger, did you?"

Rose's voice was soft. "No."

Jolie backed the truck up to the tie rail next to the front steps and looked over at the woman. "The genetic fuckup he was born with screws up most of the body. It happens to one in a hundred million. He talks to several others, all over the world, through the Internet. They've even gotten together.

One screwed-up bunch, and yet, the most powerfully positive people you will ever meet."

The black tornado exploded through Jolie's window and bounced all over inside the cab. Nothing was safe from Pink's tongue and excitement.

Rose laughed, fending off the wild tongue and happy face. "I guess this means mommy is home."

Rocket kicked open her door. "She must be off her feed." The black terror bounced out of the door and back in faster than a person could say out. "Usually, she's at least a little happy to see me."

16

CONDITIONS

The east hills softly glowed with a pink halo. Jolie had always loved this time of the day. Only a few of the birds were awake. The coyote trotting along the far edge of the wagon yard only peeked at Pink and Jolie as they stood on the porch. Jolie wasn't sure if it was the same one who crossed every morning or there were others. She could feel Pink lean against her thigh. The dog had never shown an urge to chase another animal. Watch? Undeniably. But never twitched to chase.

A piece of the large dark hole of the open barn door separated and started across the yard. Dot veered toward the back door into the kitchen. Minutes later, she stepped out onto the porch with a steaming mug to her face.

Jolie side-eyed Dot as they came even. "I saw the UPS guy yesterday as I was coming back."

Dot hummed in acknowledgment. The steam from the coffee swirled around her face.

"I guess you've been getting some work done with Sydney around."

Dot's grunt was low and quiet.

"I noticed the ring's been used lately."

Dot sucked on her mug gently.

"I found a spot on Stonewall. I think someone has been beating him lately."

The sound of sucking coffee only paused. And then resumed. Jolie watched out of the side of her eye. The darker skin around the woman's eyes crinkled and closed to a slit. The wet reflection became dark. Jolie knew Dot was watching her.

"I think it's time for you to move back to Los Angeles."

The responsive growl was deep but insincere. "I be moved out by Tuesday."

Jolie turned to face her. "You owe me twenty-seven thousand for food and rent."

Dot spat her coffee back in her mug. "You so full of shit. It be less than eight. But you owe me forty-eight fo' all da work round here."

The words intensified, but the temperature never raised.

Jolie leaned her nose and mouth into the side of Dot's face. "I guess I'm going to have to take your sorry ass out to the ring. Beat the shit out of you. Unless you tell me what the hell you two been up to this last month and a half."

Dot's mug lowered as her head ground around. Their noses touched and stayed. "Oh shit. Dat all you want? Why not ask? We tell ya."

The eyes locked, and Jolie squinted. "Then why didn't you tell me before."

Dot pulled back and looked at Jolie's mouth. She turned her head back to her mug of coffee. "You know you gots a big mouth."

"Born with it."

Dot shrugged her face and shoulder. "I tell you. You tell Rose. Dat Sydney's job."

Jolie thought a moment and sucked the last sip from her coffee as she stood. "About liking girls?"

Dot flinched and looked over as Jolie walked behind her.

"That horse done left the barn years ago. But she's only seventeen. That makes her underaged if you start sniffing down that trail. Is there any more coffee left?"

Dot's teeth clenched. "You need to make more."

Jolie could hear the last mouthful of coffee in Dot's mug flick into the wagon yard. The quiet, fuck, was softer.

They sat on the steps. Hardly a hand's width between them. The fresh coffee steam carried a whisper of Chicory from Dot's private stash. Dot drank left-handed Jolie right.

"How long she know?"

Jolie furled her lips and looked across the yard to the big horse in the corral. Stonewall didn't like the cramped quarters of a stall. So, until they rebuilt a couple into one, he was content outside. "She said a few years, but I got the impression she always knew."

Dot's head bobbed. "Mothers be scary dat way."

Jolie looked over. "Think your mother knows?"

Dot watched the sky. The touch of pink on the small cloud was now bleaching out to just white. "I think momma still trying to figure out why I always get in trouble at school fo' beating on da boys." She looked over and then down at the road map of scars on Jolie's left shoulder. The black sports bra was a y-back with nothing hidden. What little meat she had on her bones was stretched thin and stitched together with scar tissue drawn even tighter.

Jolie breathed in noisily through her nose and sighed. "I sure wouldn't want to be seventeen these days. And I damn sure wouldn't want to if I were a lesbian. Just dealing with today is hard enough."

Dot looked at the barn. "It ain't so bad out here." Her head ground around. "I gots a woman to beat on. Steel to beat and grind. And who don't love being kissed awake by a slobbering dog?"

Jolie snorted softly and leaned over to bump shoulders. "Mutual."

Pink squeezed between them and then settled down with her front paws hanging over the top step. As she laid her head down on her legs, her lip-flapping sigh said it all. She was content between her two mommas and ready for a nap. The large, long tail thumped loud and slow on the boards.

Jolie upended her mug to find only a drop. The hand and mug dropped to hang between her knees. "Did she say anything about her father and what he does?"

"You mean about his skimming money off government jobs, doing shitty construction, or killing homeless people and prostitutes?"

Pink and the two women looked up at the voice.

Sydney silently crossed the porch barefooted and sat next to Dot. "Or are we talking about the canned hunts for blacks and Cubans from Miami at a quarter-million and up?" She looked over at Jolie. "Yeah, I know. It's why Dad and Mr.

Nyack want to find us." She looked down at her coffee. "Mom and I are sure they want to kill us." She put her mug of coffee on the step, pulled her knees into her arms, rested her chin on her knees, and looked out toward the trees past the corral. "Damn… I don't even like coffee."

Jolie looked at Dot, who nodded. Jolie quietly stood and walked to the barn. A couple of minutes later, she walked back with two small boxes in her hand from Dot's private stash of special tea she kept for Fernando, the farrier.

Showing the two boxes to Sydney, her voice was soft. "All you have to do around here is ask."

Sydney looked up, her eyes awash, as she pointed at the box of herbal green tea. Jolie could see the slightest quiver in the lower lip.

"Anything in it?"

The voice cracked. "Honey?"

Jolie nodded and took up the mug. She looked at the almost white liquid and flicked it out into the wagon yard.

Dot reached out and took Sydney's hand. The two sat quietly as slow tears dragged their ways equally down white and black cheeks. Sydney sniffed quietly. Dot responded with a juicier long sniff, ending in a full forearm wipe.

Jolie placed the mug next to the girl. Two tea bag tags hung over the handle. The scent of spearmint and chamomile whispered in the air. Jolie sat back down on the other side of Dot and Pink.

Dot rocked as she shoulder-bumped her friend.

The gray head appeared in the light of the barn door. Baby stood silently, sensing the morning.

Jolie whispered. "Maybe if we don't move…"

"Ma, ma, maa—mee. Eee, ee."

Dot snorted. "Well, it was worth a shot."

Jolie stood. "Big breakfast or workout breakfast?"

Dot tossed the last mouthful. "Mike's not here yet."

Jolie snorted. "Mike has his own damn kitchen. And any more guff out of you, I might just move over there. I could live in his big-assed microwave oven."

"He needs the walk. Just because he be Mr. Bionic man with fancy new hips, don't mean he'n jus' lay around now."

"Someone talking about me again?"

They all turned at the deep voice. He had abstained from using canes for a pair of walking sticks.

Rose stepped out of the front door with two mugs of coffee.

They watched as Mike deliberately navigated the three steps to the porch. He leaned his walking sticks against the wall and took the offered mug. "Thank you. It's all I've been thinking about this last hour." Turning, he looked at Jolie. "What were you saying about breakfast?"

***

For once, Jolie enjoyed sitting outside the ring. After breakfast, she had run over a hundred arrows through her new cammed compound hunting bow. The bow probably wouldn't work on a four-hundred-pound pig, but they built it to drop a deer or elk at twenty yards.

The cam action helped ease the strain on the pull. But it was holding the bow and the strain on the left shoulder. She knew she was still not back to full strength since the doctors had rebuilt it from the shoulder blade to the elbow, but not hunting for meat bothered her. She could afford to buy all the meat the ranch wanted to serve, but all her life, rifle, bow, dogs, and knife put the food on the table. It had been so since her grandmother had shot deer and bear from the camp where the corral now stood.

The genuine surprise was Sydney. She had run some arrows through a lightweight bow at summer camps as a scout but had never seen a compound hunting bow. The first couple of weeks, the inside of her left arm was raw from the string. She had happily chased more arrows than hit the target or even the hay bales. But slowly, over the summer, as she settled into the skill and the targets got replaced twice a day, she had also graduated to the larger, more powerful bow —the bow Jolie eventually wanted to use.

Mike looked over at her, slowly rolling her shoulder. "Do you want me to go get you an ice pack?"

She reached over. "I'm good. I don't want to miss any of this."

He leaned in with a smile and a frown. His growl was low and quiet. "Have you been telling young Sydney secrets about Dot?"

Jolie laughed through her nose as she looked over with a smug smile. "Just kick the bells, would ya?"

He laughed and kicked the hanging cluster of cowbells.

Sydney came out but stopped short of the center. As Dot closed the gap, she was one step off. Her weight was on her left foot instead of her right. Sydney feinted toward Dot's head. Dot ducked—putting even more weight on her left foot. Sydney spun and swept the foot. Even though Dot was starting to jump out of the way, Sydney's shin caught Dot's Achilles tendon and heel. As the two feet rose, Dot laid out and landed on her butt.

She jumped up and glared at a laughing Rocket. Sydney had scored with a sucker's move. They all knew she would never get to use the move on Dot again, but each score was a confidence builder.

For over a month, Rose had massaged and iced Sydney as she stumbled her way into the art of the ring. As Rose rubbed, Rocket talked, and Sydney learned.

Rocket waited for the next move. She knew Dot would be watching now, which is a distraction.

Rose leaned over Pink, her arm draping to let her hand play with the large ears. "If you want, I can massage your shoulders before we turn in."

Jolie turned and looked at her with curiosity.

"What? I pay attention." Rose chuffed. "I'd offer to rub down Sydney, but even after this beating, she would never admit she's sore. Between the horses, Dot teaching her blacksmithing and fighting, and now the archery on top of it all, I see her grimacing when she gets up in the morning. She's been hurting every day. But I've also watched that little muffin-top she had as it disappeared. She's in better shape than I ever was. Even when I needed to be."

Jolie raised her eyebrows. "You haven't been lying around and eating bonbons yourself. I think those bib overalls are getting kind of loose around the middle. Pretty soon, you're going to be digging through Sygh Dot's stash of fighting leggings."

Rose chuffed. "No thanks. Those days are long gone. But

I'd like to learn archery. Not to go hunting or anything, but just… Well, it looks fun."

"And to have something to do with Sydney?" Jolie's look was warm but passive.

"Yeah. That too."

Jolie nodded. "It is, but it also puts food on the table. I'm up to my new forty-pound pull, but Sydney is already running hundreds of arrows through the seventy-five-pound bow I'll need to be pulling to stick meat in the locker. Once she got the hang of it, she's become a beast. I've been watching the targets. They're all shot to shit, but only the centers."

"BAM! That's what I'm talking about." Sydney pranced around the ring as Dot slowly rolled over and glared at Rocket.

Rocket held up her hands and shrugged. "What did we miss?" She looked over at Mike with his fist up to his mouth as his chest jiggled in laughter.

Rocket backhanded his shoulder, and he laughed harder.

Dot lowered one eye. "You in fo' it now, missy."

Sydney stood over Dot and dropped onto her shoulders—flattening her to the mat. She reached back and grabbed a foot into her elbow and hauled it up. Dot tapped her knee.

"Jus' you wait, Rocket. You gonna be in a world o' hurt."

Rocket waved her hand at Dot. "All talk. We just watched you get taken out by an unranked. Time to hang it up, Dot."

They all laughed. Even Pink's tail thumped in appreciation of the event.

RIDING

Stand in the stirrups. Let the saddle bang your butt, but have your legs bent a bit to be shock absorbers."

Sydney followed the hot walker pole around at a canter. Jolie watched her legs stiffen, and then the jar of the canter would break the locked knees, and Sydney would bounce off the saddle. "Your legs need to be the same half-bent all the time. Try to keep your head the same and the pole steady. Just let your legs keep your body in the same place all the time."

"They said this was going to be fun..." Sydney circled again. Her focus was slowly becoming locked on the pole.

The small girl in the full helmet poked at Jolie's hip. Her stubby fingers continued to poke as she stumbled through her question. Jolie looked down.

"I can... do you... Should I get Princess... I can show her."

Jolie smiled and squatted. Tina—Patina—was one of her favorite students. The flattened pie face with pumpkin freckles was never without a smile. Even the one time she fell off her pony, Princess, she got up laughing and asked if she did it right. The full padded helmet had protected her head but not her arm. The pink cast was back atop Princess before two weeks were over. Nobody knew if she would ever grow past her four-foot-six height. But Jolie saw the Valkyrie heart only restrained by her Down's Syndrome, congestive heart failure, glaucoma, and her need to sleep twelve hours a day because of the chemotherapy and radiation. Whatever life she had left, she would live at full tilt.

Jolie adjusted the helmet. "Sweetie, do me a favor and go get Princess. I think you showing her as you ride alongside her in the arena will work. Okay?" She gently gripped the tiny shoulders and let her go.

"Ya… You got… You got it, Missy Rocket." She gave her a ham-fisted salute and raced off to fetch her pony.

Jolie looked toward Rose. "And that is why she is my favorite student."

Rose could see the glint of wet under the broad shade of the black brim. She swallowed any thought of a reply. It would have only squeaked, anyway.

Jolie unlatched the gate and walked into the hot walker corral. Slowing the horse, she unhooked the snaffle. "We're going to do some team riding in the arena. Just walk her over." She smirked. "For that, you can just keep your butt in the saddle."

Sydney only nodded. Her thighs were vibrating from the strain of new training.

Rocket smirked under the hat as she guided the horse toward the gate. Her right hand snuck in a couple of comforting strokes along the neck of the horse before she turned them loose.

Rose and Pink joined her as they walked toward the distant new arena. It stood unfinished, but enough that Norm would let Rocket use it for her students. Jolie liked the raw wood, but she knew everything would eventually get a coating of sparkling white paint to go with the red roof motif.

"Her legs…?" Rose hesitated.

Rocket side-eyed her. "She'll get it. Just let the Mighty Tina work her magic. She's only the size of a minute, but she has her ways."

Rose chuckled as she realized Pink was walking to bump her leg and then Jolie's leg and then back to her leg again. The dog seemed to herd her flock of women. She looked up at Jolie, looking down at the same behavior. "Is this part of the training about Sydney… or about the little girl?"

Rocket's brim rose to expose a fence of glistening teeth. "Which little girl?"

As they walked into the large arena, they stepped up onto the seating surrounding the dirt in the middle. The arena was technically the official size of an indoor polo field. But Jolie doubted there would be anything more than mock skirmishes played by any of Norm's clientele. But it lent itself to Rocket teaching some girls western barrel racing and roping.

They sat in the dimmer section at the top of the bleachers. The massive beams reached from behind their heads to the spider web of beams supporting the center of the building. Jolie hoped nobody cut off the ends of the large wooden pegs used to join the beams. They were a match for the large, oversized barn on her ranch. A barn her grandfather paid a camp full of Mennonites to come and build from entire trees brought down from Oregon.

The teacher and mother watched as the quarter horse and small pony matched their strides around the perimeter of the arena. Only as the two riders approached their half of the building could they hear the coaching coming from the small girl.

"That's it, Cindy. Up and down. Your legs do the work, Cindy. Let your body rest. Just like my legs. They are just rubber bands, Cindy."

Rose chuckled.

Jolie looked over. "Cindy?"

Rose nodded. "There's a little girl, about four, in our neighborhood. She can't pronounce Sydney, so it comes out Cindy."

They watched the two riders lap the arena time after time. The small girl even started waving her right hand at Sydney's legs. Finally, she was close enough to reach out and hold her hand for a moment on Sydney's knee—pushing up and pulling down. And then they separated as she watched the young woman grasp what she had been shouting at her.

Rose noted Rocket stiffen and sit up straighter. "What?"

The wide brim slowly moved back and forth. "That little whisperer. She just broke through to Sydney. As they come around, watch her head. No more bouncing. Just a smooth wave up and down like gentle waves rolling on a flat ocean. But it's Tina. We've been working on her confidence to control her pony. Ponies don't like being controlled, and doing so with only her knees is a difficult skill. She didn't think about it when she guided Princess over next to Junket —something ponies certainly don't want to do is ride close to a much larger horse. But did you notice, the reins were hanging loose in her left hand. She was only thinking about getting close enough to work on Sydney's knee." She ground her head around with a gigantic smile. "I only wish her father was here to see it."

"So… today is a good day?"

Jolie nodded and leaned back into the row of benches behind them, resting her elbows behind her on the bench. She smiled warmly without teeth as she watched the two on the horses. "Today is a fucking marvelous day."

She leaned back forward. "If Sydney remembers it tomorrow, I think we ought to take a trail ride over the weekend. I've got a valley she might find interesting. And who knows, maybe we might come back with some meat." Her smile gleamed lustfully.

18

CHANGE GUARDS

Camp Omega wasn't always what they would call busy, but there was always work. The dark hair was filling in over the swastika tattooed on the back of his head. As Steve raked his hair with his fingers, it still felt strange after five months. He had shaved his head, exposing the tattoo, since what would have been his junior year in high school. After six years of always looking for work, the camp recruited him with the single stipulation—remove the tattoo or grow your hair. The camp and who gathered there was one thing. But to advertise it was another.

As the FAX came through, Steve pulled the sheets. Grabbing the codebook, he marked up the sheets to the relevant information. He then called up the day logs of which employees were active and their locations. The men on the payroll were in a blue panel, the volunteers in red. Noting the relevant information on the sheets, he took a last mouthful of coffee and took them to the main office.

Steve knocked lightly on the doorjamb of the open door.

Alex looked up from the paperwork on his desk. He blinked and motioned with his head. "Yeah, Steve."

"Request from Delta, sir." He stopped at the desk and passed over the FAX.

Alex read through the highlighted area. His response was cold and quiet. "Shit. Sykes and McConnell." He dug his thumbnail into the paper and looked up. "What are we hearing from them?"

The redhead swallowed hard. "Not much of anything. In the last report, they were just north of Los Angeles. A place called Santa Paula. It's near Ventura and Santa Barbara."

"But they haven't found them?"

"No, sir."

Alex glanced over at the wet bar and then back at the FAX. "Okay. I'll take it from here." He looked up as he felt the large door silently close with a final dull click.

He scanned through a shortlist of trusted, competent, and deadly employees, the ones not paid by the camps. Their paychecks were more black ops than the CIA ever thought.

Sykes and McConnell were at the top of the list.

Alex took another slow pull on his coffee as he stepped through the list name by name. He reached over and dialed a number he had known by heart for a few years.

The voice on the other end was crisp starch and eager. "Delta Camp."

Distractedly, Alex asked for the camp commander. He knew the caller identifier would dispel any delay or smokescreen.

"Adams."

Alex leaned in toward the list on the screen. "John, I got your request. I'm assuming the good senator wants to go hunting."

"Yes, sir. He's asked for a two-person hunt this coming weekend."

"What are Styles and Track up to?"

Alex could imagine the man frantically thumbing through his smartphone. "Styles is down here teaching advanced tactics of sniper... um... it looks like he's out at the long-range. So I'm guessing they are learning about the mile drop."

"Track?"

"Home in Atlanta for the next month."

Alex leaned back in his chair. "If we need to pull Sykes and McConnell for the good senator..."

"And his plus one..."

Alex's eyebrows pushed up. "Oh, I thought it was just a double target. But he's bringing a friend?"

"Fully vetted, sir. He was out here last year on a hunt of his own. It seems like the junior congressman likes to play with his kill the night before."

Alex smiled on one side. "Male or female?"

"He likes them on the tender male side. We pulled a young boy out of an alley in New York for him. They will be in the special suite in the secure cabins. All twelve cameras will be active."

Alex smiled with genuine lust at the sexual nature and at the ongoing nature of having high-definition video in vibrant living color. "Good, good. So round up Styles and have him clean up and head for Atlanta. The boys need to go get read-in before Sykes and McConnell pull out."

"Will do, sir."

Alex didn't know if he had hung up before the camp commander or not. He didn't care.

1 9

BREAK

The guard clumsily padded the paper towel on the inside of his thigh. The coffee had dribbled down the thermos lid cup to spread on the stain where his pee occasionally leaked. Getting old was not something Horus relished at only forty-three. All too often, he imagined bending down and peeing himself or farting in bed, only to be cleaning the smeared turd in the morning. Laughing after more than a few beers had its own problems.

Horus knew he should see about buying some of those Depends he saw advertised on the TV, but he wasn't sure how to size them without trying them on. At least with the lacey black panties he bought from that mail order, he knew the size. More importantly, nobody could see him ordering women's underwear, and the stretchiness he liked so much took care of the rest. He only wished he dared to wear them while he was working. Instead, he only wore them when he was alone and masturbating to the old worn-out titty magazines he had found left in the apartment when he moved in.

He looked up.

If there were five or more of the same oversized black passenger SUVs, he could fantasize about the President of the United States being in town. But he recognized Alex Nyack's black Suburban. Rumor had it he bought the same custom model from the dealer in Washington, D.C., who supplied the Secret Service. Nobody could confirm it, but it sounded like something the man could and would do.

With tiny rolls of damp paper towel still stuck to an all-too-obvious wet spot spreading at his crotch, Horus stood and stepped out of the small guard shack at Majestic Estates. In the Atlanta summer humidity, the dark, damp crotch matched his armpits and the capital *T* down the back of his shirt and pants.

The large truck never even slowed down. The large blond man behind the wheel was always in a hurry. Too busy to deal with a guard at some silly gate. Horus heard the man's radio vibrating the metal that wasn't part of the bullet-proofing. It was the same talk show Horus was quietly listening to on his cell phone when he was sure the closed-circuit camera was off.

He only saw the face of Alex Nyack through the front windscreen. The tinted side windows were well past the limit of the law.

The SUV hit highway speed through the gated community. Alex knew the golf carts that usually dotted the streets sat in their garages—replaced by tall pitchers of afternoon high-proof feel-good juice. Most of the large wall-hugging screens in the dens and living rooms exposed large swaths of green grass just down the road where none of the residents had a membership.

Turning right, he muscled the four-ton beast around the curved driveway and to a halt. The deep growl of strained hinges echoed the shudder of the dying engine.

The idea of a locked front door was nothing Alex considered. In all the years he had been around Stanley, the door was open on a Sunday. Golf, football, basketball, or baseball, fifty-two Sundays a year, Stanley was in his custom-fitted lounger. A can of beer on the side table balanced the half-full rocks glass. Separating the two was the remote to the television filling the wall. The wall angled seven degrees to prevent any reflections from the wall of windows and the swimming pool outside. Even someone walking past could cause a tirade. Sports were the only shows the man watched, and only on Sunday as he slowly became poached in alcohol.

Alex chose the window side as he walked past the small table. Picking up the remote control, he hit the red power button. "Shut up."

"HEY! I was—"

Alex cut him off. "We got a ping. They're in California, just like we thought."

Stanley was still pointing his spread hand at the wall of television. "Where?" He looked at the remote.

Alex lateralled the remote to the oversized leather sofa. The remote hit leather twice and came to rest on the fake Persian carpet filling most of the room. "Up past Santa Barbara." He sat on the giant coffee table made from a single slab of a two-thousand-year-old cypress tree. Alex's living room housed the only matching table. They had contracted to have them made after the first successful manhunt. The senator had given them cause to celebrate with many other trinkets of wealth. Falling a protected bald cypress tree in the middle of the Okefenokee Swamp had only been a small start.

"Up past Santa Barbara covers a large territory." Stanley's eyes wandered and then focused again.

"Just like I told you, Sydney called Bunny. Bunny said she could almost feel her girlfriend's tongue through the phone. I told you they were fucking. Anyway, she didn't talk long enough to get a good triangulation, but she told Bunny they were hiding out at some ranch near the town of Los Olives or something. At least we have an area."

Stanley tried to sit up, but his hand slipped on the leather arm of the chair, so he gave up. "What now?"

"I'm sending Track and Jim out to nose around. If anybody can track them down, it would be those two."

Lukas Track had served with the US Marshal office until he became a liability risk. Namely, taking payoffs from individuals looking for people in the witness protection program. Track had been their semi-inside person for the unsuccessful raid to kill Rose and Sydney when they hid in the Okefenokee bottoms.

Jim Piles served longer with the marshals but had gotten caught. For which he served a shortened sentence in minimum security at a Louisiana facility. He had been their go-to person, recruiting the senator and other powerful people.

"When?"

"We found them flights on Wednesday. From what

Sydney told Bunny, they've been there a couple of months with no plans to leave."

Stanley wiped his face with his hands and frowned at his friend. "Why would Bunny tell you this?"

Alex's shoulders sunk as he looked at his partner. "Is it just the booze, or have you been this stupid all along? Bunny will do anything for me. She likes my dick more than she likes your daughter's tongue." He stood. "Go clean up. We need to go down St. Marys way and figure this all out."

Stanley fumbled to standing but turned at the doorway to the hall. He braced himself against the one corner, frowning back at Alex. "What's in St. Marys besides gas?"

Alex rolled his eyes. "Track bought a place there a year ago. It was closer to Omega Camp and only a short haul down to Delta Camp for the hunts. Jim's coming up from Omega. They just finished a couple of hunts with some homeless. They're replacing Styles and McConnell. They're coming back to do a double hunt with the senator and a junior congressman. Besides, Piles is the best we have if they need to be taken out from a distance."

Stanley shrugged his face as he turned down the hall. He mussed to himself, "Homeless. Good easy money."

BREAKING TRAIL

Jolie pushed at the small pieces of meat leftover from the large steaks the night before. The juice turned the minced onion golden. The bits of bacon provided the fat, and the minced jalapeño peppers added green and heat.

Rose rested her chin on Jolie's shoulder as she hugged her waist. Her eyes closed, and she breathed deeply through her nose. "Oh, Mama, I'm back in my childhood. The only difference would be the meat."

"What would your mother use?"

"When beef was cheap at the market because it was past the sell-by date, she would make jerky. When she made a dish like this, she would chop a handful and soak it overnight in water and tequila. The results are machaca."

Jolie snorted. As Rose stepped back with a frown, Jolie pointed at the upper cupboard above the refrigerator. "Open that."

Rose hesitated and then opened the cupboard. Her eyes

grew large as she realized the large square plastic bags were blocks of jerky. "Beef?"

Rocket buzzed her lips. "Don't swear in this house. Elk, deer, and I only wish wild boar. There's another five hundred pounds down in the root cellar."

Rose turned. "You have a root cellar? What do you…? Where?"

Rocket pointed the whipping whisk out the window toward the barn. "Right out there. Under the wagon yard." She turned to the large bowl and began beating the dozen eggs.

"How do you get to it?"

Rocket was having fun. "Through the pantry."

Rose opened the pantry door and turned on the light. Wooden shelves lined the small, well-lit room. She had fetched many supplies from the pantry in the last months. She saw nothing new.

"Hey, while you're in there. Could you fetch me the pepper mill on the middle shelf?"

Rocket listened for the reaction. She knew the mill was obvious but set back against the wall. Once pulled…

"Holy shit."

Rocket kept whipping the eggs. "Now push on the wall. But be back in a few minutes. Breakfast is almost ready."

She saw Dot and Sydney coming in from the barn toward the back door. Pulling a second low-wall iron fry pan from the drawer, she put it on the next burner and turned it on high. "Sydney, can you fry the tortillas while Dot rewashes her hands?"

The girl stepped next to Jolie and ripped open the bag of tortillas. "Where's mom?"

Rocket watched Dot at the sink. "She's down in the root cellar fetching a jar of peaches."

Dot snorted, and her head ground around. "Really? You turned her loose in the candy store?"

Sydney looked from one to the other and back. "Candy store?"

Jolie nodded and jerked her head at Dot. "Yell down there and have her bring a couple of jars of peaches. We can make an upside-down cake for dinner."

Dot nodded and disappeared into the small room of the pantry. They could hear her yelling to Rose about the peaches.

Sydney looked hard at Jolie and started toward the pantry. Jolie stopped her. "Your tortillas are going to burn. There's plenty of time for secrets after breakfast."

As Jolie poured the eggs into the large iron skillet, they could hear Rose's excited voice talking to Dot as they came up the stairs. Jolie turned to Sydney and wiggled her eyebrows. "I'll show you the other secrets from the barn end of the tunnel. But after we eat."

Rose set the two glass jars of flat sliced peaches on the counter. "Who sells peaches sliced flat? No, forget that. Where did you get all those canned fruits and vegetables? I don't think you have time to can a batch, much less shelf after shelf of everything down there."

Jolie stirred the clotting scrambled eggs, meat, and vegetables. "You're right. But we know people who grow the food and can it. We need the food, and they need the money. It's a win for all of us. As for the peaches, I would have never thought of it, but Jeannie Krebs has won tons of blue ribbons with her peaches. She and her husband only have about twenty trees, but they're the most spoiled peach trees ever. She shared the secret of her success with my mother, and we've been buying her flat sliced cooking peaches since then. I think it's the brandy she puts in every jar." She raked the scrambled eggs out onto a platter, and they walked out to the front porch and table.

Rose looked across to the mist, blanketing the sins of the valley. Only the treetops and taller buildings peeked above the fluff. "It's too bad Mike is missing this." She sat and pulled her chair to the table. "Surfing at the break of day seemed a major part of his youth."

Jolie served herself some scrambled eggs and grabbed a biscuit. "Dawn bombing was more than just his youth. Until his last ride, it was how he started his mornings. Erin would pack snacks for breakfast, and we would hit the sand by four-thirty. Most of the time, he had waxed his board the night before. Car to water was only a few minutes."

"Erin was his… wife?" Sydney looked up from the thin film of strawberry jam on her biscuit.

Jolie nodded. "High school sweetheart. Her older brother played football with Mike. She was the pest who had nothing better to do than hang out near the older boys. Mike treated her like a human being. About the time he finished college, she was just starting. They would surf at dawn and then go study after. She was premed, and he was learning the ropes of property management the right way."

Rose's one eyebrow rose as she shoved what she was

chewing into her one check. Covering her mouth with her napkin, "There's a wrong way?"

Jolie took a breath through her nose and stretched her neck. "Early on, he made gas money by fixing shacks into almost houses. The owner of the company also dealt drugs and other stuff. He finally got his rewards about a year ago. But Mike got out and went to school. I don't know what the property management degree is, but he also got a degree in business management."

"Huh."

Jolie looked at her with wide eyes. "Huh? That's it? Just huh?"

Rose waved her hands in defense. "No. I'm not belittling his degrees… But the rest explains why he…" She glanced over at Sydney. The girl was watching passively. It was her mother's play.

Rose took a sip of her coffee. Softly putting the mug down, she cleared her throat softly. "When we first arrived, I felt I owed someone an explanation about why we were here. Mike quietly listened. He had no questions other than for clarity. I thought maybe he didn't believe me or something. But now… I think he had already been there and didn't think it out of the ordinary for us to be here looking for help."

Jolie watched Sydney. The girl could become the best poker player in the world. There wasn't a twitch, jerk, shy, or movement near her mouth. "What do you think, Sydney?"

Sydney sat still, looking at her plate, with her hand and half a biscuit hovering in the air. She looked up after a few seconds. "He's a nice guy."

Rocket snorted. "That's it? Just, he's a nice guy?"

Sydney gently set the biscuit down, and slowly wiping her hands in her napkin, she looked at Dot. "How bad will she hurt me if I try to beat the shit out of her?"

Dot leaned back in her chair. This wasn't some smartass bluff or whack comment. She studied the young woman and then glanced at Rocket. "Which would you like to do? Go with them on the trail ride for the next few days, or spend some weeks in traction while your bones knit?"

Rocket realized something intensely serious was going on, and she needed to dial back her Rocket and just be Jolie. "I didn't mean anything serious. I was just looking for more insight into how a seventeen-year-old girl might view the old man. I've known him most of my life. To me, he's the big brother I never had. But for you, he's old enough to be your grandfather or uncle. That's all I was asking. Is he nice? Does he just ignore you? Does he talk to you like you were an adult or a kid? Just the simple stuff..." Jolie realized her hands were hovering in the air, palms out. She gently brought them down.

Sydney looked at her mother. There was nothing on either face Jolie could read.

Sydney stood, mumbling, "I need to brush my teeth."

Jolie watched her walk deliberately into the house. Thinking, she looked to Rose for answers, but Rose was looking at the table and her plate and her mug and the table, searching for her own answers.

Sensing Jolie's quiet, Rose looked up. She sighed softly through her nose. "I don't know. I really... this time, I don't have any answers." Her hands slipped into her lap, and she caved in on herself.

Jolie looked at Dot. The two quietly stood and cleared the table, leaving Rose to sit in her quiet.

JOLIE PICKED up the box stacked full of waxed cloth bags full of cast-iron frying pans. She took a deep breath and let it out slowly with blown cheeks. The day had started screwed up and didn't look to be getting better. Turning, she almost ran into Sydney in the doorway to the root cellar.

The box slipped, and they both grabbed.

Jolie flushed. "Here. Let's put it down over here." As they set it back on the table, the box tore from the weight. Jolie grabbed two of the cloth bags of matching pans. "Maybe it will just work better to take more trips."

Sydney reached out and gently stopped her by grabbing her bicep. The two came eye to eye. Sydney had never been comfortable with someone as tall as her. Even when she was only five-eight, she was taller than most of the boys in her class. It sheltered her from physical abuse, but not the crueler spoken cuts and wounds.

"Look… I'm sorry about this morning."

Jolie cocked her head as a shrug-off. "Don't be. Your business is your business." She held up the bags of pans. "I need to go get us packed."

Sydney stepped aside and let Jolie pass. Turning, she grabbed the other two bags out of the box. She frowned at the weight. As she stepped out into the long tunnel running from the house to the barn, she held up the bag in her right hand. "What's in these, anchors?"

"Cast-iron frying pans." Jolie started up the stairs leading to the secret door in the barn. The door stood chocked open. She crossed the barn to the large rough-hewn table near the tack racks. She placed the bags next to other bags and steel boxes.

Sydney placed her bags next to a dozen green metal boxes with old white markings she recognized. "These are ammunition boxes for machine guns."

Jolie raised her eyebrows as she looked at the boxes and then the girl. "Yes…"

"Just sayin'. I've seen them before. The fifty-caliber Browning M2HB is a popular gun… in my dad's circle of friends."

Jolie leaned her hip on the large table. "The fifty was a popular gun, even back in World War Two. But these boxes probably only date back to Vietnam." She sprung one open, revealing the zipper-topped plastic bags stuffed with a handful of jerky. "They're still weatherproof, and the animals can't pry them open."

Sydney took in the number of containers. "That's a lot of jerky." Looking up. "How long were we going for?"

Jolie smiled. "This ride, we're only going for three or four days. This is to get you and your mom used to trail riding…" She waved her hand over the containers on the table. "And set up supplies for campsites."

"Who's going to use the campsites?"

"We are. You think I want to just sit around and work all the time?"

The girl shied her head and was coy. "Well, you do also beat on Dot… or the other way around."

Rocket waved her hand in dismissal. "Oh, that's just us two blowing off steam instead of heading into town and a bar."

"Kind of like an AA meeting?" Her eyes narrowed.

Rocket snorted. "Nah. I wasn't an alcoholic—you've seen me drink with Punchy. But I was the town drunk and slut for a while."

The girl's mouth hardened in a shocked circle. Jolie saw the disconnect.

"Look, next time we're over at Norm's place, ask him. If we go into the feed store, ask any of them. It's no secret. After I stopped riding, I fell down a long rabbit hole. There was a bottle at the local watering hole nobody else could drink from. If I woke up in the morning, it didn't matter whose bed it was."

"Because the bottle was yours or the bed?"

"Partially. But the bottle definitely, mostly because it was a custom blend of white lightning, high-test rum, and a few other liquors to up the kick. I could drink for hours, dance, and raise hell... and still find myself in my own bed most mornings."

Sydney sat on the bench. "But you said you... were..."

"A slut?"

The girl nodded.

Jolie furled her lips and looked around. Not for an answer, but a gentler way to explain how broken she had been. "I had a horse, Thunder. We were more than a team. It was like we could read each other's minds. We roped the pro rodeo circuit. I made more money during a four-day rodeo than I do training horses in a month. We were the team to beat.

"We can't see the calf in the next chute, but we could sense it. Thunder's chest would be an inch from the line when the calf broke the line. That put us in a place, a zone, a sense of no guy could take me, too. I tried to find it in alcohol too… but it was only there on the back of Thunder."

She sat heavier on the table. "And then, one day, it was a ten-grand purse. Thunder had been off the round before. I should have pulled us. But I was Jonesing for the zone. Thunder could feel it. He knew it was the final round. Less than a second separated us from the other guy. We lined up in the chute. There's a calm that comes over you and the perfect horse—no twitch, no sidestepping, and almost no breathing. It's almost like you don't need to breathe again. In the time it takes for your heart to beat a dozen beats—it's all over."

Rocket's eyes fluttered closed. She took a deep breath. It was as if she was there at that moment. But she knew how it ended.

"What happened?" Sydney's voice was little more than air.

Jolie's head came up as she took one more breath. Her eyes opened. "We broke the wire. I threw the lasso on the third swing. I was already over the top and running for the calf as Thunder set the hook. I hit the calf, flipped it, dallied, and set the hooey. I was up with my fist in the air. I knew we had set a personal best and won. But the grandstands were silent. They had seen Thunder. When I turned, he fell. The bones of both his front legs split out of his skin. He had given everything with green breaks in both legs."

"Oh, my God…"

Tears were streaming down Jolie's cheeks. "I grabbed the gun out of the doc's hand. Nobody was going to do what I needed to finish." She wiped her face. "I don't remember how I got home. I just found myself wrapped around my bottle down at the bar. I never rode again."

"But you ride now."

Jolie rocked as she nodded. "I had seven years to think about riding. But it was Dot who got me on a horse again."

Sydney laughed and snorted. Then honked another snort at having snorted. "But Dot doesn't ride."

Jolie pulled her head to one side. "Nope. Doesn't ride and doesn't shoe horses. She pounds out the most beautiful horseshoes, but she won't put them on."

Sydney's brow furled. "Then how did she get you to ride again?"

"One day, she had really beat the crap out of me. She had me in a sleeper hold. Her fist was inches from my face. She told me I had a choice. I could let her beat my face ugly or get on a horse and ride. So I did."

Sydney leaned over and lightly grabbed Jolie's chin. She moved it left and then right. "Hmm, it hardly shows."

Jolie gave her a bad rendition of the evil eye before neither one could keep a straight face.

As they sorted out the packs, they started to laugh again.

Finally, Jolie pointed at the other end of the bench, and they sat. "So what was going on this morning? Your reaction had nothing to do with this morning or here."

Sydney sat quietly, looking at the bench and picking at the rough wood. "Mike."

"What about him? Did he say or do something?"

She looked up and around the barn. "No. He's nice. That's just it. He's nice. He sits and listens and doesn't try to solve my problems. He doesn't make any advances…" She jerked to look at Jolie. "Boy, did that come out wrong. But what I mean is… he doesn't try to take my hand, or run his fingers along my shoulder, or hug me. It's like he knows…"

"That you're gay?"

She nodded and then shook her head. "Yes… and no. It's not like that. It's like he understands how I don't like to be touched." Her shoulders slumped. "Not by guys."

Jolie rocked her nod. "He's incredibly intuitive. I've known him since I was in high school. He's family, but he rarely hugs me." She thought a moment. "I guess I need to learn just to give him some hugs instead. I know he can use them. I don't think he will ever be over Erin. And I guess I won't either."

Jolie listened to the bellows roar out in the forge. She knew Dot was wrapping up the morning smithing and would be in soon wanting lunch.

"So where do you think guys touching you comes from?"

Sydney shrugged her face. "Guys. Since I started growing these and passed about five-six, guys keep trying to find reasons to rub against me, or grab me, or just straight-out touch."

"Your breasts?"

She snorted tiredly. "Tits, ass, legs, arms, hair, you name it."

"Well, you are strikingly good-looking…"

"And that justifies—"

Rocket cut her off. "No. That is not what I said or meant. Nothing justifies anyone doing anything without your permission. But what have you done?"

"Nothing."

"No. I mean when they touch you? What have you done? What do you tell them?"

Sydney folded in on herself. "Nothing. Eventually, they just leave."

"Did anyone try to rape you?"

There was silence. The girl was stone. Unmoving.

Jolie sighed. "I'm sorry. You don't have to…"

Sydney gently shook her head with her eyes closed. A single tear squeezed out and traced an inch down her cheek. She shrugged her shoulder up and wiped it away. "It's okay." She took a few breaths. "A couple of times."

"And…?"

The girl just nodded.

"Did you tell anyone? Your mom?"

The eyes closed as she rowed her head gently back and forth.

Dot noisily dumped a box of metal on a bench in her grinding room. "Lunchtime."

Jolie reached her hand out midway. "Come on. Let's get some lunch."

As they walked toward the large open barn door, Sydney slipped her arm around Jolie's waist. Laying her head against Jolie's, she hummed. "Thanks."

"No problem. That's what this ranch is all about."

ACHIEVING BALANCE

But why weigh them?"

Jolie looked up at Sydney, and Rocket flashed across her eyes for only a second. Jolie licked her lower lip, curled in over her teeth. "Because…"

Dot called from where she was leaning in the doorway to her grinding room. "You can't tell her."

Jolie frowned as Sydney and Rose turned. "Why not?"

Dot sipped on her mug. Jolie didn't want to know what was in the mug at three in the afternoon.

Dot licked succulently at her lips and smiled. "Same be like me. You show me, you show her." She pushed out the fist and mug. "Go on." She nodded her head forward. "Show da girl."

Sydney turned, palms out, with a funny look on her face. "Okay, show me. I guess."

Jolie led her toward the pile of loose straw bedding. She pointed. "Stand here and face Dot."

Sydney stepped onto the spot and turned around. The

second she turned, Rocket pushed her sideways. She side-stepped and stood looking at Jolie, smiling innocently. "Wha...?"

Dot chuckled. "Jus' pay attention. Class ain't start yet."

Rose sat on the bench and hugged Pink. They just knew the show was going to be fun.

Jolie walked to the table and hoisted a bag full of iron pans.

Dot shook her head. "Uh, no. I said show no hurt."

Jolie moved and picked up a twenty-five-pound bag of oats. She looked over for Dot's approval. The woman was nodding her head with her face buried behind the mug. Jolie could tell from the crinkles around the eyes that the mug was hiding an evil smile.

Rocket grabbed a tie rope, whipped two round and a hooey. The bag now had a cauliflower head to grab onto. She took it to Sydney. "Here. Hold this in your left hand."

As Rocket moved to her right side, Sydney moved the weight to her right hand. The bag hung heavy just above her ankle.

Rocket watched the right shoulder as it crept upward. "Comfortable? Not too heavy?"

Sydney shook her head. "Nah, it's—"

Rocket pushed gently. Sydney stepped, stumbled, and fell into the pile of straw.

"What the hell?"

Rocket put out her hand and took the oats as she helped the girl up. "Now stand here as I said. But this time, hold the bag in your left hand."

"Why?" She glared at Rocket as she slipped back into Jolie. "You're just going to push me again."

"How you goin' ta school wid attitude?"

She turned and glared at Dot, who was looking about the upper reaches of the barn. She snatched the bag from Jolie's hand, stepped back to the spot, and moved the bag to her left hand.

Jolie watched. The girl was standing with her moccasins slightly wider apart. The left foot turned out slightly, supporting the weight of the oats. The left shoulder started to rise and draw more toward the neck. "Ready?" And she pushed.

Sydney rocked but didn't step. She smiled.

Jolie smiled back. "You think you didn't fall because you knew I was going to push you again."

"It worked, didn't it?" Her smug look turned to horror as Rose stepped over and pushed her left shoulder.

Jolie caught her. "Your mom didn't push you hard, did she? She didn't have to. You were already half falling over before she pushed."

"But the bag was on my left side…"

Jolie saw the realization flood across her face. "So your body was compensating by trying to move the weight or your whole center of gravity to the centerline. Which meant, halfway into my arms."

Sydney stood breathing through her nose. Jolie waited through the blinking. She knew the girl didn't see the straw on the ground. She was going through the whole lesson on packing a donkey, mule, dog, or person—the weight needed to be even—always.

Out of the corner of her eye, Jolie noticed Dot smile, throw the last of what was in her mug out onto the barn floor, turn, and walk back into the grinding room. The fun part of the lesson was over. Now came the details. And for Dot, she'd rather be grinding or pounding. She had no time for riding.

Jolie walked back to the table. She put their clipboard over the face of the scale. Placing a bag of pans on the scale, she moved the clipboard so only Rose could see the weight.

Rose looked and nodded.

Jolie removed the bag and picked up an ammo box from the floor. She placed it on the scales and exposed the numbers to Rose. Turning to Sydney, she smiled. "Which is heavier?"

Sydney smiled. She had carried out most of the ammo boxes filled with jerky packs. She pointed at the bag of pans. "The pans."

Jolie smiled and turned to Rose. "How much did the pans weigh?"

"Thirty-eight pounds."

Jolie moved the clipboard. The scale stood at forty-nine pounds.

"No way." Sydney stepped over and started to pick up the ammo box. "What the…?" She opened the box. The box was packed to the top with 30-30 bullets. She looked up at Jolie.

Rocket chuckled. "I cheated. But the box of bullets and the box of jerky look the same because they're the same box…Just not the same weight."

"So we weigh it all."

Jolie smiled her winning smile and nodded.

"The bags of pans weigh the same. The boxes of jerky are also the same. But the pans are a small package for thirty-eight pounds. The boxes of jerky are the same size, but only a third the weight. So, we pack them in weight groups. With the groups, we can keep balancing Baby's packs as we drop off the sets." She pointed at the sets of tin plates, utensils, and mugs. "We need those stacked in sets of four plus a cooking spoon and spatula." She pointed at a large cabinet against the stairs. "Root around in that cupboard and see if there's anything else you might want to cook with."

The girl stood and blinked.

Jolie went back to sorting, then stopped and looked at the girl. She wasn't moving, just blinking with an empty look on her face. Jolie called down the barn. "Rose?"

The woman backed a wheelbarrow, heaped with waste, out of the distant stall. "Yes, dear?"

Jolie smiled inwardly. *I must admit, she's a self-starter.* "How much have you taught Sydney about cooking?"

Rose put the wheelbarrow down and put her hands on her hips, thinking. She shifted her weight onto the other foot. "Sydney, you get your own breakfast…"

Sydney narrowed her eyes at Jolie. The growl was deep, quiet, and pure teenager loathing. "Cereal."

Jolie tamped down her Rocket. "Do you slice fruit on top?"

"Bananas and strawberries." Her teeth clenched through every vowel.

"No raisins?"

"Dad won't allow them in the house. Not even in the cereal."

Jolie blinked. Rocket looked down the barn at the distant woman who was already wheeling out her sixth stall of muck for the day. The tall rubber boots slapped at her legs just below her knees. Twenty-some years separated mother and daughter along with the realities of turning tricks to survive or pouring cereal into a bowl.

Rocket's head ground around and looked at the door to the grinding room. "Dot." She raised her yell to a scream, scaring the three doves out of the hayloft. "Dot!"

Dot strolled in from the sunshine through the large barn doors. Her voice was casual. "I'm right here." She stopped shoulder to shoulder with Rocket as she gingerly sucked on the warm mug.

Rocket frowned and growled low. "Are you day drinking?"

Dot passed her the mug. Rocket looked inside and then took a cautious sip. Her smile spread as she stepped over and passed the mug to Sydney, who looked at the mug like it had cooties or poison.

Rocket softened to Jolie. "If you're afraid of germs, drink near the handle. Careful, it's hot."

Sydney took it hesitantly. She kept her eyes on the two women as she took a sip. Her eyes shot to the mug and then looked back up at Jolie, laying her arm across Dot's shoulders. Both were smiling.

"Oh my God. What is this?"

"Dat be bone broth. Mostly elk, but some deer and a slow contractor or two."

Rose only caught the last as she walked up behind Sydney. She pulled the glove off her left hand and reached out. Sydney playfully pulled the mug out of reach and took another sip. The mother leaned in and growled. "Don't make me sic Dot on you. Now share. I know a few contractors I'd like to reduce to bone broth." She took the mug and sipped. "Oh goodness. When's dinner?"

Rocket crossed her leg and planted the toe of her rubber boot in the dirt. She side-eyed Dot. "Just as soon as Sydney rustles up some stew."

Rose laughed. "Oh lord. Can we just order pizza?"

Sydney stole the mug back. "That's my line."

Rocket bent her head forward to only look out of the top of her eyes. Her growl was her most evil. "Dot only likes anchovies on her pizza, no cheese. It makes her fart."

Dot stepped back and back-kicked Rocket's butt. "That's evil. I don't fart. I be a princess." She turned with her finger on her head. She waved at Sydney to follow.

Jolie laughed at the spinning rendition of a music-box ballerina. "Yeah, princess bull farts."

As Dot slung her arm over Sydney's shoulders, she called back. "You time in da ring is gittin' closer."

Jolie looked back at Rose. "Really? You never taught her anything about cooking?"

Rose slung out her hip with her fist buried in defiance. "Honey, before I married Stanley, I was barely one step above TV dinners and street tamales. When I made dinner, the phone was my friend. Most of the dinner dates, I measured a quarter or less of the plate and only ate some of it. Nobody wanted a fat call girl."

"And now?"

Rose walked around the table and headed for the barn door. "I'd love to talk, but I think I'm late for my class." Her pace turned into a scurry.

TRAIL CRAFT

The light was glaring as it bounced off the barn door at the south end. Only Baby seemed unfazed by the brightness. The moment the wooden rack with its large pack bags on each side raised off the ground, Baby kept trying to get underneath. She was ready to go. She acted like an excited puppy since Jolie had set up the packing table and the rack. One sniff and she knew she was going to be going with them.

Mike had shown up at the first break of daylight, as promised. Neither Jolie nor Dot had beaten his soda biscuits. Jolie pulled out the huckleberry jam she hid behind the large jars of sauerkraut in the root cellar. The delivery of elk and buffalo sausages had arrived from Montana, and Mike had picked up a five-pound pack at the meat locker the previous afternoon.

Breakfast had been a festival of flavors and delights. Only Rocket knew it would be the last fancy food they would have until they returned. Trail food was hardtack, jerky reconstituted or a stick in the fist, eggs the first day, flapjacks the second, and field kill the rest. For all the size of Baby's packs, Rocket's trail rides were sparse and utilitarian.

In the past, the pack animal carried more dog food for the pack of six or eight dogs. Once Rocket had killed, dressed, and skinned the deer, elk, or pig, the pack was for coming home. The longest getting home had once been two days with a wounded dog with a field-stitched gash in her leg. The dog proudly rode between the two packs of the five-hundred-pound sow and her three suckling piglets.

Monte, the pack donkey, had stood patiently as she slit open a fifty-pound bag of dog kibble and let the pack jockey for food and water. Only his left ear twitched in irritation as she and her mother winched the large pack and dog off him. When Rocket said it was okay, he walked to his stall and the waiting food and water. At bedtime, and after weighing the monstrous pack and dog, Jolie slipped him a can of oats and a long, loving brush-down. The bath would come for both when they were awake enough in the morning. She had sworn never to pack a burro with that much weight again. How he had carried his own weight those two days, she couldn't imagine.

She laughed at Baby's tail as she scampered ahead. Her tail was more like a propeller or a dog's. It was always moving, always happy, and always random up, down, or the sides. Baby was always happy when she was going somewhere and not tied to anything or anyone.

"She's a happy one."

Jolie smiled a broad, toothsome smile and nodded her Storm Chaser hat. The broad brim kept most of her face in the shade, but only the twinkles shined out from her eyes. "She was almost a bargain."

"Almost?"

She glanced over at Rose. "They dropped her off with a ton of prime alfalfa for my taking her off their hands."

"How much is alfalfa?"

Rocket chuckled. "Less than a couple of hundred. But if it had gotten out, the pack station would have shot their happy little jackass… Well, business would have suffered more than the ton cost them." She smiled over at Rose, who was still working out the logic.

"But then, why is she almost worth it? I mean, she cost less than free."

Rocket chuffed. "Next time she wakes us all up because she's hungry or wants attention… I'll let you go take care of her."

Rose started laughing. "Is this like poking your husband and telling him it's his turn for the two o'clock feeding?"

Jolie looked back at the tall teen girl calmly riding as she took in everything. She smiled at Rose and nodded back. "She didn't suffer."

Rose sighed. Her smile softened. "I couldn't ask for a better daughter." She looked back for a long second. "What's missing?"

Rocket grimaced. "Missing?"

Rose smirked. "You only train younger girls, don't you?"

Jolie's eye sockets narrowed into pits of deep space. The response was drawn. "Yes…?"

Rose chuckled. "Don't do older teens. Getting the ear things out of their heads is major surgery. But with Sydney, music isn't a big deal as much as reading is. But the headphones give her headaches. And the little earphones are worse. If you ever catch her staring into her phone, it's a book. She and social media don't get along, either. Too many torment gays on social media. Many end up committing suicide."

"But she doesn't have a phone."

"No. The FBI, or whoever they really were, took them away. They said we could be tracked by our phones."

The wide black brim nodded up and down. Rocket could feel the extra-thick weight of the satellite cell phone in her hip pocket. Mike had given her the phone, but then they had encoded the chip. If you didn't have the code on your phone, you couldn't find her. And with the satellite, there was no cell tower to find her through. But even out here in the back hills where there was no cell reception, all Jolie had to do was swing up the antenna and dial up the nearest satellite for an untraceable conversation.

Jolie peeked back at the young woman coming into herself as she rode in awe of the nature around her. Rocket could tell Sydney had forgotten she was on a horse; she was just floating through the hills.

She turned back to find Rose had been watching the same. The woman had a soft but sad smile.

"If she likes to read so much, I'm surprised she hasn't found the library in the back of the house."

Rose started to chuckle. "Oh, Madre de Dios, she has. She always has at least six books on her nightstand."

Jolie's eyebrows raised into the brim of her hat. "I haven't seen her read…"

Rose snuffed softly. "Ever notice her going to bed around eight-thirty?"

Jolie nodded. "I'm not far behind. Sometimes she's in the barn before I am. It's still a jolt to find a teenager up and digging into the work without being told."

Rose shrugged. "You haven't asked for any rent for putting us up. We both know our mucking the barn is one chore you can always use a hand with. But no. The books. I'm sure she has knocked out more than a couple of chapters before I check in with her before turning in. I don't know how fast she is, but I've noticed thinner books are back on the shelves the next day. I think if we're here until Christmas, she'll have finished your library. Back home, the county library lets her check out a dozen books at a time. They barely make it through the week."

The trail widened as it leveled off. Jolie looked back at the topic of conversation. "Hey, Sydney?"

"Yes, ma'am?"

"There's a small patch of grass on the right of the trail about a half-mile up. On the left are some rocks to sit on for lunch. Why don't you practice your stance and ride on ahead? We'll meet you soon, but you have lunch in your panniers."

The young woman thundered by in perfect form and glanced back with a large smile. She knew she was making her teacher proud.

"She's learned well. I might have to teach her roping next."

Rose chuffed. "Riding, archery, hand-to-hand combat, and knife fighting. Now roping? What next? Pig hunting?"

Rocket looked over. "Only if we see an easy target on the third or fourth day. But once I turn Baby loose, no. The horses don't like packing the extra weight a boar would provide unless you two are willing to walk out."

"Explain 'walk out.'"

Rocket smiled with a pearl fence. "It will seem like we're a long way out from the ranch." She pulled up the horse, and Rose did the same. Rocket pointed down the mountain. "You see the high electricity towers dropping over the ridge there?"

Rose held her hand up to shade her eyes. It took her a moment, and then she nodded. "It looks about twenty blocks or so."

Jolie laughed at the woman's humor. "Yes. About a mile and a half. Once you get over that ridge, you are exactly between our house and Mike's house. Turn left or right, and you're about a half-mile to home or the better biscuits."

Jolie turned in her saddle, sitting on only one thigh. She pointed at a pair of two small, sharp peaks. "Those two spires, the white settlers would have called squaw tits. But the Californios had a better name—*Las amantes.*"

Rose looked at her. "Not 'Los'?"

Jolie shrugged. "Guess not. I guess the Californios liked lesbians more."

Rose side-eyed Jolie. "Are you going to explain them to Sydney, or am I?"

"Tia Rocket can do the heavy lifting." They both looked at the black dog running back down the trail at them. Jolie turned. "Uh oh... the babysitter found us."

The horses and donkey nibbled at the chaparral as Pink

jumped from scent to scent. The overlook was everything Jolie had promised. The view even provided a thin line they could think of as the ocean. As Sydney and Rose watched, Jolie looked in the sack Mike had packed. Rocket smiled and reached in. Pulling out the wrapped object, she chuckled. "Bye-bye sandwiches."

Sydney and Rose frowned. But Sydney cocked her head. "Mike said something like that when he made them. I thought he was just being goofy Mike. He would wrap them up and stick them in the bag, saying bye-bye. So what are they?"

Rocket smiled as she passed them out. "Thin slices of elk steak, some"—sh opened the sandwich—"looks like Havarti cheese, pickle relish, stone-ground brown mustard, jalapenos, some Ortega chilies, and lettuce on Mike's biscuits."

Rose bit into hers, chewed, and covered her mouth to talk. "But why bye-bye?" She hummed as she chewed.

Rocket held the sandwich to her mouth. "Say bye-bye to the last good meal until we get home. From here, it's trail food." She opened her mouth wide and took a large bite. Her eyes slid shut, and she hummed. She paused at the second bite. "If I could sneak a few of these into the prison, I'd be visiting my soul sister every month." Her eyes opened at the silence from the other two. "Waff?"

Rose peeked at her daughter. "Care to unpack that sentiment?"

Jolie washed her mouth with coffee in the thermos. "Sentiment?"

Sydney shrugged her head to one shoulder. "Smuggling

contraband into a prison, soul sister, and something about a regular basis." She looked over at her mother for confirmation.

Rose pushed out her lower lip and nodded. "Yeah, that about covers it."

Rocket sat up. "Easy, except there's nowhere for Mary to keep any food. The food in prison you survive on. Period. Mary will never get out to experience good food again. But if I could bring her even one, I'd go every day they let me."

"Which is only once a month."

Rocket nodded and took a smaller bite.

Sydney continued. "The twentieth."

Rocket stopped chewing and stared at the girl. There was no challenge or duplicity. The young woman had just made a statement. Rocket chewed slowly as she thought through the last three months.

She swallowed and sipped some coffee. "How do you figure the twentieth?"

Sydney sat up with a sigh. Her eyes danced across the sky, hopping from tiny cloud to bird to just the blue. "We got here on a sixteenth. Three mornings later, you got up and left at three in the morning. You didn't take Pink. You got back just before dinner, took a long shower like you were washing off something that doesn't wash off. The next month, the same routine, but you took Pink. Last week, you didn't take Pink. I don't think they let you bring her every time."

Jolie looked down and thought. After raising the brim so only the thinnest crescent of her eye showed, her voice lowered. "They don't. Every other month, I work with the dogs the inmates are training. They're training service dogs for Posttraumatic Stress Disorder and Traumatic Brain Injury. The dogs can sense when their person needs to calm down before they even start to blow up. They're the perfect trainers because most of the inmates have the same problems."

"And your soul sister?"

"Mary was my cellmate for seven years. The first two didn't count. But along the way, she saved my life, and I took the fall for something she didn't need. In theory, we should have killed each other. There were white gangs and black gangs… but we weren't part of either. So we became our own gang. In the last two years, we started helping others learn to read. So we built a tribe of a mixed breed…" Her voice drifted off as the brim of her hat drifted down and to the side. She was back there or elsewhere.

Rose and Sydney sat quietly, finishing their sandwiches. A silly simple name… and so much raw understanding.

STASH FOR ANOTHER DAY

N o. From the other side." Rocket stood and pointed.

Sydney frowned as she looked at the bag in her hand. "But there are bags on both sides…" She looked at Rocket, glaring at her. She could almost swear the two glints of light under the dark of the hat were glowing red. She had forgotten her shirt was red, but it shook her, and she moved around Baby to the other pack. On top of the pack was a bag of iron pans, just like the bag in the other pack. She pulled it out.

Baby sidestepped only a couple of inches and settled. Her sigh was wet and juice as her loose lips buzzed.

Jolie pointed at Baby's head. "See. Now she's happy."

Sydney held out the bag, but Jolie didn't take it. Sydney withdrew the bag an inch or two as her shoulders drooped. She could feel a lesson coming.

Jolie smoothed her hand along Baby's face as she stepped closer to Sydney. "How much does the bag weigh?"

Sydney closed her eyes and sighed deeply. "Thirty-eight-pounds… Same as the larger provision bag." The moment she said it, she knew she shouldn't have gotten ahead of the lesson.

"Don't be a smartass. Be smart. Being an ass is Baby's job. Being a smartass is Dot's job. What's your job?"

Sydney looked down at Rocket's moccasins. The small patches, tattered beadwork, and worn sections showed the years and miles. She mumbled softly.

The black hat appeared tipped under her face. The blue eyes were flashing, but not from anger. "Don't mumble. Don't ever mumble again. You're a grown woman." Rocket gripped her shoulder and stood her up straight. Her right finger and thumb pulled Sydney's chin up. Their eyes were inches apart. "You're not just any grown woman. You can ride a horse and shovel their shit. You've learned how to beat iron and grind knives. In fact, you're grinding your own knife, and it's not a sissy little city girl knife. You can drop a target with an arrow from fifty yards, which means you can probably drop a suckling pig from thirty feet. You can almost beat Dot or me in the ring." Rocket's finger flashed up almost to their noses. "I said, almost."

Rocket stepped back and pointed at Rose. "Three months ago, you two showed up scared and lost. You were a whimpering spoiled child from Atlanta who could barely toast bread, much less cook a breakfast. Now here you are. Twelve miles out on a trail ride and getting ready for your first night in a cozy down feather bed with fluffy comforters." She smiled and winked at Rose. "And getting ready to cook us old folk dinner."

Rose snorted. Sydney realized the lecture had turned to the deprecating humor of the weather-beaten horsewoman. Her smile brought out a mirrored smile from Jolie. Sydney realized everything the woman said was true—she wasn't the girl who had shown up on the doorstep afraid of everything, including her own shadow.

Sydney rolled her eyes. She placed the bag of pans on the ground. "Help me get the pack off Baby."

Rocket stood still, her eyes lost in the darkest reaches of the shadow from her brim. Sydney could only sense the hard eyes on her. Waiting.

"What…?"

"What's your job?" The lesson wasn't over.

"Cook." The inner edges of her hands inched toward her hips. "Hump the loads, tote the bales, slop the pigs, and whatever other shit job you and…" Her voice faded as her hands dropped and shoulders drooped. Her bluster was gone.

"What's your job?" The sound was barely more than the soft rustle of the chaparral around them. A small bird down the draw could have made more noise.

Sydney bit her lower lip as she looked at her mother, pleading with wet eyes. Rose tossed her hair and went back to pulling the saddle off her horse. It wasn't her lesson, and Rose knew it was a lesson a long time coming. She listened for her daughter. Sydney would answer for both of them. Rose wiped the tear from her cheek on her dusty shoulder. She listened for her daughter.

"What's your job?"

Sydney wiped the tear from her cheek on her dusty shoulder. "To… to learn."

The air drew slowly in through Rocket's nose. The third breath exited Jolie's split lips and gently revealed the tips of pearls. "Well, these packs ain't gonna get themselves off, are they."

They both reached for the hang loops. Jolie looked at the young woman's face set for the load. "Each pack is about a hundred-forty pounds right now. If we each take out one bundle, it drops the weight to only about a hundred. If we take out two bundles…"

"It makes for easy lifting." The girl smiled.

The black hat gently rocked up and down. "And you live to hunt another day."

Sydney reached in and grabbed a bundle. "Pull on three?"

Jolie snorted. "Just pull. I'm getting hungry, and I'm more tired than the highway to the next rodeo."

———

THE FIRE WAS NOT MORE than the size of two fists. The small but cheery light reached out but stopped short of the horses and donkey munching on the tender tips of the brush and occasional clump of grass. Jolie fed another small twig into the flame. Most of the heat came from the heaped bed of coals.

"Why not build a larger fire instead of feeding it all the time?" Sydney eyed the ring of rocks Jolie's hat could span. The fire barely fit in the center. The frying pan had covered most of all the rocks.

Jolie looked up, but Rocket flared in her eyes. "Are you

cold?" She knew how the girl wore the jean jacket loose over her shoulders that she wasn't cold.

"No… it's just…"

"Because that's the way you always saw it in the movies?"

Rose snorted. Her gaze never wavered from the small flame. "Not much camping in Atlanta." She looked up with a smile. "I did sleep out once in East Los Angeles."

"Camping?" Jolie's eyes glittered from under her hat as she fed another twig into the flame.

"I had a crush on the boy down the street. I thought it would be romantic to sleep in his treehouse. Smelling his manly boy smells or something."

Sydney had obviously never heard about this before. "How old were you?" Her face screwed up in disgust.

Rose huffed through her nose softly and looked over. "School had started, so I was probably five or six."

Jolie sniffed and smiled. Her hand fed two more twigs in the flame. "How did that work out for you?"

Rose rocked back with a melodic laugh. "It probably only got down into the sixties, but I knew I was freezing to death. The next morning, I think I had a cold and stayed home from school. When I saw him again, the romance was gone."

Sydney's eyes danced with laughter. "Gee, Mom. One cold night and it's all over. You sure were a wuss as a kid."

Rose rolled her eyes. "Not much changed by getting older, did it?" She looked to Jolie for support.

Jolie's eyes focused on the fire. She fed a couple more twigs.

Rose's voice was soft but concerned. "Jolie?"

Jolie didn't move. Her eyes narrowed as she watched the twigs burn and then just glow like embers. "A person never knows who they are until they challenge their belief. Once challenged, they either fail what they believed, vindicate, or rise above." She looked up. She wiggled the twig at Rose and Sydney. "A year ago, you would never believe you could betray your husband. Escaping with Sydney was not even in the question. And yet, here you are. Protective Mama Bear."

Jolie smiled at Sydney. "You said you played soccer and volleyball in school. Now you're a kick-ass in a ring, can shoot the bullseye out of a target with a bow most men quiver at, and cook a mean pan of chili con jerky."

Sydney smiled shyly and rolled her head to one side as she stared into the pile of glowing embers. "Don't forget shoveling shit."

Jolie waved the twigs at the dark. "And riding Buttercup."

Sydney scoffed with a laugh. "Anyone can ride Buttercup."

Rocket flared with a crooked smile. "You think so? Ask Dot to ride her."

Sydney chuffed. "Dot doesn't ride anything that breathes."

Rose barked a laugh. "She sure looked like she was riding you three days ago in the ring."

The young woman blushed in the dim firelight. "She got the drop on me…"

Rocket snorted and stuck a small handful of twigs on the glowing embers. They flared. "She didn't get a drop on you. I warned you about sweeping your foot too high. She was waiting for you. But as for riding, she won't ride any of the Broken Ride horses. But I have seen her lying on the back of

Baby in the sunshine. They were sound asleep, so technically, she wasn't riding. But she won't ride the horses because she knows each of their stories and why we have them."

"She told me Buttercup bit the guy who had her."

Jolie nodded. "She did. He was rough on her. He kicked her in the belly to make her blow out the air so he could tighten the strap on the saddle."

Rose frowned. "And he gave her to you because she bit him?"

"No." She added a few more twigs. There was no smoke from the twigs. The tiny smoke came only from the one leaf of chaparral. "No, his widow gave her to us. He took the lashing to her. But the moment he was behind her, she let him have it with both barrels in the ass."

Sydney's eye grew. "That can kill a guy?"

Jolie shrugged her eyes and lower lip. "Maybe. It sure destroyed his entire pelvis. But it also threw him against the wall. It was the six-inch peg for hanging tack that probably killed him." She side-eyed Sydney. "Pegs usually do that when they're driven through a man's heart."

"Is that why you cinch, walk them around, cinch, walk again, and cinch one last time?"

Jolie wagged her head gently. "Nah… That was the way my daddy taught me. The horse likes it and eventually trusts you enough you never get another hole out of the belt after the first cinch. My Thunder stopped swelling his belly after about the second week. He knew I'd never knee him or kick him. If he didn't want to ride, he just backed away sideways before I could put the blanket on. I learned to respect that.

Even on rodeo day. When a horse knows you respect them, they'll respect you."

"So is Buttercup dangerous?"

Jolie looked at Rose. "Not anymore. And not to Sydney." She turned to Sydney. "How many times do you think you brushed her and bathed her before you tried to bridle her?"

The girl leaned back on her elbows, her eyes large, and her cheeks ballooned. "Phew. Dozens."

Jolie waved her hand toward the girl as she looked at her mother. "There's your answer. She'd already won the horse's respect and friendship before she ever did anything more than pamper her."

The two looked at the young woman. She was flat on her back and breathing softly.

Jolie put the rest of the twigs back on the small stack. "Yeah. It's time to get some shuteye. The sun comes up earlier on this side of the ridge." She glanced toward Rose, who was already turning over on the blanket as she pulled the other half over her shoulder.

Jolie smiled. She reached back, adjusted her saddle, and leaned her shoulders and head into it. With one last look around the minimalist camp, she listened to where each horse was. She never worried about Baby.

She drew the large-brimmed hat down over her eyes, and she was back in her strange safe spot. She could feel the weight and security of the prison cell's thick concrete walls and iron bars. Her imagination played the sound of Mary's slow breathing with its funny soft poo with each exhale. She drifted into the dark with the knowledge they locked the cell door, but Mary would wake even if a guard walked by on their almost silent crepe-soled boots. Safety and protection would let Jolie sleep until just before daylight.

Baby's ear twitched. Something small rustled through the underbrush. A wild pig rooted up the draw. One of the horses shifted its weight as they slept. Sydney rolled over and snuggled up on her saddle com pillow. A barn owl floated silently overhead—hunting.

THE LARGE MAN slid into the booth. He sat in the middle, out of habit. His slender partner slipped into the other side and slid over to the wall. He half-turned to watch the entire café. They were creatures of habit and had grown used to who liked what during their five years working together.

Piles' hands were slender and delicate. Without his watching, the right hand straightened the paper napkin—precisely two inches from the edge of the table. The silverware was a quarter inch from each side and touching spoon over knife next to the fork.

The larger man, Track, had always found it amazing the man straightened the table by feel instead of sight. "I think we're close. I noticed that guy at the gas station. His pupils grew when we showed him the photos."

Piles' eyes moved back to the booth. He thought about what his partner had said. "I noticed the same with the waitress this morning. I think they either moved through here or are nearby but only come to town occasionally."

Track noticed the waitress headed their way. He pulled

the two photos out of his shirt pocket. "We'll work the small towns around here for a while. See if we can pick up a trail."

The young woman spread her one hand across the apron over her dress as she put down the two menus. "Good evening gentlemen. Can I start either one of you with something to drink?"

24

HOG RUN

Jolie had extended their trail ride an extra day. She had shot a jackrabbit, so Sydney tried her hand at it. The results weren't the same. Jolie worried when the hunter showed up with her bow, but her hands, arms, and clothes smeared with blood.

Sydney stood up-trail of the camp. Her bow hung lifeless from her left hand. "I think I need your help."

Rose and Jolie looked up at the bloodied statue. Rocket stood silently. Her hand went to her back and the large knife's handle in its holster strapped to her back. The fourteen-inch blade could reach through the shoulder and slice the heart of a full-grown quarter-ton of charging European boar.

"It's dead. But I don't know how to skin it or whether to do it there or bring it back here first."

Rocket's voice eased down to the coaching Jolie. "What did you kill?"

"A pig."

Rose stood with wild eyes. This wasn't stealing the car to drive to the mall or getting her first period. This was… she wasn't sure. But it wasn't anything she expected from her daughter. "How big?" She held her hands out the size of a medium dog.

Pink stood next to Jolie. She could sense something had happened.

Sydney looked at her mother's hands. "Not that small." She pointed at the hundred sixty of Pink. "More like Pink, but bigger."

Jolie blew out her breath in relief. She had feared it was a suckling and the mother was somewhere behind—tracking Sydney. She waved her hand back up the trail Sydney had taken. "Come on, Baby. We might need you. Rose, how about you stay here and start packing the horses?"

Baby and Pink rubbed noses in the excitement of an adventure and then followed the two women. Pink's black tail whipped back and forth as Baby's was a blurring propeller, first one way and then the other.

The pig was as tall as Sydney had said—as it lay lifeless in the dirt. But the girth put the boar well over the three-hundred weight. Rocket's eyes danced with an inner glow rivaling the embers of the last few nights. She leaned into Baby's neck and hugged. "Sorry, girl, but you're going to have to work today. Your girlfriend bit off a lot to chew."

Sydney turned, horrified. "It's too big?"

Rocket laughed. "If you shot three of these, we would still pack them out." She checked the edge on her knife by running her thumbnail down the edge. "It just means we're going to have some hard work, a fast lunch, and then take the hard way home." She held her hand out. "Let me see your knife a second."

The young woman reached under the back of her bloody shirt and withdrew a ten-inch version of Rocket's knife. Rocket drew her nail down the edge.

"I honed it just before we left. It's only cut the jerky." Sydney watched with nervous expectation. The honors student had never worried about a test. This one…

Rocket stepped over and leaned into the large pig. Riding the back of Sydney's smaller knife down the shaft of the arrow, she jammed the blade halfway in and rocked it down to open the cut. She felt her way into the large wound. Her arm stood buried past the wrist in the still-hot blood. She cranked her head around and looked at the hunter. "How many steps did he take after the arrow went in?"

"None. He just looked up like, *What the fuck?* And then just dropped. Why?"

Rocket moved out of the way and nodded toward the ground. "The front hoof. He dropped straight down. He wasn't even walking. You shot him the moment he first heard you. If he had been moving, the hoof would have stretched out. The hind legs would be behind as he stretched out going down. I just wanted to know if you were still paying attention. Some people blank out on their first kill. You used the small-head arrow."

Sydney nodded. She didn't know if it was a question or a reprimand. "I thought I was hunting rabbits."

Rocket folded forward, convulsing in laughter. "Yeah… oh, shit." It took a moment for her to settle down. "I was hunting deer up in the Owens Valley, over near Nevada way.

Up popped a bunny, and I drew and fired. The large-head arrow took his head off right at the neck. Damnedest thing I'd ever seen." She strained and then pulled the arrow. It came out with a soft pop.

Jolie stood with a broad smile. "If he had gotten a step in before the arrow, he'd still be chasing you. You split his heart." She handed the hunter the arrow. "Great shot. That's the arrow you never shoot again. It goes on the wall."

Sydney stood a little taller. "Kind of like a business framing their first dollar?"

Jolie wiggled her eyebrows as Rocket skimmed across her eyes. "Now the work begins. Up to learning how to field dress a pig when you don't have a tree to hang it from?"

Sydney blinked a few times. "I guess I don't have a choice."

Rocket locked into the eyes under the hat. She pointed at the twin peaks on the distant hill. "Oh, you have a choice. You always have a choice. You see those two upright teats?"

The girl nodded.

"Those are the Squaw Teats. The original Californians called them the lovers. Just take off through the chaparral straight to those two. When you get up there, head straight down the other side and keep on going. You'd probably want to stop when you hit the ocean. Say 'hi' to your dad when they find you." Rocket turned back to the pig. Laying the smaller knife on the ground, she drew out her much larger knife. In seconds, the center of the carcass was open, and she was drawing the intestine out and onto the ground.

"That's not what I meant." Sydney took up the smaller knife and wiped it on her leggings.

Jolie paused and pointed her knife at the blood patch on the black wrestling leggings. "It does wash out, but you run the risk of slicing the leggings or worse, through the leggings and into your skin."

"Then how do I wipe off the blood?"

Rocket smiled a picket fence of pearls. She flipped the knife in the air and wiped it on her moccasin. The back of the knife led the wipe as she drew the knife across and up her calf. "Do it with the back leading, and you don't run the risk of cutting the leather." She flipped the knife over and wiped the other side as the knife drifted down the calf. She turned back to the pig. "It also helps waterproof the leather."

She pulled, and the esophagus, gullet, and lungs pulled out of the neck and cavity. She slung them over near a bush. Rocket smiled back at Sydney. "While the blood is fresh, it scares the hell out of the city slickers, too." She wiped the blade and stuck it back in its sheath on her back. "Here, help me turn this bastard over this bush."

Once they got the pig on the bush, it looked like the pig had reanimated. Jolie stepped back and admired the carcass. She elbowed Sydney's arm. "Frankenstein's monster rides again, eh? Too bad my sat phone doesn't have a camera."

Sydney's lips were furled in a half-smile as her large eyes blinked and blinked again. "He is big…"

Rocket rocked, agreeing. "More than you and me. Maybe add in Pink here." She fluffed the ear of the dog, who wasn't sure about the pig being back up on its feet.

Rocket jerked and elbowed the hunter. "Come on. We're burning the daylight we'll wish we had when we're heading to the Two Tits. Grab your knife."

Rocket showed her how to cut around the leg just a hand's width above the hoof and make the cut line from the circle to the gutting. "The rest is all muscle work. Next time Dot's beating on you in the ring, or it's after dark and you're still pounding steel, you'll know what real aching muscle is about."

Grabbing the skin near the hoof, she started working the skin off the meat. Soon they were working their fists between the meat and skin. In the cool sunshine, the sweat ran down their backs, arms, and faces. Finally, the whole skin was up around the neck, flipped over the head.

"Come on. We need water, and your momma's probably worried about what happened to us."

Sydney followed, pointing back at the pig. "But what about…"

"Nobody is going to touch it while we're around. The flies would be there even if we were there. We need the outside of the meat to glaze over. So, meanwhile, we can get some water bottles, grab some jerky, and get your mom breaking camp."

An hour later, Rose came up the trail, leading the horses. Only the bones and the pig's head were left on the ground by the entrails. The meat lay packed away in Baby's packs. The skin, rolled inside out, hung strapped behind Buttercup's saddle.

Sydney stood staring at the thick roll. Her hand passed over the end.

"What?" Jolie checked the horse's belly cinch. True to her nature, Buttercup only relaxed around Sydney. Jolie pulled the extra two holes and tied them off.

"I never would have guessed a pig's skin was so thick on the back."

Rocket leaned gently against the horse to look at the new hunter. "When we tan this out, I'm guessing we'll take two inches at the most. On some big older boars, we've seen four-inch-thick armor." She held her hand up in the measure. "Come on. We want to make the lovers before dark. Otherwise, we end up on the trail and don't make it home before midnight."

They broke through into a small clearing. Jolie pointed at the break in the chaparral. "See how the ground isn't flat?"

The two women nodded.

"That dish out of the trail is from large pigs running the trail. It'll wind, but it's headed over the ridge. You can just follow the break in the chaparral." They watched as Baby danced with her propeller tail in and up the trail. "Or you can just follow Baby all the way home. She knows where her food is." Jolie waved them on ahead.

Pulling the satellite phone from her back pocket, she raised the antenna. She pushed and held the two. In a moment, there was a click, a ka-chunk, and a ringing. "Yeah, Mike. Sorry to disturb your nap... Oh, good. Kick the plumber's ass and shoot a warning shot over the electrician's head... No, we've had a great time, but we're heading back now. I'll call when we make the crest at Twin Tits, but I'm guessing we won't be in the yard before ten. But we have about three hundred pounds of prime pig to turn into sausage... Nope... Sydney... Bow... Dropped him from about fifteen yards. Snuck up on him. She done me proud... Yeah. Thanks. See you later." She closed the antenna and shoved the phone back in her pocket as she looked around.

She thought about all the years she and her father had hunted out here with just the dogs and a knife. They would be gone for a day or three. No phone. No worries. Nothing more serious happened than her father breaking his arm or having to bury a dog, but they never thought about being out here alone with nobody knowing where they were or any way of getting help. And now she sat on that security, and it seemed so strange to use it—the common courtesy of just letting them know to expect three hungry hunters and five starving fur children.

Rocket nudged her horse and rose in the stirrups. A familiar ache was starting in her arms and back. It was an old friend she had been missing for years.

"Pig." The large toothy smile shined under the wide brim.

25

HOME AGAIN

Jolie pantomimed the previous night. "So, there I am, bent over, panties around my right ankle with my bra wrapped around my neck and elbows. And this strange male voice croaks from the dark bedroom, *Don't shoot.*"

Rose, holding her sides, squeals in laughter. Sydney is smothering her face with the towel.

"Shoot? Hell, if I still had my pants on, I would've loaded them." Jolie rolled over into the lap of the man with the basketball for a head.

Mike smiled at those laughing. "What did the doctor say, Punchy?"

Punchy kissed the top of Jolie's head and then crossed his arms over it, trying to smother or at least keep the noise down. Which only caused even more laughter at his trying to ignore the comedy. "Between the Benadryl and epinephrine inhaler, I'll probably be ready to get back to work in a couple of days. But I still need to check in with the sheriff's office to verify my new hat size. And they want to test me for sensitivity to burning poison oak."

The loud, snotty snort under his arms set even him to laughing.

Finally, Jolie rolled up to look at Mike. "So, when I called from the ridge, it just slipped your mind that I would share my bed with a strange man?"

Mike rolled his eyes into closed as he turned his head. "There may or may not have been a little scotch involved."

Rose chuffed. "More than a little. I kept smelling it while we were unpacking and wondering where my ration was. But thanks for coming over to help unpack. Just, next time, bring the bottle."

Mike smiled. "You can come visit the house anytime. The bottle never leaves the middle of the counter. There's a chip in the tile they haven't fixed, and it reminds me every time I take a drink."

Rocket growled, "There better not be any fucking tile in that house. I paid for manufactured soapstone. I know you surf bums, and I don't want any stains or chips in the finish."

Mike laughed. "Good to know my landlady is on top of the contractors… so to speak." He winked at Punchy.

Jolie sat up. "Speaking of being on top of the construction. Are you hanging around while they fix those two windows and check the dead wall plugs today?"

"Sure. Why?"

"Well, basketball head here has to go shoot the shit at the office. I figure we girls can tag along and maybe do some shopping until he figures out we're hungry and takes us to a wonderful lunch at the Crab Shack."

Mike looked at Punchy and started nodding. "And you want to borrow the Lexus because the four of you don't fit in the truck. How am I supposed to get home?"

Rocket snickered. "That's what all that metal in your pecker region is for. The walk is good for you. Unless you want to hang out here with Dot."

Dot stopped pulling and winding her twisty dreads. Her eyes glowed red around the dark centers. "Oh, hell no. The las' time he hold steel while I pound, the steel hit me chest, bounced off the anvil, den hit chest again." She pointed at her large rock-hard breasts. "And they still be all swollen up."

Sydney rolled her eyes and stood. Bending, she gathered the dishes. "This is getting too racy for my tender ears. I'm gonna pull up my pants and go do the dishes."

Even Dot snickered as they watched the young woman pad her way into the house.

Rocket's eyes narrowed as Sydney turned into the open door. She leaned toward Rose. "She's not wearing her moccasins…"

Rose's one eyebrow raised as she looked out of the side of her eye. "She started to climb into bed last night and then looked down at all the dried blood on them. A minute later, she was in the shower. I didn't hear her throw up, but she was in there a long time. This morning she put on fresh leggings but not the moccasins."

Punchy squinted, which was as close to frowning as he was going to get with his new head. "Blood?"

Rocket leaned back into him as she stroked her long, blond ponytail. "I taught her how to field dress the pig. And where to wipe the blood."

He nodded. "It makes them water-resistant."

Rocket snorted. "Keeps the tourists away, too."

He started laughing in a hacking, snorty way. "Bishop." He coughed and snorted again. "The Pro Rodeo."

Rocket's eyes lit up. "In the park." She squealed with laughter.

"That woman's face…"

Rocket nodded violently as her she beat her feet in the air. "And the husband trying to cover the two kids' eyes."

The other three just watched the show. Either they would get the story, or it would just pass into the day. Mike watched Baby playing in the wagon yard. He couldn't see any butterfly the donkey was playing with… but her antics resembled such. The smaller hooves pranced around like a spring lamb.

Dot leaned over. "She be happy she no pack today. The freezer full of meat." Her head slowly wagged as they watched the dance of gray donkey, dust, and the air. It was pure delight in the sunshine.

Jolie kissed Punchy somewhere near the mouth or nose as she pulled out of the chair. "Bus is leaving in thirty minutes. And we have a trunk full of meat to load."

Jolie was looking over the scale printout as Punchy got in the car. She glanced up. "How bad?"

He snorted as he started the car. "The usual jokes about punching out early to make it to the basketball game." He looked over with a finger point. "Jessie almost got creative. He got about five words out and then ran out of joke."

Jolie rocked her head and pursed her mouth. "Five words… That's a lot for Jessie. I'm impressed. Maybe we'll help reelect him."

They looked at each other. They knew how they felt about him. "Nah."

Punchy backed the car out of the slot and nosed it onto the road down from the vantage point of the sheriff's office on the decaying mountainside. He peeked over at the paperwork and back at Sydney. "How did the new hunter do?"

Jolie found the final scale reading on the printout. "Two-seventy-three with a seven percent." She smiled back at the quiet girl. "You did great."

Punchy's face was still screwed up as he ran the numbers. He looked at the girl in the rearview mirror. "That means the pig was about three-eighty before you stopped him with that arrow. If you were in 4-H, you would take home a blue ribbon for a hog that size." His thumb floated in the air as he watched the girl's smile grow.

Jolie turned in the seat. "The fat content was a little light, so they'll throw in some extra, and we'll have sausage to smoke by next week."

Rose smiled with a questioning look. "Which flavor of sausage?"

Rocket flared across Jolie's smile. "Mostly link, but I'm sure we can put in an order for… say, a quarter into chorizo. It's been years since I've had chorizo and eggs el primero."

Punchy leaned his head. "Feed and clothes, or somewhere else?"

Jolie leaned over the back of the seat to look at Sydney's feet. The girl crossed her legs under her knees, but Jolie saw the tennis shoes. She leaned her chin on the back of her arm on the bench seat. "Do you want new moccasins?"

The girl closed her eyes as she shook her head. "I saw you pull on boots, so I figured the moccasins weren't something to wear to town…" Her voice was quiet but faded off.

Jolie licked her lips as she thought. She only half-peeked at Rose and caught the slight shrug. With the kill, she realized she was no longer in "mom" territory. The girl had stepped into her own as a woman.

"I pulled on my shit-kickers because it's what I'm comfortable in. Like your normal tennis shoes, since long before I was as old as you, I've lived in boots. Only those seven years in prison did I wear soft shoes every day." She reached her hand out. "When I surfed, I wore flip-flops. When I rode, it was shit-kickers. Around the ranch, it's shit-kickers or mocs. Some days, it's even barefoot until I need to go clean the barn, then it's whatever I find on my feet. So, whatever you feel comfortable in, that's what you should wear."

"Even with the blood on the moccasins?"

Rocket cocked her head and smiled. "Especially with the blood on the moccasins."

Punchy pulled up the alley and parked a truck length from the large sliding door.

Jolie wiggled her eyebrows, which didn't show under her hat. "Last chance. New moccasins or boots? It's all on the ranch's account, and what you just put in the meat locker bought you a lot of credit."

The girl paused and then shook her head. "No, I'm good. I don't think boots would be good in bed."

Punchy paused halfway out his door. He glanced back with a lecherous grin. "You never know. Especially with Mexican rowels."

Rocket slugged at his escaping arm and looked back with wide eyes. "Ignore the horny old goat in the barrel."

Sydney frowned. "Mexican what?"

Rose rested her hand on the girl's leg. "You know the little wheels on cowboy's spurs? The vaqueros have the same wheels, but they are a mass of little sharp spikes."

"But why would that be good in bed? Wouldn't it tear up the sheets?"

Roses eyes grew huge, and she glared at a now giggling Rocket. She furled her lower lip and patted Sydney's leg as she opened the door. "We'll talk about this when you're older." She pushed her daughter out of the door.

Her forehead stopped at Rocket's brim. She gritted her teeth as she growled. "I'm going to kill your husband."

Jolie laughed. "Not married yet. Just living in sin."

The two women walked with arms around the other's waist as they followed Sydney past the stacks of hay and bags of alfalfa. Long blond ponytail under a black hat and a long black ponytail clenched with a Navajo squash blossom of silver and turquoise. The giggles were pure naughty schoolgirls.

The shopping was casual with a handful of needed shirts, socks, and a couple of on-sale insulated barn coats with an eye toward winter. Jolie knew from experience that every city slicker near rural would snap up anything insulated when the weather turned.

Jolie pulled a dozen-pack of rough-out gloves from the rack. She showed them to the youngish man behind the counter, ringing them up. "What do you hear?"

The redhead wagged his head with a disgusted look on his face. "They're undersized weird, and the stitching pops. They're made in Korea, and they haven't gotten a good grip on what they're for. Grab eight pairs of the Rio Grandes, and I'll match the price. But they'll last five times longer."

She put the bag back and grabbed the work gloves she usually bought. She dumped them on the counter, then turned to Rose. "Grab anything you see you might like. I gotta go take a pee." Turning back to the redhead. "I don't know where Punchy is, but he's probably also got some stuff. I'll be right back."

She walked down the hall and quietly pushed into the women's toilet.

The whisper was in the last stall. Jolie stopped, listened, and Rocket took over.

"It was awesome. The pig was enormous, and I got him with the first arrow. Rocket taught me to skin him, and then… Bunny, someone is here. I gotta go. No… I gotta go. I love you, but—"

Rocket kicked the stall door open. The girl screamed and tried to scramble up the wall away from the sight of the black hat over burning angry eyes.

Rocket snatched the phone in a sparkling pink phone case. She held it to her ear. "I know where you live. If you tell your father anything, I will come find you, and then it won't be pretty. You got me?" She listened and then hung up.

She shoved the phone in her front pocket and then glared at Sydney for three breaths. Her voice was as cold and quiet as death itself. "Outside. Now." She turned and fished out her own cell phone. She punched the three ones and leaned against the sink as she watched Sydney slink out the door. "I don't know where you are or what you're doing, but we're leaving now." She hung up. Starting for the door, she remembered why she came in.

Punchy met her at the counter with his barber, Stan. He looked at an agitated Rocket and cocked his head in a nod at his barber. "Tell her."

Stan was a man's barber. He had a reputation for saying little and looked like he ate less. Rocket had seen him around for years. He was one of those fixtures in a small town, like a stop sign. Nobody knew when it showed up—it just felt right to be there.

He leaned in so she could hear his soft voice. His hand was barely a width away from his belt buckle, but the finger pointed behind Rocket. "These two hombres just blew into town yesterday. They ain't from California. I'm guessing back east or down south. They're looking for a mother and daughter. They done told a few the mother has kidnapped the daughter, but she's old enough to be on her own. Others they done told she was pimping the daughter. But nobody's buyin' it. But those two fit the description and photos they been carryin'. I don't know what's going on, but I just thought you should know. I don't know if'n anyone's squawked, but a heads-up is better than no head. These guys ain't no preachers spreading the good word. They're trouble."

Rocket put her hand on his shoulder and leaned in. "Thanks, Stan. You're right. The heads-up is just what we needed. And if Punchy ever misses a haircut, you call me. I'll cut his other hairs and then send him down." She nodded honestly.

His lips rolled in as his scalp wrinkled at the thought. He glanced down at Punchy's crotch and then patted his arm as he left. "You're on your own there."

Rocket fished the pink phone out of her pocket. "She was talking to her girlfriend. I don't think this is the first time."

Punchy peeled the shell off and set it on the counter. Sliding open the back, he pried out the battery, then stuck the whole in his back pocket. "Let's go. Call Manuel. We need his expertise."

She dialed while Punchy drove. The two in the back were silent.

26

TACTICS

Stanley stood at the sliding glass door. His dream had been to have the triple-expanding doors of glass open to provide an entire wall of open-air for his office. It would be like working outside, but with all the conveniences of his office. No matter how big the laptop, nothing rivaled his triple panels of forty-two-inch monitors. The tower was a server in its own chilled room. Serious, well-paid gamers could only dream of the computer he played solitaire on.

First, it was the spring with pollen. Then came the flies, spiders, fuckbugs, and gnats. He expected the summer heat, but the combined heat and humidity upset the balance of the rest of the house. He had replaced the smart system three times in the first year. In the late fall of the first year, he endured eighty-degree heat to have his open wall for almost four days. The sudden storm had drawn in moisture and high winds enough to cause a land hurricane. It took his crew over a week to replace the missing doors, straighten the track, and dry out his office. And then the custom wool carpet molded.

The python and three cottonmouths for the second Christmas had stopped the wall from ever being open again.

He turned at the chime, causing his fifty-year-old whiskey from Kentucky to slosh in the glass. The chip of ice had melted in the last pour.

He punched at the red button of the speakerphone. "What?" He noticed the caller ID. He thought about adding a "sir" or "Alex." But it was too late.

"If you were standing within reach, I would slap you for that." The man was already mad. Usually, he was only half-mad. The man lived in a world of anger and hatred. His money and power helped him to live out his darkest feelings.

"Sorry. I was just—"

"I don't give a shit. Your kid just called Bunny. We nailed it. They were at a feed and dry goods store in a town called Santa Ynez. Track and Piles are already headed that way. Your women have been shacking up with some mountain woman named Rocket. Track will get the location and then reach out to a local militia up the coast from there. They'll have weapons and armor for us, so we're good the minute our boots hit the ground. So, grab your go bag and get your ass down to Hartsfield-Jackson. I'll meet you in the first-class lounge. I've got us tickets for the six-twenty to LAX." The phone clicked.

Stanley threw the phone across the room. It came to rest in five pieces. The colored housekeeper would clean it up and get it replaced.

He looked out at the pool. The Cuban was slowly vacuuming the bottom. Stanley didn't even want to think about when he last had time to relax by the pool. He wasn't even sure if Sydney laid out or swam. He was sure Rose didn't. Her hair would get wet or something. The more he thought about the money he wasted on the house and the girls...

As he stormed past the desk, he kicked the wastebasket made from an elephant's foot. He never found time to go hunt one for himself, but he found the basket on the black market. It made him even madder that his foot left no mark on the tough hide. It felt like the theme of his life lately—no matter what he did, it was meaningless.

"I WASN'T THINKING ANYTHING. I was just..."

Dot pulled her legs up into the chair with her arms around them. "Feeling like you gots to tell someone?"

Sydney nodded.

Rose opened her mouth. Dot's flat fingers-and-thumb duckbill snapped it shut.

Dot's voice was low and soft. "And because Rocket and your mom had been there, you had nothing to say to them? They already be there."

The girl nodded.

Punchy stepped onto the porch and placed the coffee carafe on the table. In his other hand was his indestructible work laptop. He set it on the table and slipped back into the chair next to Jolie. She gently nudged her chin at the computer as she narrowed her eyes at him. He patted her thigh and poured more coffee.

"How many time we be in da ring?"

Sydney smirked. "More than I want to remember. Why?"

"How many hours you hep me pound and grind?"

She shrugged. "Hundreds?"

"What we talk about?"

The girl looked at the table, porch, her tea, the corral, Stonewall cropping at the alfalfa, anywhere but the one person who mattered now.

"What?"

Sydney's head hung as she mumbled. "Everything…"

"But I don't know nothing about no hunting. Dis, you ha' to go spill yo guts ta… what?" Dot's voice dropped to a chilling, cold wind. "Da one who's daddy aim ta kill y'all."

Sydney flared. "It's not like that."

Punchy put up his hand toward Dot. "Yes, yes, it is. It is exactly like that. Of all the places in the world, how do we have two guys wandering around Santa Ynez looking for you and your mother? Chance? They just threw a dart, and this is where it landed? I don't think so. When was the last time you called your girlfriend?"

Sydney was stone and glaring.

Rose cleared her thoughts. "When we took you to buy clothes and your moccasins."

"It was only half a minute. She couldn't talk because she was in the car with her mother."

Punchy nodded. "If they were actively monitoring, thirty seconds is enough time to get them to the Santa Ynez Valley."

Rose's eyes widened. "I hope Millie wasn't driving. She wakes up drunk."

"They have a driver now. Some guy from Dad's camps."

Rose rolled her eyes and fell back into her chair. "Oh, great. A wannabe Nazi army drone."

Punchy opened the laptop and rebooted the email. "Clyde and Muriel sent me this from their security tapes at the convenience store and gas station." He turned the laptop around for Rose to see.

Rose shook her head. "I'm not sure." She turned it for her daughter to see.

Sydney pointed at the giant of a man. "His last name is Track. His son plays on our football team. They call him 'Half-Track,' like the tank thingy in the movies. He's about six-six and over three hundred pounds."

"As far as we know, it's just the two of them so far." He looked at Sydney. "How long did you talk to her this time?"

"Only about four or five minutes."

Punchy nodded at Jolie and Rose. "More than enough time. They'll have it nailed to the feed store. They'll be in there talking to everyone down to even Chester. Once they have your name, they'll be coming."

Rose blew out a sigh. "How do we stop them?"

Punchy rolled his eyes large. His hands rose.

Rocket stiffened. "We don't."

Punchy blinked and looked at her. "We don't?"

Rocket snuggled back into the chair as she looked at Dot. The two smirked. "Nope. If it's just the two, we even give them coffee, and if it's around lunchtime... Well, it's Californio hospitality."

Rose shifted in her chair. "And what do we do?"

Dot snickered. "Help serve."

Rocket squinted over at Punchy. "When was the last time there was a shootout on the streets of Santa Ynez?"

Punchy closed his eyes as his head fell back. His eyelids vibrated with his search for one of his favorite subjects—local history. "The Rodriguez cousins in the spring of 1897. It was over one of them marrying one of their cousins."

Rocket's eyes never left Sydney's. "How many died?"

"On the street? Only about twelve. Seven more were dead by the morning."

"And the Rodriguez ranchos?"

Punchy's lips rolled. He licked his lips. "The state took control of the two hundred square miles and sold most as smaller ranches, but they kept some land for the prison, missile base, and up north, the nuclear power plant."

Jolie tipped her hat back an inch. "And this is why we invite them in. To preserve the same peace we have enjoyed in the valley for over a hundred years."

"But…"

Rocket stopped Rose with her upheld hand. "When was the last shooting in the valley? A really bloody shooting?"

The deputy shifted in his chair. "I was the first to arrive—March seventeenth at four-thirty-five. I found two bodies on the front porch, three in the living room, four in the kitchen dining room, and two in the bedrooms. By midnight, we had found nine more in the outbuildings used for cooking meth and processing heroin."

"Who were they?" Sydney's voice was only a breeze.

"Aryan Nation owned the property, but we also identified some bodies with a biker gang we didn't know were in the county. Several bodies with silenced Tech-9s were with a

Latino gang up from Ventura. We didn't know if it was a drug buy gone wrong, or they were trying to move in on the territory. Only one survived, and she hasn't said a word. But we hope if she ever comes out of the coma…"

Rocket pointed back a Punchy and then at Rose. "The point being, we like to keep the downtown quiet. The killing…" She looked back at the off-duty deputy. "Or, not killing, we like to keep to home. It's easier to control and doesn't upset the tourists."

Rose swallowed hard. "And your experience…"

Punchy's one eye nearest his soon-to-be wife opened wide. "It was self-defense." He pointed at the patches of scorched wood siding. "They lit the whole porch and front of the house on fire."

Dot snickered. "Ignorant city slickers. Didn't know squat about burning nobody out of they home. Pink here took out most." She grabbed and kneaded the dog's ear. It rewarded her with a moan and a slight roll over to expose her belly for scratching.

"Someone tried to burn you out?"

Rocket nodded. "Yup. They were hoping we'd come running out the door so they could shoot us."

Sydney snapped her fingers and laughed. "They didn't know about the tunnel."

Rose looked at her daughter and then started laughing too. "Who would have thought?"

Jolie rocked with a satisfied smile on her face. "The tunnel was put in by my grandfather a hundred years ago. But I was afraid as a little girl when my father and some men were working on it. Because I never went in, I never showed it to my best friend. So, when she and some men came to kill me, they didn't know."

Rose choked on her coffee and coughed her way clear. "Your best friend tried to kill you?"

Jolie's head barely moved up and down. "She killed my mother, and I served seven years because nobody looked beyond my pig knife in her chest. I had all the motive they needed—except greed. Celeste had that in spades. She's in the same cell I was for seven. But she's in for a lot longer."

The deputy nodded. "Conspiracy to commit murder, conspiracy to commit larceny, and aggravated assault with mitigating circumstances... she'll get out just before she turns a hundred and eighty."

Rose's eyes rolled wide. "Yup, I see it now. You do things a lot different out here in the country." She put down her empty mug. "So we invite them to lunch... but what if my husband and his partner are with them?"

Rocket pushed her brim back farther, exposing her face. "Santa Ynez, as you saw"—she pointed at the computer — "is small-town. But the businesspeople are no hicks. As you saw, they also don't have those grainy cheap cameras. The gas station's been stuck up a few times. Clyde and Muriel are a sweet old couple. Clyde likes to shoot skeet, but Muriel has more than a few large trophies from speed draw and combat shooting. Before they retired, she ran the Department of Justice weapons training battleground up in Sacramento. But when someone wants them to clean out the till, they just do it. There's a single fifty-dollar bill under a spring-loaded trigger. When it comes out first, the silent alarm goes off to the substation. The camera feed starts broadcasting, and a couple of times, deputies were standing outside when the would-be robbers finally came out. Scared old people take a long time to fumble money out of a till, you know." His smile was engaging.

Rocket leaned back onto her right elbow. "So when your husband hits town—we'll know."

Sydney shifted uncomfortably. "And then what?"

Rocket batted her eyes innocently. "Care for another trail ride?"

Sydney frowned and cocked her head sideways. "Trail ride?"

Rocket glanced at Punchy. "Close your ears, dear."

His eyes got enormous, and he looked around innocently. "Eh?"

Rocket continued. "Goats eat everything that is a vegetable. But pigs eat everything with protein." She peeked back at Punchy. "Everything but the teeth. Those just pass on through."

Punchy looked at the sky. "The State of California versus Franklin Waterman. Killed four women and fed them to his pigs. Nothing left except lying in the muck pit was a tooth. People think pigs are dirty or messy. But just the opposite is true. Give them a large pen, and they will divide it into a bedroom, dining, living room, and bathroom. They want their mud bath in the living room, but they will never soil it. They only poop in the bathroom area. And when we finished screening the bathroom muck, we had all four of the women's teeth."

"But..."

Rocket stopped her with her hand. "No buts. If they come

all the way out here, it isn't for lunch. You need to make up your mind before they arrive. So, do you want to keep running or stop them here? Punchy can only tell you certain things or hear certain things because he is an officer of the court. I'm just a rancher who enjoys riding horses into the backcountry. Anything beyond that is up to what happens. But it also depends on being ready."

Mother and daughter looked at each other. The idea was hard to grasp.

Punchy stood, picking up his laptop. "Take your time. Maybe you two might want to take a walk or something and talk. Just know this: we have nothing we can hold your husband or his men. I've reached out to the FBI, and they don't know of you, them, or what you said they do. The deal you thought you had with them was bogus. But it doesn't mean they won't be looking into them. Rather that I have no interest or jurisdiction here. It ties my hands. And tomorrow, I head back to Sacramento and school."

Jolie's back pocket pinged. She pulled out the satellite phone and looked at the screen. "Manuel is at the bottom of the driveway. Maybe it's best if you're not around."

READY

The evening made the upper reaches of the barn all but disappear except for the cooing of the two doves in the southern end. The last sunlight and early morning warmed the south-facing wood of the hayloft, and a thick crossbeam had provided ample area to build nests for over a hundred years. The sparrows preferred the holes, nooks, and crannies of the roof and overhangs. But when the barn doors were regularly open, the doves preferred the long span of the beam. Jolie's grandfather, father, then her mother, and finally her, all occasionally cleared the old nests not used for a few years to make room for new boarders. The soft cooing seemed to calm those below—four-legged or two.

Rocket, Sydney, and Rose stood at the long prep table. They broke the supplies into six bundles. "The four larger bundles we'll store at the camp stashes." Rocket floated her hand over the bundles made up of twenty-four broad-tipped and narrow-tipped arrows, hanks of thin cotton rope, an extra utility knife, a battlefield first aid kit, and a box of 30-

30 bullets. "I'll show you two more stash safes down in the north end with the larger trees for these. Dot will finish with these when she gets back this evening with more rope and bamboo. We'll drop them first and then the four at the camps. Hopefully, we have enough head start to set some traps. I know you're still squeamish about the whole kill or be killed thing, but if we can take out at least one with a man trap, so much the better." She looked at the other two. "Questions?"

Sydney pointed. "The bullets?"

Rocket rolled her lips for a couple of heartbeats. "Last resort. Your mom is better with the rifle than the bow. You've already proven you're good with the bow. But remember, they'll probably have guns if they're as intent as you say they are." She looked at Rose. "If it comes to it, you need to be thinking about saving Sydney's and your lives."

"What about your life?"

Rocket pursed her lips hard as her head rocked. "If it comes to you having to use the rifle… I'm probably no longer an issue."

Sydney shifted her weight to her hand on the table. "You mentioned bamboo…"

Jolie held up her hands like she was holding a basketball. The words were there, just not in the right order, so Rocket took over. She held up a finger. "Just a moment." She strode across the barn. A moment later, she walked out of the grinding room with a four-foot piece of bamboo in her hand.

Standing the bamboo on the dirt floor, she whipped out her knife. Placing it on end, she stopped and slid the knife back under her shirt. "I want you to learn." Looking at Sydney. "Use your knife."

The girl pulled her knife out of her back harness and placed it on the end of the bamboo. The knife was on edge at an angle with the handle below and the point up, the same way she had seen Jolie stand her knife.

"Now smack the top of your hand with your other hand. Kind of like the cutting hammer when you hold it for Dot to hit when she's splitting the hot steel."

The girl struck her hand, and the knife bit deep into the bamboo. Then Rocket made a twisting motion with her hand, and Sydney copied it and followed the opening crack down the stick. Soon she just grabbed the two halves and pulled them apart.

Jolie held one of the halves. "Split it again."

In a moment, they had four-quarters of a four-foot-long bamboo. Rocket started to reach toward her back and stopped. She grabbed one of the folding utility knives on the table and unfolded the six-inch blade. Drawing across her chest, she backhanded a swipe across the end of the bamboo in her left hand. The result was a four-inch-long tapered sharp tip.

Putting down the knife, she hefted the quartered stick in her right hand like a spear, and with her left, she extended her arm and pointed at the barn door twenty feet away.

Her arm and body spun. The short spear buried the point with a dull thud. The stick was pointing back at them. Rocket looked at the other two. "Simple, silent, and if you throw it hard enough, plenty to kill a man if you hit the lungs or heart. And where we're going to be, just a serious bleeding wound is good enough. The pigs can smell the blood from two miles away."

Rose blanched. "And they'll come like sharks?"

Jolie squinted one eye. "From two miles away…?" She fanned her hand in dismissal. "Nah. But you can bet there's at least one or two within a hundred yards of us at all times. They are inquisitive animals. Give them a chance at food, and they will take it."

Sydney returned with the stick. She put her thumb near the tip. "That much."

Rose frowned. "That's all that stuck in? But it was holding—"

Rocket laughed. "Nope. That's what was sticking out on the other side." She had seen the girl look at the outside of the door.

Sydney's shoulders sagged. "You knew?"

Rocket chuckled as she pointed at the large door. "Look around the door sometime. There are a lot of holes. Most of them are little more than a dent. I didn't learn to stick them the first throw."

Sydney whipped around and threw the pole. It stuck with a thud.

Rocket growled in mock battle. "If I ever find out Dot has been training you to do that, she is dead the next time in the ring."

Rose cleared her throat. "Um… let's deal with first things first before we talk about killing friends."

Jolie looked at the dark outside. "Dot will be here any minute. Why don't you two grab showers and get to bed? I'll wake you for breakfast at about four in the morning. We need to be on top of the pass when the day breaks. It's going to be a long day."

Sydney cocked her head. "Why not take two days instead of rushing a long day?"

Rocket rocked as she thought. "Because I need to work the day after tomorrow. There's a little girl who's going to make it all the way around the barrels in less than five minutes."

Rose smiled. "Goldilocks?"

Jolie smiled warmly and nodded as the truck lights curbed into the wagon yard. "There's Dot. Now scoot. The both of you."

The two slipped out of the barn in the narrow space Dot had left with the truck's bumper. They acted like two little schoolgirls caught skipping class.

Dot waved goodnight and grabbed a large bundle of bamboo out of the back. As she walked through the door, she started. Looking at the spear stuck in the barn door, she backstepped. Reentering, she laughed. "Not yours. Sydney?"

"She didn't get it through?"

"Nope. That be how I know it not you."

Rocket grabbed the blacksmith's T-shirt and twisted it close. "Have you been teaching her?"

Dot smiled and shook her head. She looked back. "How many tries?"

Jolie pointed. "Her first try."

Dot looked back with large eyes. "Damn." Her soft voice was pure admiration.

Rocket smiled broadly as she wiggled her eyebrows. "Yeah."

Dot kicked at the bamboo. "How you want me to do them?"

Rocket thought about what they might do with them. "These are what, nines?"

Dot nodded.

"Knock about six down to threes and quarter them. Don't spike 'em. We'll point them as we need to in the field. Then do the same with three more, but only a foot long—quarter half of them. And split them up into two bundles. We'll be stashing them at the head of the back valley where the chaparral is thick and the trees overhang. The shadows give excellent cover for mantraps."

"Not booby-traps?"

Jolie caressed her chest. "Boobies are never to be trapped viciously or deadly."

"What time you eat?"

"I'm shooting for four. But you can sleep in. We're leaving you with all the work."

Dot smiled. "I'll wake you when breakfast ready. I'll need the time to take care of da barn. You take Baby?"

Rocket looked at the table. "I wasn't, but I guess we better."

"I'll pack the rack and hang it. You go sleep."

Rocket hugged her and turned for the door. It was going to be a fast night before a long day.

2 8

MORNING

Breakfast at three in the morning meant a strip bar serving steak dinners. Substitute eggs for the baked potato, and you have breakfast. Stanley wondered why they called it a titty bar when the dancers walked through their three-song routine bearing little more flesh than their nipples. Most of the strippers had bodies of little more than prepubescent tweens. Stanley understood they were dancing for tips and would save the tips until they had enough to buy some oversized breasts.

Out of embarrassment, Stanley paid more attention to his phone and the news. Occasionally, he glanced over at the happy lustful face of his partner. For more than a few years, he had heard rumors of Alex and his daughter Bunny. He had chalked it all up to smack talk from guys who couldn't get a date on Saturday night with a few hundred-dollar bills in their hands. But now he could see the talk about Alex and underage girls—and probably Bunny—was true. Stanley was afraid to look down at the man's lap for fear of what he would see.

"What time are they expecting us?"

Alex shook his head and looked over, annoyed. "What?"

"What time are the guys out in the desert expecting us?"

Alex took a mouthful of his bourbon and crushed an ice cube between his teeth. "This morning. Who cares? Don't you like your breakfast?" He crushed the last of the ice cube and fished out a twenty to the blond with the side of her head shaved. The bill disappeared into the butt crack and bikini bottom. Alex laughed as the girl danced lewdly, mimicking what she knew he wanted.

Stanley picked up his phone as he stood. "I'll be in the truck." He knew he would get a good nap and be the one to do the driving while Alex slept off his drunk.

He looked back down at the half steak and an egg he was leaving. The girl danced into his peripheral vision. He turned for the door. He'd lost his appetite—for almost everything.

Outside, he stood looking at the five vehicles in the parking lot. The many streetlights lit up the broad street like noon. He speculated at the need for a bail bond agent so near to an international airport. The sketchy massage parlor advertising Japanese shower massages squeezed snuggly between a tattoo shop and an erotic bakery. The five chopper motorcycles and one on the way in front of the tattoo shop was the only advertisement they needed. It was gang territory, and someone was getting their club colors done. The new members' next stop would probably be next door for a long, slow Nuru shower massage.

Stanley looked down the street at the many other available selections. In disgust, he shoved his hand into his pocket before remembering he didn't need to click a fob. The doorhandle softly chirped as he touched it. At least some things were cleanly straightforward. With a quick look back down the street, he climbed in the backseat. He longed for the days when he had been innocently oblivious to the proclivities of the deviant. The years before Rose, or even the early years when worked hard together to make a good life. A simple life. One they could hold their heads up about. Instead of one where he was forced to do the unspeakable to protect himself and others in their depraved world they created.

He wadded up his leather jacket to use as a pillow. Even something as simple as a leather jacket he liked on a whore walking the streets of Jacksonville... he drifted off into an uneasy sleep. His sleep had stopped being restful years before.

———

THE SKY WAS a lurid canvas of pink to purple wisps of morning clouds drying in the gray of the wakening. The dark took on shades of dark gray shapes in the black as they had left the barn. The horses followed Baby as she knew the way and preferred to lead with Pink. Jolie left her choice of horse, Trace, to his whim of follow the leader. All the horses except Stonewall had been up and over the trail to the valley many times. There were other valleys, but the one Jolie came back to the most was the one she had the happiest memories of hunting with her father.

The irony of where Sydney had shot her pig did not escape Jolie. She killed her first pig on her sixteenth birthday —less than a hundred yards further up the valley. It was her birthday present from her father. They had taken only a burrow and six dogs. With or without a pig, they had told her mother they would be home for dinner. They never made it.

They found two small suckling pigs scampering through the brush. The dogs attacked them first, so her father stepped in over each and slit their throats.

Jolie then stood watch for the sow. The head dog, Hondo, triggered first. His head snapped to the thick wall of rugged chaparral. He was never wrong.

Jolie stepped over to her father's back. The large knife's handle was just above his left shoulder, where he could reach it fast. Her hand drew it as her feet turned. On her third step toward the brush, the wall separated. The back of the sow was as tall as her chest. Her eyes locked on the moving front leg. The leg moving forward caused a crease at the side of the chest. The leg and the chest were armored, but the crease was supple skin. Behind beat the large heart—three-quarters of the length of the large blade in her hand.

She bent her legs. Her arm cocked solid with the blade's edge pointing up. The pig took her second step—already at twenty miles-an-hour. The third step took the quarter-ton of pig past thirty-five, creased the skin, and drove her body onto the sharpened blade.

The chest slammed against the hilt of the knife. Jolie reached up with her moccasin covered right foot. Stepping on the handle as if it were a stirrup, she pushed her way over the back of the pig. The blade in the pig rotated. The edge sliced through the beating heart.

The pig's fourth step stumbled. Almost seven hundred pounds of pig at thirty miles-an-hour drove the jaw and nose into the dirt. The furrow stopped at her father's moccasin. A few racing heartbeats later, he smiled. She had turned his stories on the front porch into the pure reality of the hunter. The jawbone with the two curled tusks still sat on the coffee table in the library office.

Sydney turned back in the saddle as she approached the outlook under the power lines. "Are we taking a rest break?"

Jolie smiled. The peekaboo view of the ocean was only visible in the afternoon. "Tell Baby to keep going. The top is only a few more minutes."

She looked at the sky as she thought about the first time she rode up here on her pony. At the top, after they watched the sunrise, her father said goodbye and went hunting while she rode back in the new daylight. *You won't regret the wait.*

The pink was spreading along the taller inland coastal range separating the valleys from California's great central valley. Jolie knew it was just an illusion. The sun had already crested the even taller southern end of the Sierra Nevada Mountains that edged California's eastern border.

The spread bled south from Cachuma mountain. As they stood refreshing with tea and coffee from their thermoses, the gray sky blushed into a washed lavender. The pink broke into streaks of blue, and then all was a wash of blue bleached by the rising ball of fiery Phoebus.

"Wow. What a way to start the day." Sydney turned for confirmation.

Jolie's smile pulled hard to the right. She was sure she had told her father something similar. For many years she said goodbye to her father from this spot. She slurped the last of her coffee and stowed the thermos. "Now we're burning daylight." She stepped into the stirrup as she swung her leg over the saddle in one smooth motion. She wouldn't mention it was her birthday because such would lead to explaining which one it was.

She called to the black shadow dancing from bush to bush. "Pink. Hiza." Turning forward, she called to Baby, who was already at the edge leading down into the valley. "Take us in, Baby."

As they started down and the trail widened, Rose fell back alongside Jolie. Jolie looked at her with expectation.

Rose thought a moment. "Hizzle? As in Snoop Dog?"

Jolie laughed. The rapper's made-up words were common in prison. "The word is Hiza. It's Japanese. All her commands are in Japanese. My uncle, who breeds the cane corso, was a code buster and forward spy during the war."

Rose frowned. "Vietnam?"

Jolie chuckled. "You kids. Everything is about you." Her smile grew large. "My father and Jinx were on Corregidor and Midway, spying on the Japanese. After the war, Jinx married a woman forced to be a bed hostess because she was part Korean."

"So, the word means *come*?"

"Actually, it means knee. Like the command to heel, but the choice is up to the dog. So, the way we use it is more like just come."

She looked down at the large black dog walking between

the two horses. Pink had never had a problem walking close to the horses. It was the horses getting used to Pink wandering in and out of their legs.

ALEX WOKE up with a sour look on his face. His eyes were razor slits. Stanley could see the raging headache of the hangover. The man had worked hard for two hours on the strip joint's bourbon supply while trying to get at least a blow job from the strangest of the three strippers. Only the bourbon had worked on the man. It had taken three tries and a drunk pee on the side of the rental to get him in the backseat.

Stanley, for a hundred miles, had regretted walking away from the rest of the steak. Now, the only accommodations were sagebrush, sand, and the occasional yucca plant seared brown by the summer heat.

Stanley touched the icon on the GPS for restaurants. The next food was seven miles before them or the closed half-burned building two miles behind. He looked at the visage in the mirror.

"Help is five minutes away." He lied.

Alex's head weaved as he looked around at the desert. "Gotta pee."

Stanley pulled over. The SUV was almost stopped when he heard the door open, followed by the sound of vomit.

Stanley waited with his head against the still cool glass and his eyes closed. If this was any harbinger of the fate of this trip, it wasn't looking good. But then, the last ten years had been a shitshow spinning down the toilet. So what else was new?

ROCKET TUGGED at the rake of foot-long bamboo knives securely lashed to the drawn-back branch. Rocket fed the dirt-colored twine through the ring on the top of the stake. The steel stake held the ring a foot off the ground. Rocket pulled on the twines looped end. She pulled the loop over the stake on the other side of the trail. There was only about an inch of sag.

"Perfect."

She looked at Sydney. "You played with all the horses. Where is the top of their heads?"

The girl held her hand above her head. Rocket walked through the twine. Pulling the pin on the branch, it released the deadly rake of little bamboo spears. The branch and rake cleared Sydney's hand by only one more hand's width.

Sydney ducked and held her hand and then looked at it. "Damn! Warn me next time."

Rocket pointed. "Put your hand back."

Rose's eyes grew as large as her daughters. The rake was vibrating at the end of the branch over the middle of the narrow trail. The height was where a man's chest or head would be if he were on a horse.

Rocket pulled the loop off the stake. "Pull the branch back and reset the pin. We'll reset the trap when we come through again." She looked at the other two. "We gotta go. There's one other tree that might work."

Sydney and Rose both smiled as they chorused. "But we're burning daylight."

THE "COLONEL," like Alex and Stanley, had never served in any military. The closest he had ever come was thinking about going on a ride-along in his hometown of Apple Valley. After high school, he made money selling acid and mini bags of dope to other students.

Those who didn't have money, broke into homes and businesses and traded guns, ammunition, and jewelry for a small handful of dope. The LSD he paid money for, so he insisted on cash. By the early eighties, he found some groups didn't care where the weapons came from. Business grew. If it could fit in a van, the "colonel" was your man.

He opened the last door in the back of the underground bunker. The door hid secreted behind a large cabinet, randomly filled half-full of antique rifles, from old English fouling guns to an early lever-action thirty caliber rifle taken off the body of a Union soldier. None of the rifles worked, other than to help hide the real stockpile.

"Gentlemen." He waved his arm into the expansive room. "Let's go shopping."

ROCKET RAISED her arm and sniffed at her pit. It smelled like a long day. Her horse pulled up next to the other two. She laughed at the propeller tail already down at the plateau and about to follow the power line over the edge. She knew the little donkey was hungry and would only be minutes away from wanting dinner.

Jolie looked out toward the distant ocean. The large orange ball was already half-buried by the coast range. It wasn't a spectacular sunset because of the lack of clouds, but the usual coastal humidity and smog gave the air a glow.

She fished out her satellite phone and rotated the antenna. Bars appeared. She listened to the ringing. She knew if it made it to four rings in Dot's office, the rest she could hear from the ridge. The large klaxon horn was off a Southern Pacific train. Dot picked up with the second blast. Jolie knew it sounded like a freight train coming through the forge area.

"Jesus, what?"

Jolie laughed. "Baby is about ten minutes out and hungry. We're about forty behind her and just as hungry."

"Okay. Bedding the forge now. I be ready for Miss Princess."

"Don't wash up. We stink also. But steaks and those small potatoes grilled with chunks of onion sound good right now."

"Yes, yo majesty."

"When did you eat last? Because you sound really hangry."

"Today?"

The laughter echoed at both ends as the connection broke.

The horses started down the trail. They were hungry also.

GOLDILOCKS

The fresh white paint on the corrals and buildings was blinding. Rose was glad she had opted for her dark glasses. She studied Jolie. From the way she held her head and the pitch of the wide black brim, she couldn't tell if the woman was asleep or just driving blind.

"You never wear dark glasses?"

The hat tipped up almost imperceptibly. Rose noted a tiny glimmer off the wet eye, and then it disappeared under the brim again. The growl echoed the gravel of the road. "Never needed them."

"Any glasses at all?"

"Nope." She pointed at the large barn straight ahead. "Can you read the sign?"

Rose chuffed. "Of course. Barn three."

The smile was pure Rocket. "How about the next line?" She pulled the truck right and nosed up to the corral. She could tell the woman was still trying to make out what was below the three. The barn was only sixty yards away. But Rocket knew most couldn't tell what was there.

As they got out, Rose walked around the back of the truck and down the road. At a point, she stopped and then walked closer to the barn. Rocket snorted as she watched the woman turn and start back.

Swinging the gate open, Jolie grabbed the first barrel and roll-walked it on its rim to the starting position. She grabbed the second barrel as Rose walked up. She nodded at the third barrel.

"It's just a line."

"No, it's a barrel. That's why they call it barrel racing."

"No. The sign. Under the big three. It's just a line."

Rocket marked an X in the dirt with her boot. "Your barrel goes here."

"It's still just a line. And you knew that before I went down there."

Rocket set her barrel and looked at the alignment. Of all the decades of helping set up kids rodeo and then local and pro rodeos, she relied on her sense of distance. "Nope. Kind of. And nope."

Rose held her fists on her hips as Rocket walked back. "What do you mean nope, kind of, and nope?"

Rocket spotted the tall black man approaching. She stopped beside Rose and turned her head. "The signs are new. I'd never seen them before. But I also knew it wasn't a line." She continued toward the gate. "Good morning, Norm."

He tipped his white straw hat that matched his starched

shirt. The khakis were barely darker. "Mornin', Rocket. I believe this is your cousin Ellen?"

Rocket nodded as her hand and finger waved in the air. "Norm, Ellen. Ellen, this is the owner of this broken-down ramshackle joint. You met him briefly earlier this summer."

They nodded. Norm turned and pointed down the road at the barn. "Did you notice we finally got the signs up?"

She smiled. "It looks great. That dark green with the yellow letters really stands out. I also like how the painter shadowed the carving."

His smile turned large. "That granddaughter is finally coming into her own. She did the carving too."

Rocket smiled at Rose. "Norm's brand is the Bar Three. Some people would think it was just a line under the three. But his father used to be one of the best grooms for race-horses on the West Coast. When they race, there's a bar or gate across the front of the roll-away. The horses are coaxed into the chutes until they stop at the bar. The second bar is close behind them. When they are all in, the loader calls 'Bar Three.' The bell rings, and the front bars or gates open."

Rose nodded. "And the race is on." She looked at Norm. "Was your father one of the guys who called out 'Bar Three'?"

Norm chuckled. "When the racers were going the bar, daddy was calling four."

Rocket laughed. "He was throwing the same shit Sydney is throwing right now."

Norm smiled without teeth. "Best place to be and best perfume in the world." He looked out into the arena. "Is this the Goldilocks day?"

Jolie smiled and puffed her chest. "It is. Matt Thomas agreed to come down and do the timing no matter how many tries she takes." She looked up the road at the approaching truck. "And speaking of the hard-nosed old coot..."

The bent-over man with pure white hair crept out of the truck. Reaching back, he grabbed his two canes and a straw hat with the same wide brim as Rocket's hat had.

Rose stepped forward, and both Jolie and Norm stopped her arms. She looked at Norm, who stood proudly with a welcoming smile. As her head turned, the smile was matched by Jolie or Rocket—for once, Rose couldn't tell which personality was standing there.

The man's voice was soft as butter but firmer than his body seemed. "Greetings all. A wonderful day to be certifying one of our youngest riders." He stopped and looked around.

Jolie coughed to clear her throat or get the man's attention. "Goldilocks will be along shortly. I think maybe her mother is still harnessing her up. How are you doing this morning, Mr. Thomas?"

The man cocked his head and smiled up at Jolie. "On days like this, I feel like a spring chicken. Right before the ax falls." He twisted to see the others. "Good morning, Norm. Who's our good-looking guest?"

Rose stepped forward before Jolie or Norm could stop her. Her hand shot out. "Hi, Mr. Thomas. My name is Ellen. I'm Jolie's cousin from out of town."

The man stepped back with a shocked look. "I don't touch people."

Chided, Rose stepped back and didn't know where to put her hand. "I'm sorry. I didn't know."

The man turned. "Most don't. Well, I'm assuming the timer and all is set up in the perch?"

Norm stepped over to walk with the man, separated by a body length. "I'll go with you and make sure." His hand fanned the air for Jolie to go check the girl.

Rocket waited until they were most of the way across the arena before turning toward the barn. "Fucking old asshole."

Rose's eyes were large. "And here I thought you were just joking about the most loved man in the county or something."

The brim turned up and then resumed its standard pitch. Rocket's growl was visceral. "Not fucking likely. The man has been an ass since he got the position and certified me for my first rodeo. My father held me to his face and swore if I weren't nice to the man, he would make me skin out and butcher every pig, deer, or elk we killed."

"How old were you?"

"Six." She turned and watched the woman walking the small rider and tiny pony. The full-head helmet bobbed along barely above her mother's waist. The smile was always happy but with a hint of worry. She would never compete in the open classes of barrel racing, but it would log every run she made against every other rider with dwarfism and Down's Syndrome across the continent. Their standings posted on a controlled website. On any Sunday night during rodeo season, the riders flooded the site with their comments. Many had met each other, but they all knew each other through the website.

"How's my superstar?"

The girl's tiny face beamed. "I… I'm feeling like a champion, Rocket." She pointed at the head of the tiny pony. "We've been practicing hard."

"I've heard." Jolie looked up at Goldilocks' mother. "All the braces…?"

The thumb was straight up. "Ready to go. She checked me three times."

Jolie nodded her brim up with a slight bob. She had learned how frustrating it was to deal with a mild case of OCD. The girl's condition increased her stress. Jolie had read the girl's medical file and talked over her fitness with their doctor and specialist. The belief was it was now or not. The dwarfism of the thirty-two-pound little person was only the beginning; even that carried a handful of medical problems. Down's Syndrome carried another handful of problems. Combined, she wasn't expected to make it to high school. So, any living she was going to do needed to happen now. Tomorrow or next year had no guarantee.

Rose fed herself into the bars of the fence and sat with her arms draped and crossed over the higher bar. As she watched Jolie leading and talking the girl through the pattern, Rose noticed several other riders and what looked to be staff take similar seats around the arena.

Nobody left. The hour was a dance of Jolie walking alongside the pony as they traced the pattern. Rose noticed the mother's hand shoot to her face when the girl leaned too far and struck the rim of the second barrel with her helmet. As the girl righted and kept going, the hands lowered, but Rose knew they were not relaxed.

Norm called down from the announcer's perch. "Rocket, can you let her run one more time, but alone? And Goldilocks, you need to pep up Galahad just a bit."

Rocket kneeled and talked Goldilocks through the expectations of the next run. The helmet bobbed and bobbed again. Finally, they walked back to the starting chute. The clock reset. Rocket folded her arms. The bell rang.

The pony trotted with the same lack of haste he had every single time before. Goldilocks begged him to pick up the pace. As they came to the first barrel, Rocket leaned her weight onto her right leg—into the curve. She held her weight on the inside leg until they had cleared the barrel.

The pony trotted to the second barrel and the left-hand curl. They leaned so tight to the barrel Goldilocks' helmet rode the rim all the way around. As they cleared the barrel and headed for the center and third barrel, the girl leaned as far forward as she could. The pony responded. As they hit the third barrel and the second left-hand turn, the helmet clanged and rode the rim. But before her mother's hands could rise to her face, the tiny girl let out a yeehaw worthy of a seasoned cowboy.

As they cleared the final barrel, the entire arena could hear the tiny voice. "Take it home, Galahad. Take it home."

The fence of the arena exploded in cheers. Win, lose, or draw, the little girl was one of them in spirit.

As the cheers settled down, the arena silenced. Now there was only one voice that mattered. The soft drawl had people holding their hands up to their ears to hear.

"Four minutes, forty-three seconds. Goldilocks and Galahad are certified."

Jolie walked past Goldilocks' mother. She knew Goldilocks would be agitated for a short time while she was taken off the pony. The bracing that allowed her to ride was also a prison. They would need alone time. As they passed, Jolie smiled with a thumbs-up. "I think I need some yogurt."

Goldilocks' reward for doing good at something—even as innocuous as a doctor's visit without a temper tantrum—was a small dish of frozen yogurt at the YoYo shop.

As Norm and Mat Thomas finally descended the stairs from the perch, Jolie smiled at Norm. "He didn't fudge those numbers, did he?"

The old man glared. "I've never cheated on anyone's certification. The day I do, I'll retire."

Rocket flared, but Jolie pushed forward. "Well, thank you for coming out today. It means everything for her to ride in the fall rodeo. She'll finally have some numbers to put up with her friends on the national standings."

He waved it off. "Well, I don't know anything about that. But she needs to lean over that damn pony's head more. He thinks this is a pansy-prance in the park or something."

Rocket sighed. "Yeah, we'll work on that."

The man crept across the arena, on his legs and canes, toward the gate and his truck. "See that you do."

Rocket growled quietly. "Fucking old asshole."

Norm tipped his head back, stretching. "You think Mike will be ready come October?"

"If he doesn't certify, I'm going to be tanning his hide with the pig we got the other day."

Norm frowned as he looked down at her. "You went hunting?"

Rocket pointed at Rose. "Ellen's daughter dropped a big sow with a narrow head arrow from about forty feet or so."

"Jeez. What bow?"

"A hundred-forty-pound cammed compound recurve with a seventy-five-pound pull. The one I still can't pull." She smiled up at him. "Yeah. She's a beast. And getting even better with knives."

Norm's shoulders and arms shook. "You hang out with scary people, McGee."

She looked back, and the smile widened. "Yup. And one just qualified to race in the rodeo."

30

LUNCH

Stanley pounded on the door. The cheap brass nine rattled on its two nails.

"Go away."

Stanley leaned in toward the door. The housekeeper glared over her cart from three rooms away. "Alex, it's almost eleven o'clock and checkout time."

"I'm still sleeping."

Stanley realized the childish giggle was coming from the room, not somewhere else. The man had gone back to the bar last night. There was nowhere else he could have hooked up with a girl. The entire fart in the road comprised a gas station, the bar, the motor lodge, and three closed buildings. The nearest house was an eighth of a mile out in the desert behind the gas station. It was anybody's guess if it was occupied or even habitable. It seemed in better condition than many of the shacks housing multiple generations of people around the Okefenokee Swamp.

Stanley walked down to the office and noticed a car sped by. He chuffed to himself. *Traffic.*

He drew out his wallet. "I guess he's going to be sleeping late this morning. Is there any place around here I can get breakfast?"

The man's eyes roamed everywhere but Stanley's face. He waved his hand. "Bout ten or twenty minutes thet away." The man's thin hair stood straight up and looked like it hadn't seen a comb in years. It seemed to follow whichever direction one of the man's eyes tracked.

"I don't remember seeing any restaurant yesterday."

The man's face popped as he pushed back the three dollars in change. "Taint no sign. Just look for the jet fuel tanks lined up on the desert side. Carnita's is across the road."

Stanley remembered the fuel tanks. He had wondered if they were for sale. He crumpled the bills in his hand and shoved them in his pocket. "Thanks."

"When he be out?"

Stanley turned.

"Lupe only here till she go pick up her kid at the school."

Stanley shrugged. "Couple of hours maybe."

"He best no be in there with that furner girl. She only fifteen, but she has the clap so bad she her own cheer squad."

Stanley sighed. "I think he's just sleeping."

"Jus' sayin'. She didn't come home last night. I don't care, but he best go see a doctor."

Stanley grimaced. "I'll tell him." He pushed his way out through the sand-pitted glass door. Some days he felt like a truancy officer.

Forty minutes later, he sped past the motor lodge going the other way. The notice from the health department dwarfed the "closed" sign in the Cantina's window. The closest breakfast was the other way, about ten minutes past the motor lodge. The fuel tanks weren't for sale, but the guy had most of the parts for a light Sherman tank. Pushed, he admitted it was just the shell.

While he drove, Stanley called Lucas Track.

"Track."

"Lucas, it's Stan."

"What do you need, Stanley?"

"What have you found out about where they are?"

"They're at a ranch about twelve miles out of town up in the hills."

"Have you been up there?"

"No. Alex didn't tell us to."

"Well, I'm telling you to. Go snoop around and get the lay of the land. We'll probably get in after dinnertime."

"Where's Alex?"

"Sleeping off a drunk with a fifteen-year-old with more diseases than all Atlanta. Now get to it, or we're going to have a problem with you."

The metallic snip of the call hanging up pissed Stanley off more than the blatant disrespect. If things didn't improve, there might be more holes dug in the desert than they had intended.

He nosed the SUV into the small roadside café.

"Mus' be lunchtime."

Sydney frowned. The knife blank in her hand sliced into the bed of coffee grounds with a soft crunch. "How do you figure?"

Dot leaned against the doorjamb. The barn doors were both wide open. They could see most of the wagon yard. The large black SUV eased around the hard corner and into the yard.

Sydney stepped over and stood next to Dot, watching the mysterious vehicle pull in next to Rocket's beat-to-shit truck.

Sydney had forgotten about the slight ding sound in the grinding room a couple of minutes before. It was soft and meant to be missed by someone other than Dot or Jolie. The trigger was the same kind of metal detector buried in a road and attached to a streetlight. Nobody other than Mike walked or rode a horse out this far. And Mike would come over the back trail or up from the barranca or his home.

Dot's voice was soft as butter but with the hard bite of cyanide. "Think it them?"

"I'll know when they get out."

The tall man squeezed out of the door.

"Yup. Showtime." Sydney looked down at Dot's expanse of rippling muscle barely covered by the wrestling top. "I take it the house servant and barn sweeps are dressing in sports gear this year?"

Dot laughed and nodded at the even skimpier black sports bra advertising for Everlast with a body-hugging harness holding a large knife up the girl's back.

Sydney laughed. "Time to break out the jean shirt the servant starched."

Dot leaned in and sniffed loudly. "Yeah. Shower too."

Sydney reared in mock shock. "What about you?" She leaned in to catch the heavy stink from mucking stalls, pounding iron, and grinding more blades.

Dot smiled a picket fence of large teeth. Her voice dropped into a perfect southern drawl. "Time for the three-corner offense. Give 'em what day want ta see, an' sucker 'em in fo' da kill." Her smile sent chills down the younger woman's spine. Dot continued. "Why, us colored barn keeps and servants up in the big house always smells skunky, don't ya know."

Sydney's eyes grew large as they rolled. "Oh, great. Now I have to keep from laughing too."

Dot pushed her. "Go shower in mine. Towels be in da cupboard. The pink one mine."

Dot watched Jolie come out onto the porch. "Shit." She knew she had to hurry. She ducked into her small groom's quarters and grabbed one of Mike's jean shirts. The extra size gave her the slop she needed. She pulled her head of twisties back into a ratty bun and stabbed two long chopsticks in the knot. She checked her face for grinding soot among the dark brown freckles splattered on the cocoa face.

She started and stopped. She looked down at the calf-high rubber boots slapping at her legs. She smiled and headed for the big house. All her fighting was mainly performing a stage act. This was the first time she would play a part so disgusting to her, yet, so important.

"Sorry, Missy Roberts. Dot jus' be sleepy today. I gots da barn mucked. An' I start yo noonday."

Jolie narrowed her eyes at her partner. "Jobs are hard to

find these days, Dottie. Just be mindful of that when you're fetching our meal." She turned to the two men. "We don't have any of that there sweet tea, but Dottie is the best house servant in the valley when it comes to laying out a meal. You two care to join us?" She smiled sweetly. "Dottie hasn't poisoned anyone in at least a month or two."

The scrawny weasel of a man started to make excuses. The larger was looking around for a way to back out.

"Hi, Mr. Track. What are you doing here?"

The man whirled to find Sydney dressed in jodhpurs, English flared pants, and a starched shirt. Her hair was in a tight French curled bun. The riding crop and helmet were under her arm. She bounced up the stairs and stopped near Jolie. "That horse froze on the three-rail fence and the brush hedge. I'm not sure you got your money's worth." She turned back to the still-stunned men and frowned. "Are you out here to buy a new horse?"

The man stumbled. "No. No… We were out here looking at some property. The agent suggested we come talk to Mrs. Roberts. We didn't even know you were out here."

She acted bored at whatever the man was saying. "Mmm, whatever. Say hi to Half-Track for me." She turned to Jolie. "Do I have time for a shower before we have lunch?"

The still-damp skin and wet hair didn't escape Jolie's eye. "Of course, dear. Take all the time you want for a shower. Dottie is having one of her"—she made a motion of drinking with her thumb and hand—"lazy days. So I'm guessing it might be an hour before we see any food."

She glimpsed back at the two men as she sashayed inside. She snapped the riding crop along the tall boots for effect.

The men started at the gunshot sound. Jolie's fake smile pulled sideways in amusement at the reaction.

Track opened his door and held up his hand. "We need to go look at some other properties. Maybe when we're out this way again, we'll take you up on your gracious offer."

Jolie waved her best rodeo queen wave. "Well, you have no idea what you're missing." She watched as they rumbled down the pitted driveway. There was no coming or going from the ranch that was fast or smooth. Only those who knew took the smoother back way, usually reserved for pulling the horse trailers. The Broken Ride was more interested in the slow approach than some stranger's comfort.

Rose and Sydney came out of the open front door. As they came alongside, Rocket slid over the façade of the friendly Jolie. "Who's the weaselly guy?"

Rose's head vibrated softly. "I don't know him. But if he's with Track, he must be deadly. Track is Nyack's dirty-work guy. If they have any problems, they send Lucas Track." She locked eyes with Rocket. "I think he's one of a few who genuinely has some military background. But I don't know how much or what kind."

Rocket fished the satellite phone out of her back pocket and thumbed the antenna up. "Time to keep track of them." She turned and paced the long front porch, making several phone calls.

Sydney's attention was intent on the woman with the phone. Her head jerked to see Dot. There wasn't her usual smile on her face. Sydney went back to watching Rocket quietly talking on the phone like she was checking in on a fresh load of hay.

Dot shifted. Sydney twitched. "I don't know which is scarier—fighting her in the ring or her being quiet on a phone."

Dot looked at the young woman and her mother behind her. "If that be about you, you best be in the ring instead. If she quiet, it be time to run."

Dot looked around and then down. Pink was standing next to her leg. Dot realized how much she was surrounded by the same deadly aura—a quiet Rocket and a matching silent dog.

31

DAWN TRAIL

Pink moaned as she rolled over into the spoon of Jolie and the blanket. The dog had recently been splitting her time between Jolie and Dot. Jolie even considered maybe it was time to head to Montana and let Pink pick a niece or nephew to help with the ranch. Anything she picked would be fine with Jolie or Dot. The joke was happy Pink, happy ranch.

The satellite phone pinged again. Jolie opened one eye, finding it still dark and dawn a long way off, so she rolled over. Because the ping was the default ring tone for strange numbers, she knew it wasn't someone she knew, and she would never answer the phone to some obnoxious computer named Heather, Binky, or Jake from some company she never cared about.

The phone pinged again in the dark. Jolie slapped the small table with her hand. "Fuck. Find the phone, Pink."

The dog groaned and rolled in to snuggle closer.

Jolie pushed. "Get my pants."

Pink looked at her, looked at the black window, and groaned. She rolled, dropped, and rebounded onto the bed—dropping the sought pants on Jolie's face. The heavy phone clunked against her cheek.

Jolie laid back and thumbed up the antenna as she used her other thumb to open the phone. "What time is it?" She hadn't recognized the number, but she knew it was in Buellton.

"Four-twenty. Good morning, Rocket. I do hope this is the right number at this hour. This is Jessup Goertzen down at the Best Western. Clancy said that Norman said if the four gentlemen from somewhere with a thick accent my wife can't understand were to do anything unusual, I was to call this number straight away." He cleared his throat. "I do hope I dialed the right number."

"Yes, Jessy, you called the right number. How is Anais doing?"

"Well, you know we're getting up in our years, but I think she's determined to cook again for the barbecue this year. Her sauce is always a winner."

"Yes, yes, it is. Tell her we're looking forward to it. And thank you again for the phone call. So what are they doing?" She knew the man never slept in the night. He was planted in the easy chair in the office, watching old movies to improve his English.

His groan told her the octogenarian was turning in his chair to look at the activity in the parking lot. "Well, it looks like they are moving out. The two new men who checked in last night look like they packed for a month's stay. They have several long black bags." His breathing eased. "What ya think?"

Turning on the nightstand light, Jolie swung her legs over Pink and sat on the edge of the bed. She was glad Punchy was gone and out of the line of danger this time. "I think they're up to no good. Thanks again, Jess. I need to go feed the horses."

"Always a pleasure, Rocket."

She closed the phone. She'd call Mike and warn him later. Or just let Dot do the warning.

She stepped out onto the landing. "Rose, Sydney, we've got to go."

Jolie pulled on her trail jeans. The most worn-out and comfortable of her sports bras lay next to the scabbard and knife on top of the tall handmade chest of drawers. Any dark T-shirt would be the right one for the day or however long this hunt took. She had no reservations about the outcome. This hunt was about survival. She only hoped the other two felt the same.

As she pulled on her tall moccasins, the main room lights went on, and she heard Sydney walk past the door. "Sydney, can you put the large skillet on the burner at medium heat, please."

"Yes, ma'am." The moccasins beat a quick tattoo down the stairs softly.

Rose almost ran Jolie over at the door. "I'll slice up the elk roast if you want to start the eggs."

Jolie smiled and jerked her head in a sweep. "Just like a roping team. I need to go wake up the horses and Baby and feed them."

Rose nodded her head as she stepped down the heavy stairs. "Then we'll get the food while you get the horses."

Jolie opened the front door. "I'll be back in fifteen."

Dot had the three horses lined up at the rail. She had flipped the feeding trough around properly last evening. Baby was eating in her stall like a pampered princess.

Dot pointed at the three saddles on stands. "Rose's saddle won't fit her nice like, but it fit flatter on Buttercup. The bedrolls be clean. I washed last week. There be water bottles, jerky, an' trail mix in da saddlebags. I do a couple more trail canteens when I get 'em up."

Jolie shook her head and smiled. "When did you get up?"

Dot rolled her eyes down and closed through a blink. "I heard yo phone ping an' Pink fart."

Jolie narrowed her eyes at her friend.

Dot snorted and looked at her with one eye. "I be hand-polishing since three."

"You need to get better sleep."

Dot shrugged and harrumphed. "So dis be it?"

Rocket flittered and glowed in Jolie's eyes as she ground her head over to her shoulder. "Round five."

Dot nodded at the mixed martial arts reference. She had spent several years fighting the fifth round, which is only for championship matches, instead of the standard three.

She ran her fingers up into her thick head of twisties. "Fo' all the marbles." She looked up. "Think they ready?"

Rocket flared. "Once it starts, they won't have a choice. Either they push all in, or they won't leave the valley."

Dot took a deep breath and sighed slowly. "What about you?"

Rocket knew all the implications. She had been cleared of killing her mother, but the stigma of seven years in prison was still there. What happens in the back valley must stay there. "Punchy said he had his fingers in his ears and never heard a thing. Other than that, I'm ready to help in some restitution."

The dishes were left where Dot told them. The horses were saddled and tied at the hitching post. Baby stood to one side.

The leather scrunched as they mounted. Jolie whistled the bright birdcall of a bobwhite, a bird that wouldn't be in the back valley. Sydney called a soft seagull, another bird that wouldn't be in the valley to confuse them. Rose made them smile with her clacking call of a crow. Once was come, two was they were okay. There was no call for help. For that, Rocket had explained to just scream. No need for deception.

They turned the horses. Rocket nodded to Dot and held her hand up with all fingers spread in a five. "We'll call."

Dot pulled her new satellite phone from the back of her leggings. "I'll let you know when they start up."

"Keep Mike away until it's over." They both knew Mike and his company had a vested interest in the back valley. It was best if he didn't know about any activities construed as breaking the law.

SYDNEY BROKE AHEAD and dismounted while the horse was still moving. Jolie smiled as they rode by. Her student was genuinely taking to the practical riding skill and the cowgirl flair.

As Baby and Pink passed, Sydney carefully pulled the cord and slipped it over the stake. The first tree trap stood primed and ready. Her horse was moving to catch up before her leg was over the saddle. Apart from the business of the day, she was enjoying the confidence in her riding.

Jolie set the second trap. As she walked toward her horse and the others, she worked on explaining one or two extras she had been thinking about on the trip over the ridge. She paused for water, running some in her hand for her horse to mouth. The other two dismounted and followed suit.

"I've been thinking of a couple of loose ends. If we survive this, a couple of things need to happen. First, strip the bodies of all personal stuff. Somebody can identify even a money clip. If you're comfortable doing so, strip them completely. Afterward, slice open all their fingers and thumbs lengthwise. Probably crosscutting the feet is enough. We can figure out what to do with their clothes later, but burning is probably the best."

Rose winced but asked anyway. "What about their faces or teeth?"

Rocket realized she hadn't thought about dental records. "Probably a ten-inch cast-iron skillet would do the job."

She turned to Sydney. "You still with us?"

The young woman looked around in the scrub oaks. "It doesn't look like anyone else is here to protect us." She sobered. "Yeah. I'm here."

Rocket looked back up at the ridge. "Okay. Dot called two hours ago. That means those four will be coming over the ridge just about any time—if they know how to ride. What's been bothering me is the ridge." She pointed up. "If they really are ex-military, they will probably leave one of them up there if they know how to shoot long-range. It's close to a mile, and most couldn't hit something the size of Stonewall over that distance. But just in case, we'll leave the horses under a short cliff that overhangs from the ridge. They can't see it from the ridge, but it and the trees will protect the horses. From there, we can split up. I'll take the first camp."

Rose's eyes narrowed. "No. This is my fight. We're here because of me. I'll take the first camp."

Rocket could see Sydney's eyes turning wet. The girl leaned over and, with one arm, hugged her mother. The hug was longer than just a thank you. It carried all the things that hadn't been said for too long a time.

"Okay, Rose, you take first camp. I'll take the north side. Sydney, I think the best spot for you would be the small rise on the south side. But careful. Find some thicker chaparral to hide you if there's a sniper. And just in case, as we pass the second stash, you can grab the extra arrows. You might need them."

32

SLIGHT DELAY

Dot shook her head at the mess on her larger anvil. The one with the extended horn for getting into deep cavities. It also was her favorite for shaping wrought iron. The end was as small as her finger. She could gently pound curls and leaves on the point. She once pounded out a set of copper drinking mugs before discovering the copper tasted like crap with beer or scotch. The mugs became a winter wreath of leaves for her mother. Dot never told her why she had played with copper.

Now she had to clean up the mess on the anvil before doing some work, which could be problematic.

A couple of hours before, Dot had called Rocket to let her know the men were heading up the trail. And they were— three of them.

Angry at the delay, the three had been brutal in their haranguing and final dismissal of their friend. They told him they would go ahead, and he was to follow when he figured out what he was going to do.

The large man knew he could never fit on a regular horse. His gaze fell on the giant Friesian horse, and he knew he had found the four-legged truck to haul his size and weight over the mountain. He only needed to find the colored barn tramp to help him.

"Hey. Where you at?" The barn was huge, awfully dark, and nothing he was comfortable with.

Dot stepped out of the next to the last stall. "Yes, sir?"

"Hey, come down here."

She pointed at the empty stall. "No, sir. I be working here, sir." She took a step back into the stall.

"I need… Hey, where's the saddle and stuff for the big horse?"

She stood in the middle of the clean and empty stall. There had never been a single straw of hay or dropping in the stall in twenty years. But it was all the way back in the scary darkness of the barn. She smiled as she listened to the man rummaging around where light spilled in through the open door. She knew if he thought to open the second door, the light would fill the entire barn. Fear of the dark was his first problem. Fear of the scary dark woman was his second. Dot hummed to herself softly as she danced with the pitchfork. She had only thoughts about using.

"Hey, hey nigra girl. I'm done messin' around here. I needs to be up that hill right now." He kicked at the lower slat on the first stall. "Now y'all come down here and help me saddle this damn horse."

She stepped sideways, halfway out of the stall. She slowly counted to six before he spoke again.

"Come on. Get on down here and help me."

She stared at the business end of the pitchfork. Her thumb worked the tips. The rounded tines were dull for separating hay and manure, not sharp for penetrating skin and muscle.

She calmly leaned the tool against the wall in the alleyway of the barn. There were better ways to delay or finish the man. Dot stretched and flexed her hands as she shuffle-walked her way the length of the barn. "I'za comin'. Too much work fo' little ol' Dottie. I jus' work, work, work. Ain't no rest for ol' Dottie."

She stopped in front of the man. She slowly looked up his body and finally to his face. She bent backward with her fists in the back of her hips.

"Man alive. You do be a big'un."

His face contorted with time lost. He wasn't excited about getting on some horse. But how hard can it be? He knew how angry Nyack would be about the delay of his backup. Track was his number-one guy whenever the man personally ran a manhunt. He relied heavily on Track's eight tumultuous years in the army and then as a mercenary for one of the larger private contractors in Afghanistan. The man's dishonorable discharge for brutality and suspected criminal activities got him hired by the contractor. His lack of morals or compassion was what drew Nyack to hire him. His eagerness to please Nyack kept him close to the man and in the core of their enterprises. Horses were not a part of that.

He turned to leave the dark, scary barn. "Just find me the saddle and stuff." As an afterthought, he turned at the large door. "And stick them on the big horse outside." His shoulders relaxed as he stepped back into the sunshine.

Dot watched the man. She knew his fears, physicality, and his weaknesses. She smirked as she turned to find the right saddle. The one they had figured out to either burn or give away. Stonewall hated how it sat.

She grabbed a tissue-thin shabrack blanket and the saddle. The thin blanket would guarantee contact between the saddle and the sensitive back of the nearly one ton of thoroughbred and Bashkir mix. The rest would be up to Stonewall.

She snatched snatched the large hackamore off the peg. She slung it over her shoulder and saddle.

"Stop dawdling and get the horse fixed up." The man banged at his hand that held his cell phone. Holding it high, he watched to find even the hint of a bar. The screen never even flickered.

Dot smiled as she opened the gate enough to slip through. The gate hadn't been latched since they let Stonewall into the softer corral. The foundation of the corral was a foot of coarse ground field rubber. This was covered with a blanket of fine mesh to prevent the fine soft dirt on top from seeping down and making the ground hard. Jolie had the corral rebuilt to soften the landing of the inexperienced riders. The enormous horse could feel the softer dirt bed. It was the best he would get short of a grassy field.

Dot slung the saddle over the long-nosed anvil in the farrier's station. The anvil was higher than most, with the long, narrow nose pointed out toward the corral. It was Francisco's set up for when he came to shoe the horses or just work some wrought iron magic. Or teach Dot about curling and leafing the rods he brought her to practice on.

She glanced at the man still wandering around in circles with his phone held high. She smiled. She knew he was almost three miles from finding any regular cell service. He crossed through the forge area, grinding room, and into the barn.

Looking out the barn door, she watched the man and his cell dance. She needed to pee. She remembered there was some coffee in her mug. Sticking it in her microwave, she used the bathroom. The coffee was almost gone, and she finished reading the article on a new up-and-coming knife maker. She heard the man calling.

She rinsed out her mug and left her hands wet.

Grabbing the curry and brush, she walked out of the barn. She ignored the sour look on the man's face.

"Where did you go?"

Her head ground around as she mentally slow-counted to four. "Well, I haz ta pee. Yes, sir. Dottie haz ta pee." She stopped and looked at the curry and brush in her hands as if they had suddenly appeared. "Oh." She looked up with a broad smile. "And I fo'got deez." She held them up for the man's approval.

The man's eyes were large but grew even more—score two more points for Dot.

"Yas, sir. Dottie gotz ta brush down horses before a blanket." She turned and made her shuffle look like the hardest trudging she could endure. Yes, sir. She was working hard for the man. Her smile was small and tight as she entered the corral and trudged back to the farrier's pit.

She put down the brushes and picked up the hackamore. Turning, she pulled the carrot out of her back pocket. The large horse had already nibbled off most of the green top. She fed the rest to the horse as she slipped the hackamore up over his head and nose. She leaned in as she raked his jaws with her fingers and nails. "I'm sorry. But if it be any comfort, you jus' be you. I give you extra treats if'n you fuck him up good."

"Hey. Girl. What you doing? Get the horse saddled."

"Yas, sir. Rat now, sir. Jus' gotta brush him down."

"Fuck that shit. Just get the damn saddle on him and make it fast."

She stepped out from around the horse as she tied him to the rail facing away from the farrier's area. "He no like no blanket and saddle on a dirty back. He get all grumpy like." She twisted up her face and screwed her eyes wonky.

"I don't give a shit. It's just a dumb animal. Get the saddle on and be done with it." His face flushed like he had spent several hours in the sun.

Dot was hoping for a stroke or heart attack, but it looked like maybe it would take someone bigger than her to get the job done.

She spread out the shabrack on the horse's back. She couldn't see on the other side and had to cross under the horse's head. Each time she stroked his jaw. He knew who loved him.

The saddle was luckily the sparest saddles on the ranch. The fenders were little more than the belts to hold the stirrups. The back jockey and skirt cut short to accommodate a horse with large hips. Even the front fender extended little beyond the gullet. The cantle and pommel swells were cut low with no horn. The saddle was cut for only the personal taste of an expert rider. A weekend warrior, much less a newbie, stood no chance at staying mounted.

Dot grinned at the man watching her as she heaved the saddle up and onto the back of the one-ton land mine. Reaching under, she cleared the cinches and pulled them snug. She leaned against the wide belly and waited.

"What are you waiting for?"

Dot smiled as she held up a single finger.

Stonewall bloated his belly and let out a long, loud, and juicy fart punctuated with a fourteen-inch patty of fresh green poop. As Dot pulled the cinch, he farted again. She fed the tongue in and tied it off.

The front cinch secured, she pulled the stirrup and fender back down. Checking all the points, she nodded in completion.

She turned to the man, who was hesitant to enter the corral. "He all ready, sir." She held out the ends of the hack-amore reins.

The man stood with his hand on the cantle. There was nothing but the short gullet for him to grab. The act seemed beyond the man's mental agility.

"Git over here and give me a hand up."

Dot bit the inside of her cheek. She stepped over and, bending slightly, laced her fingers and cupped her hand for his boots. Her hands floated inches above where his foot was sculling the air.

"Damn it. Lower."

Dot squatted lower, but her hands stayed at the same height.

"Lower."

She squatted more.

"No. Damn it. Move your fucking hands lower."

Dot's eyes and mouth matched. "Oh…"

Her cupped hands dropped a few inches. The man rocked back, and his boot slipped into the hands. Dot braced for the man's weight.

He teetered on the side of the saddle. Dot hoped for him to tip over and crash to the ground headfirst.

He swung his leg, and his foot found the other stirrup. Dot could tell he was perched on top of the saddle—pinched between the cantle and the pommel. The man's face was pinched as well. He had no knowledge about saddles and didn't know if the fit was right or dreadfully wrong. His first time in a saddle and first time on a horse. His body mass was centered twenty-two hands above the ground.

The ground or apron in front of the farrier's pit had never been disturbed. The hardpack provided stability for the horse being shod. It also gave support for the farrier to move the heavy anvils and forge in and out as need arose. Falling wrong from seven or eight feet could prove disastrous. But with most who came off wrong on Stonewall, it wasn't just a fall.

Dot stepped back and swung the gate wide. "Well, thar ya go, cowboy."

Hollywood was a strong teacher. The large man kicked his heels hard into the sensitive horse's belly.

Dot smiled at the explosive results. First, the back end twitched up and forward. The sound of the man's nose and face crushing on the horse's neck was distinct and recognizable to the former fighter. Doubling the resulting damage came a half-second later. Stonewall rose on his hind legs, the neck finding the man's face and nose again. The rotating body was well over ten feet in the air.

Dot recognized the sound of breaking shoulder and ribs as the man crumpled into the dirt—right shoulder first. The body flopped flat with a whoosh of blown dust.

Stonewall stood his ground. He was waiting for Dot to remove the tack.

As she slipped the saddle and ghost fart of a blanket off the calm horse, she heard a moan. She stepped back, still holding the saddle. The large man unfolded. His eyes were crossed, and he wobbled, but he stood, weaving in place.

Stonewall turned his head. Aimed. Then let go with both nine-pound shoes.

Dot couldn't tell if the cracking was from many ribs shattering at once or the sound dinner-plate-sized hooves make as they collapse a large man's chest.

The distance to the tip of the pointed anvil was less than a blink of an eye. The tip shone where the man might have been holding his phone.

Dot put away the tack, added a half-can of oats to the feed trough, and threw a half-dozen carrots on the alfalfa.

She pulled the new satellite phone from her hip pocket. Turning up the antenna, she began typing.

Man #4 met Stonewall. You have 3.

Dot looked down at the anvil. She figured it would be better to clean up before lunch.

33

A GOAT ROPE

I don't care what the hell is keeping him." Nyack looked back down the trail. "Track can take care of himself. If he ever learns to keep his hand off his cock."

They had stopped just down from the crest of the ridge. The thinking was to not present a silhouette on the ridgeline. The truth was, they couldn't see the valley from the ridgeline, so they had stopped on the false ridgeline, which left them outlined to the valley below.

Piles stood with his large binoculars, slowly scanning for any movement. His voice was low but also muffled. "My guess is, they will be where the trees thin out, and the brush is thick but in clumps. The horses should stand out." He scanned the valley, following what appeared to be the largest trail. In a storm, the trail would become the flash river, flushing anything in its way. He had seen his share in Afghanistan. The Taliban loved setting up kill boxes along them because the American soldiers preferred walking up the softer, wider, and easier trails.

The movement was slight, but the light color of cloth stood out against the dun colors of the sand and summer bleached chaparral. "I've got one. It looks like they are hunkering in."

"What about the others?"

He never flinched or looked away. "Still looking."

Nyack gathered the reins. "Well, take out the one soon. We're going down."

Piles lowered his binoculars and looked at the whole layout. "She's about fifty yards past where the sand trail clears the trees. There's a large dark clump of this grease brush on the left. She's in the clump before it. I'll try to take her out before you get there. If I get her, I'll follow it with a shot from my Glock."

Stanley tried to get up a second time. The third, his hopping timed right with the horse sidestepping toward him. He smiled as he adjusted to the saddle. It seemed as large as an easy chair. He kept his knees tight against the wide parts of the saddle.

Stanley nodded toward Alex as he started down the trail. As he rode, he wondered what had made the wide trail. The whole trail seemed wide enough to drive a jeep on. But there wasn't anything you would need to drive back here for. The idea of brushfires was beyond him.

The wide trail continued left at the bottom of the decline, but the horse tracks turned right up the narrower trail. Stanley looked back up the trail. Nyack was almost a hundred yards behind him. He waved his arm toward where he was turning and heading up the narrow trail.

Nyack's wave back was little more than a dismissal.

Stanley seethed. So many times. So many dismissals. It was as if Nyack viewed him in the same category as Meal Team at the gate. An ignorant disciple happy with the menial scut work. Like cleaning up after their hunts, fixing their books. Arranging the proper bribes. Everything that might soil Alex's hands.

Stanley urged his horse forward. Something he had control over. Something that did his bidding. Something going…

Too late, he noticed the movement on the trunk of the tree. His head only had time to turn and watch the branch swing out from its release.

The cluster of bamboo daggers came apart on impact. Even Piles at the lower ridge started from the scream. The shrill tenor of the voice told everyone whose blood was drawn first.

Rocket shifted and caught the eye of Rose across the small valley. She held up two fingers and her thumb. Slowly, she drew in the thumb. Rose held up a peace sign and then flipped her hand with the index and pinky held up. Rocket smirked at the old sign of heavy metal rockers, but equally the sign many at rodeos used for the horns of a bull hooking a slow rider or clown.

Rose jerked. As Rocket frowned, she heard the shot from high up on the ridge. Her eyes scanned and found the curl of smoke. Well over a half-mile. The man was no weekend warrior.

Rocket scanned where Rose had been. There was no movement. And then Rocket remembered only she and Sydney had been packing the first aid fanny packs. Rocket had meant to say something, but they had left the ranch in a hurry. She dropped low and scrambled around and through the chaparral. The ache in her left shoulder reminded her of the last time she received a bullet. She was keenly aware of a skilled rifle searching for her.

ALEX WALKED his horse up the narrow trail until he found Stanley's body moaning in the sand. Alex studied the daggers of bamboo sticking from the face, neck, and chest. Already there was a large pool of red soaking into the sand. He could tell Stanley had turned his head at the last moment. The branch trap would have caught him straight on, but the foot-long stakes stitched from one side of his head and neck through to the other.

Alex didn't think about whether it was out of friendship or just that he didn't want to keep listening to the moaning. He drew his Desert Eagle and fired, the concussive fire echoing in the valley. Birds flew from trees as four-legged animals twitched and scurried, and his own horse reared at the noise. Pulling the reins from his hand, the horse fled back the way they had come.

Alex watched the dust of the retreating horse. "Fuck 'em."

He crossed over under the trees, making his way slowly up the narrow valley. The canopy of the scrub oak would shield him from the man on the hill.

PILES HAD SWITCHED from the rifle's scope back to his adjustable binoculars. He pulled back to watch almost a hundred feet of the valley bottom at a time. If he saw something with a flick of his finger, he could draw down on less than twenty. He had set his rifle for three-quarters of a mile —but looking at the meter in the binoculars, he saw the more distant shot would be only thirteen hundred yards. He adjusted. He knew the local woman in the black hat would try to get to Stanley's wife, Rose. He had recognized the Mexican silver hair brooch on the black ponytail.

A few small tweet birds flew up from some chaparral up the canyon. He studied the canyon wall. It was already in noonday's shadow, but nothing was moving. He raised his binoculars and scanned for the large black hat.

A twig snapped, and he looked over at the canyon face again. His eyes stepped from section to section. The soft granite sand was too slippery to walk in on the steep side. But he thought about Stanley's daughter. He had not found her hiding place. Tactically, he knew the three places he would have deployed her to. But she had not shown up. He wasn't sure, other than the long black hair, same as her mother, what he was looking for. He didn't like it.

He returned to looking for the more dangerous of the three—the local who probably hunted in this valley.

He was just gently zooming in when, at the edge of his view, he saw a movement. He almost missed the woman as she ran across the sand wash of a trail. She had removed her hat. Her shirt wasn't white but more of the light dusty color of the late summer brush.

He didn't even try for his rifle. He knew a snapshot at this distance was useless. Better to track her and wait until she wasn't moving about. He followed her movement through the brush. As he had figured, she snaked through the brush to the same quadrant he had dropped Stanley's wife.

A mourning dove flew up from a bush on the side of the ridge and flew across the valley. He narrowed his eyes behind his yellow-tinted Beretta glasses. He knew he saw more in the shadows than without the glasses. Once again, his gaze stepped down the side of the canyon. One eye examined quadrant at a time. Nothing was moving. It was just the bird shifting to the sunny side of the valley with the gentler valley-type slope. The steep, slippery slope was his defense.

He hunkered down behind the scope and rifle. He scanned, with one eye in the scope and his other eye open to the area where he had dropped the woman. His open eye locked on the large bush with the upright snag on the left side. He brought the scope and rifle over to bear on the clumps of bushes. Behind the smaller bush, with a dark center, he saw what he thought was a foot.

He grabbed the binoculars, found the bush, and zoomed in. The foot pulled back out of sight.

He centered the sightlines on where the woman's body mass would be and squeezed the trigger. The closest branches of the brush twitched.

The blonde leaped from the closer bush and ran toward the larger hiding woman on the ground. Piles pulled the center of the scope to the center of her back and squeezed the trigger.

The blonde spun in the air as she crashed to the ground—a direct hit.

Stiles raised his head from the scope to get a better look. He smiled at the blonde splayed out in the sand.

The triple wings of the broadhead arrow sliced neatly through the man's neck. The massive energy drew the arrow through. The feathers tore out the rest of his artery and throat.

Gagging on the blood now flowing down into his throat, he turned. Sydney stood fifty feet away. Her uphill leg half-cocked into the steepness. A second arrow rested, notched and ready in the compact hunting bow. Her face was passive granite.

The man coughed once, spraying blood over his rifle and binoculars. He rolled back, leaking from his neck and mouth.

<hr>

SYDNEY STOWED THE ARROW. She faded back into the brush and started making her way carefully down the cliff. The knife-edge of a trail led back from where she started. It took advantage of shadows and brush.

Once down near the flats, she wove her way toward where she remembered seeing her mother last—large bush on the left with the crumbling boulder on the right.

Sydney saw Rocket sprawled on the sand with her shirt a bloody mass. Dropping the bow, Sydney squeezed between the bush and boulder. The fist to her jaw, from behind the large bush, surprised her. She stumbled and fell, landing on the still body of Rocket.

Alex stood over her and hit her again and again. "You little shit."

Sydney held up her arms, protecting her face.

The man slapped at the arms and the sides of her head. "I let you at my Bunny. And you ruined everything."

Bracing against Rocket's body, Sydney lashed out at the man's crotch—but only hitting his thigh as he reflectively flinched.

He jumped on her lap as he still beat her where he could. He slapped across her chest with his left hand. "Is this what you think Bunny liked?" He backhanded her head and hands, knocking her backward over Rocket's lifeless body.

The enraged man grabbed at his crotch. "I'll show you what Bunny liked." He unbuckled his pants and drew down his zipper.

From the side of her swelling left eye, she could tell he dressed commando. And the fighting had aroused him. She whimpered.

"Mommy?"

The man glanced back at the other body lying on the sand. "No such luck, bitch. If she ain't dead yet, she will be soon." He grabbed at her leggings.

She squirmed and tried to kick, but he was sitting on any hope of kicking him off. He slapped at her head again. Her shoulder and right arm draped over Rocket. With one hand, he grabbed at the side of her leggings, and with a heave, he tore and pulled them off her hips.

She shuddered and whimpered, small mewling sounds of fear and hopelessness. He leaned in on her.

His eyes burned with pure hatred and lust for violence. His breath smelled like the swamps he used for his pleasures. "We're going to have fun now, little girl." He grabbed the bottom of her shirt and pulled up, tearing the fabric and exposing her sports bra and leather harness. He didn't notice. It enraged him far beyond noticing anything out of the ordinary.

Sydney's right hand searched under Rocket's shirt. The handle cocked to one side by the blade pinched between the ground and Rocket.

The man's hand tore at the leggings, pulling them and panties as one. Heaving up, he pulled them down past her knees, exposing her legs and crotch. But before she could move, he was back down on her knees and leaning in. He groped her breasts.

Sydney felt the slight roll of the body under her. The knife moved.

The man's face smashed into the side of hers. She could feel his sweat.

His growl was pure animal as he guided his penis between her thighs. "Ready?"

Her head snapped to his, and her growl was equally animal. "Go to hell."

Her hand shoved the knife up through Rocket's shirt. Her training defined the tight arc. The pommel didn't stop until it was flat against the man's neck. His eyes shattered open like a window blind breaking.

Sydney followed his face back as he tried to breathe. The

sham of the frail little girl was gone. The voice growled from hours spent in the ring against Dot and Rocket. There never were any tears wetting her eyes or cheeks—only calculations.

"You may be wondering why you can't catch your breath. But right now, your lungs are sucking on two full pounds of high-grade Damascus steel. The hardness is sixty-four because it's needed to kill pigs like you. But before I pull it out and let you breathe your blood, I want you to know—after today, maybe not tomorrow, or even next year, but someday, when they have long forgotten about you… I will hunt down your wife and daughter, and after I tell them all about you, I will use this knife again."

She could see the fear take over his eyes. She leaned in close.

"Ready to go to hell?" The blade slid out as the neck sucked into a kissing sound. In the corner of her eye, she could see the smoothness of the blade was almost clean, except where the bullet had gouged a groove and removed a bit at the edge. But she wiped in on his chest for effect as she pushed him over backward.

He grabbed at his throat, but there was nothing to grip. The body sucked the blood straight from the carotid artery.

Sydney leaned back against Rocket.

The voice was little more than breath. "Check your mom."

Sydney looked at Rocket. The woman's eyes were open. She pushed her chin out as the eyes closed in a slow blink of pain. Sydney stood, pulling up her leggings. She laid the pig knife next to Rocket's hand.

The pulse was light but there. Sydney rolled her mother

over. There was one bullet hole showing on both sides of Rose's thigh. The wound was beginning to ooze. The other was high on her side. The bullet had torn the shirt, cracked at least one rib, and exited near the woman's right breast. The bloody mess on her head came from the knee of a rock she had struck when she fell.

Sydney pulled open the first aid kit. Not knowing what else to do, she wrapped the two leg wounds with four-by-four pads on each hole. The hole in the back she cleaned as best she could and taped squares over both holes. She wrapped Rose's head before dragging her into the shade.

As she worked, she could hear Rocket moving. She looked back. The knife was in the hand of an expert. Rocket was cutting the clothes off the dead man's body as she sliced him up.

Sydney ran to bring back the horses. She held the canteen to her mother's lips.

"Not like that."

Sydney looked back at Rocket.

"Wet a rag or a piece of her shirt for her to suck on. If you pour water down her throat, you risk her inhaling it. A person can drown that way." She held up the man's hand and cut long grooves down each finger. By nightfall, the split fingers would be useless for identification.

Sydney drew her own knife and cut off a chunk of her mother's shirt. Folding it, she wet it and held it to Rose's lips. The mouth suckled on the wet. When she stopped, Sydney returned to examine Rocket.

"You're shot."

Rocket smiled crookedly and held up her knife, showing

the small hollow where the bullet had carved the groove on the blade. "The knife absorbed most of the energy, but the bullet still cracked some ribs before it found its way into the sand."

She looked at the woman who today had proved herself as a warrior. The spoiled little girl at the beginning of summer was history. Rocket pointed at the body of the man, now cut up and naked. "What about the guy up top?"

"I didn't take the time to strip him and cut him up. I knew I needed to get down here."

Rocket's head nodded. "Later." She nudged her chin toward Rose in the shade. "What about your mom?"

"I dressed the bullet wounds. Both passed through. But she hit her head. She's still out, but she took a little of the water."

Rocket's steam was fading fast. "We're going to need help to get out of here. I can't help you lift her, and I'm not sure she could ride out, anyway."

Rocket tried to pull her phone out of her pants, but her arm wasn't working right.

"Here. Let me do it." Sydney pulled the phone and thumbed up the antenna. "Who do I call?"

Jolie closed her eyes as she thought. Call the wrong person, and there would be questions, or worse. "Push the two and hold it until it rings. Mike."

Sydney stood from reflex, looking for cell service. "Mike… it's Sydney. They're shot up… Mom hit her head and is still out." She looked back at Jolie.

"I think they could get a helicopter down at the first camp."

"Rocket thinks the first camp is clear enough for a helicopter… yeah, the one just… um… south of the heavy growth of trees." Turning, she looked up the trail. "Both… I'll take the horses back."

She turned and looked up the ridge. "Oh. Okay. Well, tell Dot I'll help her when I get back tonight… I could hike back here with Baby or something." She looked back at Jolie. "Okay, I'll tell her." She collapsed the phone and stuck it in her back pocket.

Jolie's hand was grabbing at the air. She held the phone out to her. "Dial one-one-one."

She handed her the ringing phone. They both could hear the recording and then the beep.

"Honey. I need to go see a jerk in Los Angeles for a bit. I love you but come home soon." She handed Sydney the phone and looked with a question.

"Mike said they might have a helicopter that would work. But it might take an hour."

Jolie's nod was slow and languid. "Go strip the others and cut them. There's a short piece of pipe in my saddlebag. No teeth."

Sydney stood unmoving. Jolie looked up.

"Problem?"

Sydney's lower lip furled and belled. She took a breath through her nose and looked down the trail. "My dad."

Rocket crept back in and nodded. "Help me down there. I'll do him while you do the one up top."

Sydney stood looking down the trail.

"Syd?"

She looked down. Her upper teeth bit at her lower lip.

"No. I've got this." She returned from the horses. She rolled the iron bludgeon in her hand. "After all, he did come to kill us." She looked back at her mother.

Jolie roused. Rocket got her on her hands and knees and waved one arm. "Syd… you don't have to prove you're tough. We know you are. But if you do this to your own dad, you will never stop seeing this shit in your dreams for the rest of your life. Believe me, I know."

The young warrior stood looking down the trail and then turned to help the older one to her feet. "My job is to learn." She looked into the pained eyes. "Show me on Mr. Nyack first. Then I'll go get one of the cast-iron pans." Sydney looked shyly out of the side of her eye with a half-smile. "We're burning daylight."

Rocket reached over and leaned into Sydney's shoulder. She gave it a long, firm squeeze.

3 4

SHORT FLIGHT

Mike looked at the driver's license. The photo was the best he had ever taken. The rest of the Georgia license was someone else. He looked up at the little Jerk. The doctor beamed. He held up his license. The crooked smiles were the same.

Mike leaned over and read the name on the license. "Hah! Finally, a name even your wife and kids can pronounce." He pointed at the license. "But it says here you're now a proctologist instead of a micro-neural space-cadet surgeon."

The Jerk flipped his license around and glanced at the name. "Yeah, well, I'll take Piles over one-third of a Three Stooges laugh. Nyack, Nyack, Nyack."

Mike turned to Fernando, the happy farrier. "You going to be okay with this?"

The man thought as he bounced the plastic card on his thumbnail. He grimaced. "Are you sure we're flying in First Class? I mean, if it is First Class, I guess I can put up with being called Stanley." He looked up with a sad smile but a twinkle in his eyes.

Chester strolled down the hall. His haircut was fresh but went well with his sport coat and slacks. Only the extra-wide boots seemed oddly out of place. The tall, solid-built man smiled broadly, which pushed his eyes out of sync. The brown one slewed left, and the blue stayed firmly right.

Mike nodded. "Well, Mr. Track. You look like a million bucks."

The eyes rolled in different circles. "When's the flight?"

Jerk looked up and smiled. "After the best sushi in Westwood."

Fernando frowned at Mike. "You said we're going to a steakhouse."

Mike smiled. "We are. And that is also the best sushi in Westwood."

"Ladies and gentlemen, we'll start boarding for anyone needing assistance or extra time."

"Okay, we will take any active military, VIP Members, and those seated in First Class."

Each man shuffled up to the podium and held out their ticket. The gate checker took it, scanned it, and the machine beeped.

"Welcome aboard, Mr. Nack."

Mike smiled. "It's pronounced Nyack… just like my yak."

The woman smiled blandly. "Yes, sir. Nyack."

She stuck her hand out to Chester and then looked up. She blinked.

He bent forward. "It's pronounced 'track.' Just like keeping somebody on track."

She chuckled. "I've got three kids. I can relate."

He smiled back. "I have two dogs and a cat. I have no idea."

The four looked at each other as they wandered down the jetway. Their smiles were small but spoke volumes.

The flight attendant's smile was friendly. His Clark Kent glasses gave a solid support to his face. The kind of person you could trust if the plane were going down, and they said it would be all right. Mike noted the name tag. "Is this where I say, 'Home, James'?"

James' smile grew wider. "Only if your home in Atlanta. Because the plane going to Rio is over there in the next gate."

Mike smiled and turned down the aisle.

Chester ducked his head and stepped in. Standing with his head cocked by the ceiling, he smiled. "What's for dinner?"

James hesitated. "Not enough?"

They both laughed.

The four men had hardly spoken the entire flight. Mostly they slept. James served breakfast, but it wasn't enough for any of them but the Jerk. He usually ran all day on crackers, peanut butter, jelly, and celery. A good day in surgery was when he had time for leisurely wolfing down a protein bar and a cup of coffee.

All four thanked James on the way out the door. He had been a gracious host, but a red-eye is a red-eye. The deli was opening as they walked by. None said a word; the four just ground to a halt at the menu board.

Mike scanned the board and moved to start the line. "Who cares. They have coffee."

Four happy stomachs later, they stood in the furthest corner of the top deck of the parking structure. Only one car separated the four black SUVs. The matching license plate brackets were from a Chevrolet dealer in St. Marys, Georgia. The four men stood with fobs in their hands.

Each, in turn, found their vehicle. The Jerk turned to Mike. "Ain't habit nice?"

Each had the route to the chop shop in Florida after a gas-up in St. Mary's. They would each use their credit cards for the fuel. After that, they would drop off the radar.

As they each paid with the right man's credit card and passed out of the parking structure, they turned south with thoughts of fresh seafood dancing in their heads. Late lunch would be on the Gulf coast after handing the keys to the chop shop.

THE CORPORATE JET lifted off from a small field north of Tampa. The four men in the back never woke up as the plane put down in Little Rock, Arkansas, refueled, filed flight plans, and lifted off for Los Angeles.

Late in the morning, they sat in the Jerk's back yard, finishing a leisurely brunch of shrimp burritos. Their eyes danced with the small flame burning the credit cards, driver's licenses, and wallets of the men they never met.

Jerk leaned toward the man he always thought of as his uncle, Mike. "And just like that, four men disappear from the face of the Earth."

Mike drew in a deep breath through his nose and let it out slowly. "Kind of like the witness protection program. But just enough to worry their friends and partners."

Chester furled his lip and uncrossed his eyes. As his head turned, the left eye looked down. "Except we get to protect the best people."

Mike held his fist out, and Chester bumped his off the top.

Fernando swallowed his last bite and washed it down with coffee. "What about the FBI? What happens with Rose and her daughter?"

Mike shrugged and ground his head back and forth. "Beyond my pay grade. If you think you have the *cajones*, you can ask Rocket. Last, I know, she set Rose up with a computer, and the woman spent three hours stripping money out of accounts and routing them offshore. Rocket said she watched her route through different countries, in and out of numbered accounts, all attached to shell companies. Never once did she consult anything written down. The woman had it all in her head."

Chester shifted. "So, all the companies and stuff ceased to exist?"

Mike chuckled. "Where's the fun in that? Everything is still there except most of the money. If the feds find it, there's little left except for the evidence of what was there before."

Fernando laughed. "But it also looks like the four guys stripped the assets and skipped the country."

Mike smiled broadly and shot him with his finger and thumb.

Jerk's eyes were huge as he thought of what it would take to memorize multiple eighteen-digit numbers and what company they belong to and in what country… it made him dizzy.

Mike frowned at his nephew. "You okay, Jerk?"

The surgeon waved him off. "I'm fine. I was just thinking about Rose." He looked up at the confused face. "I mean… she's single now…"

Mike glanced back at the man's house his wife let him think he was the king of. "Maybe, but you're not."

The other two men laughed at the dig.

Jerk laughed with them as he waved his hand back and forth. "Actually, I was thinking of her mind. Memorizing all the information. No wonder it worried her husband."

"Scared shitless is more like it." Chester's eyes rolled around and then focused. "How much do you think she left in the accounts?"

Mike thought. "What's your base tax rate for the feed store?"

"Twenty-eight. But nobody pays it."

Mike looked at the surgeon.

"I have accountants for all that."

Mike nodded. "Yeah, but…"

"I think it's about thirty-six or seven once you're over a half million. But as Chester said, there are deductions, depreciation, investments, long-term versus short-term, and the list goes on. Why?"

"But the marginal rate is thirty-seven, and if you don't

contest and take the standard deduction, the actual is somewhere close to twenty-six. So, I'm guessing, her being as smart as she is, that's what she left. What the IRS will want to capture."

The Jerk flattened his lower lip. "Like I said, one hell of a mind."

Mike laughed. "I'd offer her a job, but she might just turn around and buy me out."

A sparrow of a redheaded woman came to the sliding door. "Jerk, the hospital is on the phone."

He looked back. "Okay, tell them I just got up, and I'll be with them in a minute."

Her face was passive stone, but she didn't move.

He peeked back. "Okay, okay, maybe I'll need to call them back."

She turned and then looked back. "Mike, there's also a livery car parked out front. The driver has been waiting about twenty minutes. I gave him coffee. I didn't want to disturb your breakfast."

The Jerk laughed through his nose as he stood. "Me—it's right now. Uncle Mike—it's 'let's not disturb his breakfast.'"

Mike rose with a smile. "Jerk, I've been telling you since you brought her home—your wife loves me best."

Jerk stood with the others. "Gentlemen, it's been a grand time. Let's not get together and do it again in this lifetime." He turned to Mike as they followed the other two. "I think we'd like to keep Jolie and Rose, at least until after the weekend. I can send them home with the service. I asked for Joaquin for you guys, so he'll know the way when he brings them. I'll keep them until I can send them home with the car stocked with champagne."

Mike slung his arm over the smaller man's shoulders. "Just keep me posted. And thanks for helping out with this."

"What's family for?"

In the kitchen, Mike bent over for a buzz on the cheek from the redhead. He always knew she was a keeper.

35

HOME

Sydney stared at her new driver's license as she moved the syllables around in her mouth. She sighed and looked out the window. The car almost seemed standing still. The countryside didn't move unless she looked down at the low brush alongside the highway. In the distance, there was a squat tree. Occasionally, she could see a few cows.

Her breath fogged the window. She breathed on it more and then wrote out her new name. It would take some time.

Rose reached over and touched her knee. Their eyes met. "You can just use Kim or Kimmie for short."

Sydney vibrated her head as her lower lip smiled sadly. "No. Kimiko is fine. It's just the Takayama I keep stumbling on."

Rose snorted softly. "Try *Rōzumarī*. I'm going to go nuts trying to remember the lines over the oh and I. And softening the center to make it a softer, soft *a*, instead of just a soft *a*."

Sydney's eyes twinkled with teasing as she reached out

and touched her mother's knee. "You can use Rose or Mari for short."

The four laughed. Dot leaned up against the door in defense. "Try gettin' hung wi' Doobahoottie at four pounds three ounces."

Rose's eyes flew wide. "Oh, that's not an actual name."

Jolie laughed as she raised her left leg and pushed her boot against the opposing seat. "Oh, but it is. I've seen the paperwork."

Sydney's gaze bounced between the two women. "What kind of name is that?"

Dot's stone face suggested her sincerity. "Haitian Cajon slave. It be my great-great-grandmother's name."

Sydney's face screwed up as she tried to clear her eyes. "How do you shorten that to just Dot?"

"I be always punctual. When I start fighting, I end fight by"—she hammered her fist a quick pound in the air—"dotting ta other's eye. The name better than Dorothy an' flying monkey jokes. So I keeps it."

Pink stepped into Jolie's lap. Her nose was streaking the window.

Jolie chuckled as she ruffled her constant companion's head and ears. "She knows. From herein is home."

Sydney whipped her head around to all the windows. "Here where?"

Jolie looked at her and then to Rose for an explanation. Or if they had dropped Sydney as a baby. Jolie turned back and joined Pink, looking out the window. She pointed to the small herd of a hundred or more elk. Pink smiled with a large, flat, slippery lick across the face.

Rocket waved to get Sydney's attention. "See the elk?"

"Those are elk?" She smiled, thinking about all the meals the summer had provided. "They look delicious."

Rocket chuckled as she pointed to another large group. "Those are tasty as well. They call them cattle. That's part of the five thousand head Jinx runs. They're mostly Hereford, or white-face stock with some Angus, Charolais, and Beefmaster mixed in for bulk and muscle. The Angus gives them the hump on the shoulders, also a toughness to withstand the weather. The Beefmaster builds the butts and hind legs for better prime ribs." She turned her nose back to the cool glass. "Recently, a few bison got on the property, and two were bulls, so Jinx made them feel at home. To winter over, we need all the hardy stock we can get. And it doesn't hurt us at the auction house either."

"Wait. You're saying this is all yours?"

Rocket snorted an expanse of a smile. "No. I'm saying it's all family. Jinx is the closest I ever got to family. He and my father were sewn together during World War II. Jinx grew up in a small town in northern California called Moss Landing. It sits just south of Watsonville, known for large truck farms. We probably had strawberries or lettuce from there. To the south is Castroville, where the artichokes come from. Back at the start of the twentieth century, the Japanese owned the truck farms. Dealing with all the farmers, Jinx became fluent in speaking and writing Japanese. After the war, Jinx married a Japanese gal. They wound up here on the ranch my father bought for them. It's theirs... his... well, you'd need to have Mike explain it all and how it works. But for all anybody else gets to know, you're Jinx's wife's only surviving family and you've come to take care of him in his old age. Try to keep up."

Sydney sensed the humor. "How old is he?"

Jolie smiled as she leaned back into the seat. Her eyes were on the large wrought iron statue in the middle of the turnaround driveway. "Let's see. Dad would have been… um… a hundred and one this year. So, I think that makes Jinx about a hundred and two."

The man was standing on the edge of the porch with his hands on his hips. Other than the wrinkles, the smile looked more like an eight-year-old on his birthday.

Rose leaned toward Rocket and growled like a cougar. "Is that his son?"

Jolie looked at her uncle. It had never dawned on her that most men past eighty no longer had salt and pepper hair. She smiled as he waved. He looked, moved, and acted young enough for a woman like Rose to have a wandering eye.

"Jinx. And as you will find out, his wife is still a strong presence in his house."

Sydney slipped her California driver's license into her pocket. "That's why our Japanese side."

Jolie shot her eyebrows up once as the car glided to a stop. "With your round faces and strong epicanthic folds on your eyes, you're either Asian or Mexican. If anybody is still looking for you, they'll be looking for Latinas. Anyone with a Japanese name won't be on their radar. So, it's up to you what you want to be—Japanese or hunted. You need to choose right now." Her hand froze on the door handle.

Sydney and Rose looked at each other. Their discussions had wound long into the nights. There was no witness protection. The FBI couldn't find anyone. The funds in the bank accounts barely covered the taxes owed. So, if they were going to drop off the face of the earth, it was to be now.

Sydney stuck her hand out. "*Kon'nichi wa.* My name is Kimiko."

Jolie shook her hand with a warm smile. "*Kon'nichi wa.* I'm your Aunt Jolie."

Sydney laughed. "Oh, fuck that. I've killed my pig. You will always be Auntie Rocket."

They looked at Rose. Her hand was on the door handle. She pulls it up, and the door swung out. "Screw you dawdlers. Mari needs a hug."

Seeing a black thundering herd of large puppies round the edge of the barn, Pink shot out the door. She met one of her nieces and the mass of bouncing puppies halfway. Pink barreled through the six puppies only to find another wave rounding the barn. Within seconds, they were all rolling around in the mock battle of happiness. Jolie shook her head and huffed a short laugh. She knew how Pink felt. Home.

Dot rolled her eyes as the others tumbled out of the limousine. "Don't mind old Dotty. I'z just fetch the bags."

With a warm smile and a bolo tie, the tall driver leaned down so he could see in the door. "No, miss. That's my job." He offered out his hand.

DOT AND KIMIKO slowly circumnavigated the large statue. The wrought iron rods appeared and then blended with visual movements like snakes or the whole sculpture breathing.

"Every piece is flowing into the next. It looks like I'm watching an almost frozen waterfall… but it's moving horizontally."

"I seen Fernando's work, but this be his best. He capture Thunder's soul and Rocket's spirit. Everything here explain the rodeo rider she was."

"But why is it here?"

"Jinx never had no children. Jolie be his only daughter. All her growin' dey come up couple times a year. Den, for seven years—nothing. Dis away, he come out here and be wid her every day."

Dot could see the wet in the young woman's eyes. She had never known such intense caring. But Dot knew she would learn.

"Ready to go check out your new smithy?"

ALSO BY BAER CHARLTON

The Very Littlest Dragon: NEW Editions
(All-new full-color ebook, a paperback with
coloring pages, and a full-color Collector's Edition hardback)

Stoneheart — Pulitzer Nominee 2015
Angel Flights
What About Marsha?
Pirate's Patch
Flat Surf

JOLIE "ROCKET" ROBERTS SERIES
Dry Bridge of Vengeance – Book One
Dry Ridge of Redemption – Book Two

THORNY WALLACE SERIES
Death in the Valley – Book One
Light to Light – Book Two

SOUTHSIDE HOOKER SERIES
Death on a Dime – Book One
Night Vision – Book Two
Unbidden Garden – Book Three
Boomtown – Book Four
One Day Under the Grass – Book Five
Southside Hooker Series: Books 1–5 Box Set

(Collector's Edition hardback & ebook available)

I Drink Coffee and Make Shit Up
One Writer's Journey Without Signposts

BAER CHARLTON

ABOUT THE AUTHOR

Bestselling author Baer Charlton graduated from UC Irvine with a degree in Social Anthropology, monkeyed around for a while, and then proceeded onward with a life of global travel, multi-disciplinary adventure, and meeting the memorable array of characters he would come to describe in his writing. He has ridden things with gears, engines, and sails, and made things with wood, leather, and metal. He has been stitched back together more times than the average hockey team; his long-suffering wife and an assortment of cats and dogs have nursed him back to health after each surgery.

Baer knows a lot about many things in this world. History flows through his veins and pours out of him at the slightest provocation. Do not ask him what you may think is a simple question unless you have the time to hear a fascinating story.

You can find more at
www.mordantmedia.com